CHAPTER ONE

'I have something to tell you,' Indigo said as her sister Violet placed a huge slab of gooey chocolate cake in front of her.

'Something worse than losing your job and your home?' Violet said, scooping up a drop of chocolate icing with her finger from her own plate and popping it in her mouth.

Indigo let out a small sigh. Was it worse? In many ways it was wonderful, exciting news and she couldn't look at it as a bad thing, she refused to do that, but she couldn't deny she'd had a little cry when she'd found out. The timing couldn't have been worse. No job, no home, temporarily living with her sister in her tiny one-bedroom flat in Salisbury. It was far from ideal. But at the same time she couldn't help but be ridiculously happy about the news too.

'I'm pregnant.'

Violet's face went through a hundred different emotions in a matter of seconds. Indigo wasn't sure which one her sister settled on but suddenly she was leaning forward and hugging her. 'Oh Indy.'

'I know.' Indigo hugged her back, tears forming in her eyes.

'I'm so happy for you,' Violet said.

Indigo smiled into her sister's shoulder. It was the perfect response. No, 'What are you going to do?' or 'Are you going to keep it?' or 'How could you be so stupid?' or 'How do you intend to raise a baby with no money?' Violet had latched onto the most important response. Indigo was going to have a baby and that was gloriously happy news.

Indigo and Luke had tried for a baby for years so when she'd finally got pregnant, they'd both been deliriously happy. They'd read all the books, discussed a million different names, they'd even started painting the nursery. And then there was the car accident. Now the baby was gone, Luke had left her and her life was in tatters. She had been completely heartbroken over losing the baby so this was still wonderful news, despite her current circumstances.

Violet pulled back. 'Wait, is this baby from that gorgeous man mountain you had that one-night stand with two months ago?'

'River. Yes, there hasn't been anyone else for me, not for over two years.'

'Oh wow.' Violet paused. 'Did you not...'

'Yes, we used protection. He was adamant about that. Gorgeous man mountain has super-powered sperm. Rubber is clearly no match for the incredible man mountain sperm,' Indigo said.

Violet giggled.

It was somewhat ironic that she and Luke had tried for

a baby for so long and one night with River and she got pregnant, despite using protection.

Indigo took a big bite of the cake. After all, she was eating for two now. And, judging by the sheer size of River Brookfield, the baby would be huge too.

'There's this too. The email arrived about two hours after I'd found out I was pregnant.' Indigo slid the piece of paper across the table towards her sister.

Violet picked it up and read it. 'Oh wow, this is—'

'Terrible timing.'

Living the Dream was a wonderful initiative that had been set up to give people work experience in the jobs of their dreams. Working in a hotel all her life had made Indigo want to work in some of the most glamorous and prestigious hotels in the world, the ideal place being the Beverly Hills Hotel in Los Angeles. It had so much history and all the old movie stars had stayed there. She'd applied to Living the Dream months ago but the waiting list was long and she'd almost forgotten she'd done it. Then the day before she'd been offered a six-month placement at the Beverly Hills Hotel.

'This has always been your dream. What are you going to do?'

'It's funny, that simply isn't a priority any more. This baby is. I've deferred it for a year because who knows where I'll be in twelve months' time. But right now I don't have the money to fly out there or stay there anyway. Making a life here for me and my baby, getting a job and a place of my own seems more important.'

Violet nodded. 'I get that. So what's the plan?'

'Well, I need to tell River. I'm not expecting marriage

and forever with him, it was a one-night stand. And he might not even want to be a dad, but he deserves to know,' Indigo said.

'Do you even know where to find him?'

Indigo smiled. 'Fortunately he spent most of the night we met, before we got to the most incredible sex of my entire life, talking about this holiday resort he owns in Wales.'

'Wait, that's where you spent the night?'

'No, he has a flat in Bristol, he said he stayed there when he was doing his studies. But he lives in Wales at this amazing glamping site called Wishing Wood, where there are these luxury fairytale treehouses throughout the woods where people can come and stay. Each one is different, but they all have bedrooms, kitchens and bathrooms, some even have hot tubs and chandeliers. It sounds magical and he was so proud and excited to talk about it. It's near a place called Skrinkle Haven. It's on the south coast, overlooking the sea. I've looked it up and it's about a four-hour drive from here. So I'm going to drive up there tomorrow, tell him he's going to be a dad and then try to persuade him to give me that job he promised me the night we met.'

'I'm not sure the purple hair is the most professional look when going for a new job,' Violet teased.

Indigo touched her Cadbury's-purple hair. Indigo's friend, Joey, had persuaded her to dye it the previous week, telling her if she was going to stand out from the crowd, then she might as well do it in the best possible way. Rather than hiding away, she should take people's breath away. Impulsively, Indigo had let her do it. She'd already lost her job because of her appearance, she didn't have anything else to lose.

'I don't know, from what I've heard of this place, it's like a magical fairy wood. I could be the resident fairy. I'm sure I'll fit right in,' Indigo said, sounding a lot more confident than she felt.

'Well he gave you that baby, I think a job is the least he can do,' Violet said.

'I'm going to take some clothes, see if I can stay up there for a few nights. If he wants to be involved with the baby, we'll probably have a lot to discuss. If he doesn't I might be back tomorrow night.'

Violet opened her purse and took out fifty pounds. 'Stay in a hotel tomorrow night, I don't like the idea of you driving eight hours in one day.'

'I can't take your money,' Indigo said.

'You can and you will. You have to think of your baby now, not just you.'

Indigo thought about it. She had the tiniest amount left in her savings, which might stretch to a B&B for a night but not much more than that. If she had to stay for a few nights, she'd need Violet's gift. 'I'll pay you back.'

Violet waved it away. 'And if he doesn't want anything to do with you, you come back here the day after and you can stay as long as you need. We can raise this baby together.'

Indigo smiled. 'Thank you, but I'm not sure how Max would take that news.'

Violet's lovely boyfriend had been really good about not being able to stay over for the last week or so as Indigo was now sleeping on his side of the bed. Violet had been staying over at his for a few nights, but as the baker's she worked at was less than a thirty-second commute from her flat and a two-hour commute from Max's house, it wasn't ideal. Staying with her sister, as lovely as it had been, was definitely not a long-term solution.

'He'll just have to get used to it,' Violet said.

'Thank you, but to say I'm cramping your style is an understatement and having a baby here would change your life completely. No, the sooner I can get a job the better and then I can try and get a little flat of my own too.'

'You'll always be welcome here.'

Indigo smiled. 'Let's see what tomorrow brings.'

Despite Indigo's optimism the day before, tomorrow, now it was here, was filled with doubt and nerves and worry. Her stomach was churning so badly the poor baby was probably wondering what the hell was going on.

She had been following signs for Wishing Wood for the last half hour, and as the distance lessened with each signpost her anxiety grew until it felt like an almost tangible thing sitting uncomfortably in her stomach.

The night she'd met River played over and over in her mind, as she tried to find some clue as to how he would react to this news.

She'd been in Bristol celebrating a work colleague's hen night. He had been there celebrating a friend's thirtieth. They had hit it off spectacularly when they'd met in a club, the friends they'd arrived with quickly forgotten as they talked non-stop. She'd been in fancy dress, like all her friends. She had been wearing a cat costume complete with green feline contact lenses, so he'd never seen what her eyes were really like. That had been truly liberating. For so long she had avoided men, kept her head down because she didn't want to hear the comments or see the looks they gave her. River had treated her like a normal woman, flirting, laughing with her, touching her, making love to her, and, after two years of not even being kissed by a man, it was incredible to feel wanted and desired again.

He'd told her he didn't drink, which surprised her. Most men his age would be going down the pub most nights and downing several pints. But that declaration was even more surprising when, after an hour or two of talking, it became quite clear River was getting more and more drunk.

He'd realised it too, eventually, when it'd been too late and he had been furious. Evidently his so-called friends had spiked his drinks for a laugh. At that point, he'd decided he better go home before he did something he regretted. And partly because she hadn't wanted the magic of the night to end and partly out of concern for him she had gone back to his flat with him. She'd had no intention of going to bed with him, she just wanted to make sure he was OK and to spend some more time having wonderful conversation with a lovely man. But as soon as they walked through his door, he'd kissed her, which had very quickly led to clothes being removed, which had led to him making love to her three times over the next few hours in what had turned out to be one of the most magnificent nights of her life. He'd fallen asleep in the early hours of the morning and she'd run away.

She'd known that when he woke in the morning with a hangover from hell, sleeping with her would most likely be one of the things he would regret. It would have been awkward, he would have made some excuses, promised to call her and then didn't. She wanted to remember the magic of the night before as just that, not have it tainted with his reaction to it the next morning. Especially if he'd woken up to see her eyes. She couldn't bear to witness the look of revulsion, not when he'd been looking at her with such adoration when he'd made love to her. 'Witch' and 'freak' had been just two of the names she'd been called in the last few years. She hadn't wanted to see him to have that reaction.

After the car accident where she'd lost her baby, after Luke had left her, after the swelling and bruising had disappeared, and she'd slowly started to get back to normal, she'd been left with a surprising consequence. The pigment in one eye had very slowly faded away. It was quite rare, the doctors told her, but not impossible that this kind of thing could happen after an eye injury. It was nothing to worry about, they said, it didn't necessarily mean she would lose her eyesight too, but it did mean she now had one eye that was the darkest chocolate brown and one eye that was the palest silvery blue. It was quite the contrast.

With only one mile to go until she arrived at Wishing Wood, she pulled over into a layby to collect her thoughts.

Because reliving the entire night she'd spent with River – talking, laughing, making love – hadn't given her any clue as to how he would react when he found out she was pregnant with his baby. Would he be angry? She'd seen that side of him when he'd realised his drinks had been spiked. Or would he be loving; she'd seen that side of him too, when she'd been lying in bed with him. Would he be dismissive, promise to pay child maintenance now and again and want nothing more to do with her or her baby?

She hadn't planned what she was going to say to him. A hundred different scenarios had played through her head on the drive down here but she guessed as soon as he saw her, and she told him she had something important to tell him, he would quickly work out what she had come for. It had been just over two months since that glorious night, it wouldn't take a rocket scientist to work out the rest.

She glanced in the mirror. She was kind of hoping she could distract River from her eyes with her purple hair. Although her eyes were the first thing people noticed, they always did. What would River's reaction be to them when he saw them for the first time? She felt sick at the thought.

Needing some moral support, she decided to message her friends in the little WhatsApp group she was in. She'd contacted them the night before to tell them she was pregnant and received mixed reactions. Joey had thought it was wonderful news. Etta was worried about how Indigo would cope on her own with no job and no home. Tilly wanted to know if she was keeping it and Vicky talked about how stupid it was to get accidentally pregnant. A definite mixed bag. Indigo had told them all what she planned to do today and that had received mixed reactions too. She'd become friends with the girls while working in a hotel in Bristol. After the hotel had been taken over and lots of people were made redundant, the five of them had moved on to different jobs but they'd stayed in touch.

She opened up her phone and messaged the group.

I'm here at Wishing Wood and I'm really nervous.

She could see Vicky was typing.

I would be too, you're about to upend this man's life.

God, that did nothing to make her feel better.

Joey joined in. **I bet he asks you to marry him.**

You can't marry someone just because you're pregnant, Tilly wrote.

Indigo quickly replied, **I'm not going to marry him. That would be ridiculous.**

He has a responsibility to you and the baby, Etta typed.

Doesn't mean he has to marry her, Vicky was quick to reply. **It's called child maintenance, much less messy than marriage. And why would you want to marry him? You have that job offer at the Beverly Hills Hotel, that's far more exciting than what any man can offer you.**

I've deferred that for a year, six months in Los Angeles really isn't on my radar right now, Indigo wrote.

You need to get your priorities straight, Vicky replied.

Any words of wisdom or support? Indigo added.

Just be yourself and I'm sure he'll fall in love with you, Joey wrote.

Indigo smiled. Joey always saw the sunshine through the rain. But she wasn't hoping for that.

Tell him if he doesn't marry you, my Marcus will be having stern words with him, Etta said.

Marcus, as lovely as he was, wasn't the sort to have stern words with anyone.

Just get in, tell him, get out, Tilly advised. She clearly wasn't seeing any sunshine in this scenario.

Tell him your lawyers will be in touch, Vicky helpfully added.

Indigo sighed and put her phone down. This wasn't helping at all. She pulled her car out onto the road and drove the short distance to the entrance. As she drove through the gates her heart was thundering against her chest. Please let him be kind, she thought. If nothing else, if he didn't want to be a dad or have anything to do with his baby she could cope with that, she would raise the baby alone, but she didn't think she could cope if he was horrible to her.

As she drove through the trees and out into a large field, she caught a glimpse of the first treehouse and she gasped. It really did look like a real fairy house with its elongated turrets, wonky windows and triangular doors. It looked magical, as if it had simply grown out of the towering oak tree it was sitting in. She could just make out other treehouses in the woods behind it. Over to the left, the turquoise sea sparkled with gold-tipped waves. It was a beautiful place and she couldn't wait to see it all. River had been very excited when he was telling her all about it.

Indigo drove up to a small car parking area outside what seemed to be the main reception. She turned the engine off and looked around, half expecting her gorgeous man mountain to suddenly appear from the woods like some kind of caveman, but there was no sign of him and actually the reception area appeared to be closed.

She took a deep breath and got out of the car.

Outside the reception, a young woman was sitting on a blanket on the grass with two little girls. The girls were giving the woman a makeover with an abundance of glitter. Indigo looked around but there wasn't anyone else in sight and, as she'd suspected, the reception was closed with a sign hanging from the door that said the staff would be back in ten minutes.

'Hello,' the woman called out. 'Can I help you?'

'I'm looking for River,' Indigo said.

'Sure, I'll give him a call.'

The woman picked up a nearby walkie-talkie and pressed the button. 'River, another interviewee for you.'

Indigo's heart leapt when she heard his voice over the airwaves.

'I'll be there in five minutes.'

'I'm not...' Indigo's explanation that she wasn't here for an interview trailed off. It didn't really matter. River would be here in five minutes and then the real reason for her arrival would be very quickly revealed.

'Please, take a seat,' the woman indicated the blanket. 'I'm Meadow by the way, and this is Star,' Meadow indicated the eldest of the two children. 'And Tierra,' Meadow indicated the smallest of the girls. Star was dressed head to toe in purple, leggings, purple t-shirt, even purple wellies. Tierra was wearing a bright blue dinosaur t-shirt with a neon-orange tutu and green sparkly wellies.

'I'm Indigo.'

'You have different-coloured eyes,' Tierra blurted out.

Indigo steeled herself for the comments that were bound to come. Children never meant any harm, but sometimes their comments could be so on the nose that they hurt, despite coming from a place of innocence.

'Yes I do,' Indigo said.

Tierra stared at her. 'I wish I had different-coloured eyes.'

Indigo found herself smiling, relaxing a tiny bit as she sat down next to Meadow and the girls.

'You have beautiful hair,' Star said.

'Like a mermaid,' Tierra said, dreamily.

'Maybe she is,' Meadow said.

'She doesn't look like a mermaid,' Tierra said. 'Where's her tail?'

'She doesn't need her tail if she's walking around on the ground,' Star said, practically. 'Only in the sea.'

'Are you really a mermaid?' Tierra said.

'I can't tell you,' Indigo said. 'It's a secret. But I do love to swim.'

Tierra let out a little gasp and then got up and sat next to Indigo, cuddling up to her side.

'Can I plait your hair?' Star said.

'Sure,' Indigo said.

'Can I do your make-up?' Tierra asked.

'Umm, girls, I'm sure Indigo wants to be presentable for her interview,' Meadow said.

'What does presentable mean?' Tierra said, opening up her large make-up tin.

'It means I want to look nice and pretty,' Indigo said. 'Will you make me look pretty?'

Tierra nodded eagerly.

'I have facial wipes over here, you can take it all off before River gets here,' Meadow said.

'I'll make you extra pretty,' Tierra said, scooping up some blue sparkly eyeshadow and covering the whole of one of Indigo's eyelids with it.

It didn't really matter if she looked ridiculous when River arrived. With her bright purple hair and freaky eyes, she already ticked that box. And she wasn't expecting River to fall into her arms and declare his undying love for her anyway. She was here to tell him he was going to be a dad. Simple as that. Maybe he would offer her a job out of duty and the need to do the right thing, but that would be a bonus.

'So are you working right now?' Meadow asked, while Tierra and Star set to work with their makeover.

'No, I, umm… lost my job.'

'Oh, I'm sorry. So many companies are struggling right now. Who did you work for?'

Indigo cleared her throat. 'Infinity Hotels.'

Meadow's eyes widened in shock. 'The most prestigious hotels in the world?'

Indigo nodded.

'Christ, this place is a bit of a come-down from that, isn't it?'

'This place looks magical,' Indigo said, honestly. 'I think it would be wonderful to work somewhere like this, and not just because I need a job.'

Meadow smiled. 'Good answer.'

'Genuinely. I've heard so much about this place, it made me really excited to come here.'

Meadow nodded. 'I love it here. Which hotel were you working at?'

'The one in Bristol. I worked there for twelve years when it was the Crystal Orb Hotel and I absolutely loved it. Then a few years ago the hotel was bought out by Infinity Hotels and… everything changed after that.'

Meadow looked her up and down. Indigo was wearing little denim shorts, bright pink flip-flops and an oversized blue flowery tunic. With her purple hair and crazy-coloured eyes, she knew she looked a million miles away from what someone who worked for Infinity Hotels was supposed to look like.

'Infinity Hotels have very high standards when it comes to their employees,' Meadow said, diplomatically.

Indigo smiled. 'The purple hair is a very new acquisition. The weird eye is new too and the reason I lost my job in the first place.'

Meadow frowned. 'What?'

Indigo watched Star paint her nails with a sparkly purple nail varnish. That was a whole messy story she wasn't sure she wanted to get into. But if Meadow worked here then she wanted to explain her side of the story of why she lost her job before the rumours caught up with her.

'When Infinity Hotels took over Crystal Orb Hotel, they were making people redundant all over the place with the lowest payouts you can possibly imagine and then hiring new people under new job titles. It was horrible because it was quite clear they only wanted what they considered to be beautiful people working for them. I worked as head receptionist and they only wanted super glamorous people to be the first port of call for their guests. I've never really ticked that box but somehow I made the cut. I can only think they just wanted someone to train all the newbies. I hated that their supposed high standards weren't about skill or experience or education, instead it came down to appearance. I started looking for somewhere else to work as I couldn't get on board with that attitude, but then…'

She paused because that was when her whole life had changed, every hope and dream had been shattered, and that wasn't something she really wanted to talk about with Meadow, not when they'd only just met. But it was part of the reason she'd lost her job.

'But then?' Meadow prompted.

'Then I was involved in a car accident and…'

Indigo instinctively placed a hand over her belly for the baby she had lost, a gesture not lost on Meadow.

'And… I took some time off for compassionate leave but then we got a new manager, Stuart Hamilton, and he was less than compassionate. He didn't want me to come back until the scars had healed, the external ones at least, and actually they healed very quickly so I had to go back, probably before I was mentally ready to do so. And he…'

She trailed off. God, she couldn't tell Meadow that. What he'd offered her was sordid and disgusting and her reaction to it was less than professional.

'I know of Stuart Hamilton and his terrible reputation around his female employees,' Meadow said. 'I'm guessing he said he'd cut you some slack if you…' she glanced at the girls and obviously amended what she'd been going to say. 'Visited his bedroom.'

Indigo nodded, relieved she didn't have to spell it out. Although having the girls there meant they had to dance around the topic, it was a relief not to have to go into too many details. 'I told him if he ever did anything inappropriate…' Indigo thought about how to word it in front of the girls without encouraging violence. She pointed subtly to her arm. 'I would break his radius and ulna and every one of his phalanges.' She wiggled her fingers for emphasis and Meadow snorted her laughter. 'And then sue the hotel and the company for every penny they had. He never came near me again but he hated me after that. He made my life hell. I was in a bad way, emotionally and mentally, and I didn't have the confidence to start interviewing for other jobs so I stayed and put up with it. The eye thing was very gradual at first, just a small spot of blue, but slowly the pigment started to fade from the rest of the eye and then it seemed to happen all at once. Stuart was horrified. I couldn't be front of house looking like this. He told me I was hideous and not the look he wanted for his hotel. Of course you can't sack someone for having different-coloured eyes so he stole five hundred pounds from the till and hid it in my handbag. Instant dismissal.'

Indigo swallowed the taste of bitterness in her mouth.

'That's horrible,' Meadow said.

Indigo liked that Meadow believed her version of events rather than the version Stuart had told everyone.

'It wasn't good. The worst thing was that I would have walked out of there willingly, I hated working there. But now I'm tainted with being fired for stealing. So far no hotel will hire me. In fact, no company of any kind is prepared to offer me a job either.'

She thought about the Beverly Hills Hotel but, as that was only a work-experience placement and thousands of miles away, it didn't really count.

'I apply for jobs,' Indigo continued. 'I get interviews and inevitably the question of why I left my last job comes up and I have to explain I got fired for stealing, even though it isn't true. If that question doesn't come up and it gets as far as references, I can only put down the hotel – I worked there for fourteen years – and Stuart has taken great pleasure in telling people the reason why I was fired. I've been unemployed for six months now, living off my savings, but a few weeks ago the money ran out and I had to leave my flat as I couldn't afford to pay the bills so… here we are.'

Meadow stared at her and Indigo blushed.

'God, sorry, I don't normally spill that whole sorry tale as soon as I meet someone. I'm normally more discreet than that. Let's go with the professional answer. I'm grateful for the experience of working with Infinity Hotels but we parted ways when I wanted to do something different.'

'I prefer the honest answer,' Meadow said. 'Star, you are doing a beautiful job on Indigo's hair. Tierra… Indigo's face looks lovely, but maybe that's enough blusher.'

Indigo smiled as Tierra opened up a tub of silvery glitter powder and started smearing it over Indigo's forehead instead.

'What is it you'd like to do here?' Meadow asked.

'Anything really. I suppose River might not want me to be customer-facing, don't want to scare the children,' Indigo gave a self-deprecating laugh.

Meadow didn't laugh. 'I can't see River agreeing to that. We all tend to muck in together here, working wherever is needed. My husband builds the treehouses, Bear sorts out all the electrics, I tend to be responsible for the interiors and accessories, but we've all worked shifts on reception, done the cleaning. Everyone helps everyone else. This is not a place where you can hide.'

18

Indigo paused. 'I'm done hiding. Two months ago I had... an experience that made me realise I'd been in hiding for too long. It was something so wonderful that I realised what I've been missing out on for the last few years. I want my life back. I want to be normal again.'

Meadow grinned. 'Normality is overrated.'

Indigo smiled. 'So your husband works here too?'

'Yes, he'll be here in a minute. Oh, actually River is here now.' She gestured behind Indigo.

'Oh. I might take you up on one of those facial wipes,' Indigo said, her heart suddenly pounding against her chest at seeing him again.

Meadow cringed. 'I'm afraid it's too late for that.'

Indigo turned and River was right there, towering over her. Christ, he looked as formidable and beautiful as she remembered. He was so huge in height and breadth. He was like a gigantic bear. She couldn't help but blush as she suddenly recalled that gorgeous weight of him pinning her to the bed, making her scream. His sapphire-blue eyes lasered in on hers and all words vanished from her head. He had dark hair that was scruffy and unkempt and she remembered running her fingers through it when they'd made love and that gorgeous dark stubble that had caused various wonderful sensations as he had kissed all over her body. She wondered if he was thinking of that night as much as she was.

She scrambled to her feet, although that did nothing to change the huge height difference between them.

Christ, what could she say? He was watching her but she had no idea what he was thinking. She would just say that she needed to talk to him. She opened her mouth to speak and…

'Daddy!' Tierra squealed with delight, standing up and throwing herself into River's open arms. He picked her up and hugged her tight.

CHAPTER TWO

'Hello my little mermaid,' River said and Tierra giggled.

'Indigo is a *real* mermaid,' Tierra whispered theatrically. 'And she let me do her make-up. Isn't she beautiful, Daddy?'

'Very,' River said, without missing a beat.

She doubted that as she had a face full of glitter and half of Tierra's make-up smeared all over her cheeks and forehead. But she had bigger things than that to worry about now.

Indigo's heart was thundering against her chest. Tierra was his daughter. Suddenly pennies were dropping into place. Meadow had mentioned her husband building the treehouses and the night she'd met River he'd talked about building them from scratch too. Oh god. Meadow was his wife. Tierra and Star were his children. Indigo had known that what she had shared with River that wonderful night was going to be a one-night stand, but she hadn't realised he was sleeping with her behind his wife's back.

Shit, bugger, fuck.

What the hell was she going to do now?

'This is Indigo. I've interviewed her,' Meadow said. 'She starts tomorrow. She can work in reception.'

'Fine by me,' River said, with a shrug.

'Wait, what? That was an interview?' Indigo said, her head spinning.

'Oh, did I forget to mention I'm the manager here?' Meadow said. 'Must have slipped my mind. I never forget a face. I went to the Crystal Orb Hotel in Bristol once. I had an interview there.'

Meadow offered out a facial wipe.

Indigo quickly took it and wiped her face.

'To work at the hotel?' Indigo asked in confusion.

Meadow shook her head. 'No, just some guy who was interviewing me for his company and using your coffee lounge. I had Star with me, she was ten months old. My childcare had let me down at the last minute and I turned up with her purely to ask the guy to reschedule. I came to the reception and I was so stressed I ended up blurting out the whole sorry story to one of the receptionists. You. You offered to take Star for me while I had the interview. Star was screaming her head off at the time so that was a brave offer but I was so so desperate for that job, I took you up on it. I went for the interview, got the job and I came back to reception expecting to find Star causing absolute chaos. There you were, with Star on your hip, she was giggling and laughing as you played with her while serving a huge queue of customers at the same time. Answering the phone, dealing with queries, checking people in, handling a complaint about noise in one of the other bedrooms, you were completely unflappable. I was very impressed. And I was so grateful for the opportunity you gave me. I'd never have got that job if it wasn't for you. I was impressed by the hotel as well, everything ran like clockwork and most importantly the staff were happy, you could pick that up straightaway. You worked there for twelve years before Infinity Hotels took over, that shows commitment and loyalty. You worked your way up to head receptionist, that shows you're good at your job. I think we would be a fool not to hire you. Be here for nine tomorrow morning and I'll show you the ropes.'

Indigo stared at her in shock. She had a distant memory of looking after one of the guests' children while she was manning the reception. What a coincidence to run into Meadow again, all these years later.

'River can show you round now,' Meadow said.

'I'll be happy to,' River said, before hoisting his daughter onto one hip and offering out a hand for her to shake. 'River Brookfield.'

Indigo stared at the hand. He was trying to pretend that they'd never met. Of course he wouldn't want Meadow to know the truth.

Indigo swallowed, hating that she was now forced into going along with the lie. 'Indigo Bloom.'

He nodded and then gestured for her to follow him.

'Can I come too?' Star said.

'Of course,' River said, holding out a hand and Star took it. He started walking off in the direction of the woods.

Indigo turned back to face Meadow, wanting to apologise for sleeping with her husband but she knew she couldn't tell her. She wanted to run away from this place and not ruin this perfect little family with her news. River was an ass for cheating on his wife but it wasn't her place to break them up. But now she had a job, the first offer of employment she'd had in six months, and she really did want to work here. She couldn't turn that down.

'Thank you,' Indigo said. She wanted to say that Meadow wouldn't regret it, but she got the feeling that at some point when the secret came tumbling out she probably would. 'Thank you so much.'

Meadow smiled at her and gestured for her to go with River.

Indigo hurried after him. She fell in at his side but she had no words to say, not least because his two daughters were hanging off him but mostly because her mind was a whirl of confusion, betrayal, guilt and anger. She settled on anger. That night had been incredible, the way he had touched her, made love to her as if she was his world, the lovely things he'd said to her. And it had all been a lie. And why the hell would he offer her a job here when he lived here with his wife? Unless he was hoping to continue having sex with her behind his wife's back. That wasn't going to happen. Every wonderful thought and memory of him vanished in an instant. Meadow was lovely and he was scum for cheating on her. How many other women had he slept with behind his wife's back?

'We have twelve treehouses here that are open to the public and a further three that are live-in accommodation for the staff. All of them are different and there's different pricing levels for each one. Some of them have more than one bedroom, some of them have hot tubs, some are big, some are small. There are treehouses overlooking the sea, some overlooking the lake, some in the middle of the woods. But all of them are designed to be luxury getaways. The houses are all self-catering so we have fully stocked kitchens in all of them. But we do have on-site restaurant facilities too for when people can't be bothered to cook. I'll show you that shortly. At the moment we are in the middle of building a further twenty treehouses which we hope to open officially for the summer. I'll show you those too.'

He was being so formal with her, there was no indication at all that she'd shared the most incredible sex of her life with him. Had it all been so meaningless to him? Just sex, nothing more.

Star ran on ahead to use a rope swing. Tierra wiggled down from her dad's arms to join her.

'Is this not going to be a problem for you?' Indigo muttered, as soon as they were out of earshot.

River stopped to look at her. 'Why would it be a problem for me?'

And then it hit her like a punch to the stomach. He had no idea who she was. Oh god. This was even worse. She had played out this scenario in her head many times – she'd pictured him getting angry, or frustrated, she'd even pictured, in her ridiculous dreams of a fairytale ending, that he would tell her he loved her and wanted to marry her – but she had never imagined that he wouldn't recognise her. She was horrified. She had such incredible memories of that night and she was just another random woman he'd slept with. One he didn't even remember. She wanted to shout and curse him, calling him every name under the sun, but she couldn't do that. She'd been offered a job and she desperately needed the money. If she was going to stay here, and she hadn't decided yet whether she would, she had to be professional.

She cleared her throat. 'I just meant because you're the owner and Meadow has just hired me without consulting you.'

He shrugged and carried on walking. 'I am the owner, with my two brothers Heath and Bear, but I trust Meadow completely. I've known her my entire life and she does an excellent job of running this place. If she thinks you're good enough to work here that's fine by me.'

She followed him, her heart and her head racing. She had no idea what to do next.

He pointed out a few treehouses and she tried to focus on them rather than this crashing disappointment. She could see, even from the outside, they were very different. They reminded her of the Weasleys' house in Harry Potter, all higgledy-piggledy, with levels of the treehouses perched precariously on top of other parts, turrets sticking out here and there in a haphazard way that somehow worked and made it endearing. They didn't go inside any of them though, as they were all taken by guests.

'Let's go over here,' River said, indicating a small brook that bubbled through the middle of the wood. He glanced down at her feet; the pink flip-flops were perhaps not the most ideal choice of shoe when walking around a wet and potentially muddy wood. 'We might have to get you some wellies. Here, use the stepping stones.'

He waded through the shallow waters and the girls splashed through too, both of them wearing sparkly wellies, but Indigo was surprised when River stopped and held out a hand to help her across.

She was damn sure she didn't want to hold hands with him. It felt flirty and wrong when she'd been chatting to his wife mere moments before. In fact she didn't want to ever touch him again. But when she took a step on the mossy stepping stone and her foot slipped a little, she quickly grabbed his hand to be on the safe side. She didn't want to fall and hurt the baby.

She quickly made it to the other side and removed her hand.

He eyed her as if she was a puzzle he was trying to work out. Maybe he was starting to remember her after all.

He stepped back away from her, scowling as he stared down at the ground. He was about to move away when he stopped. Had he remembered her? Was he going to say something?

'Oh girls, look at this.' River crouched down and the girls gathered around him, staring at something on the muddy banks he was pointing to. 'It's a newt. I think it might be a palmate newt because it has black webbing on its back feet, see, between its toes.'

'They're rare, aren't they?' Star said.

'It's rare to see them,' River said. 'Especially this time of year, they are normally in the water rather than on land.'

'He's lovely,' Tierra said. 'Can we keep him?'

'No, that wouldn't be fair, this is his home and I bet he loves jumping through puddles just as much as you do and swimming in the stream. But we can name him and take his photo, then maybe when we get back home we can look up some more information about him.'

Tierra nodded eagerly.

Despite her resolve to stay away from River, Indigo

found herself crouching down to have a look too. She'd never seen a newt before. He was a funny little lizard-type creature with large feet splayed out across the small branch he was standing on.

'What shall we call him?' Indigo said.

'What about Nigel?' Star suggested.

River smirked as he fished his phone out of his pocket and passed it to Tierra so she could take some pictures with it.

Tierra started snapping away. 'I don't like Nigel. How about Spotty?'

'They're not really spots,' Star said as Tierra handed her the phone so she could take more photos. 'More like freckles.'

'Freckles is a great name,' River said, watching his daughters with complete adoration. It was clear to see they were his entire world, which made Indigo feel even more guilty about what had happened between them and furious that he would risk his perfect family life by sleeping with her.

'I like the name Freckles,' Tierra said.

'What about a surname?' Indigo said and she watched River smile.

'Brookfield, just like us,' Tierra said and Star nodded.

'Of course,' Indigo said. 'He's part of the family.'

As she watched the girls she felt a lump in her throat. They clearly adored their dad and, while her own opinion of him was pretty low right now, she didn't want to do anything to damage their opinion of him.

River walked with Indigo on the way to the restaurant. He was hoping some of the staff would be there so he could introduce her to them.

He glanced at Indigo, her purple hair gleaming like magic in the sun. There was something about this woman that made his heart race. As soon as he'd met her, he'd felt this pull to her and he couldn't explain why. And when he'd held her hand to help her over the stream, he'd felt something, a spark so fiercely strong that he felt an immediate need for her.

But he also knew there was something else going on here beyond lust and sexual attraction. He felt like he knew her. And not just someone he'd bumped into once, it was as if he really knew her, like he shared a connection with her, something deep and powerful – which was ridiculous because they'd never met before.

He also got the feeling she was pissed off with him. She was being polite and professional, and he couldn't fault her for that, but he had the impression she was forcing herself to be civil and he didn't know why. When she was talking to the girls, who had now gone off with Meadow, she was genuine, friendly, happy to talk, but with him there was a definite edge.

He pushed open the door of the restaurant. It was that time of day when it was too late for lunch but too early for dinner so there were rarely any guests in here. But it was also the time that many of the staff would congregate here; most had finished their jobs for the day and would gather here for coffee, biscuits or whatever other lovely delights Alex had cooked for them, before they went home.

He was pleased to see a small group of them sitting at

the table, tucking into what looked like apple turnovers as they approached.

'River, you need to try one of these,' Greta waved one of the turnovers in the air. 'They are amazing.'

Lucien held up the plate and River took it, offering it out to Indigo. She took one and, after a moment's thought, quickly took another.

'Sorry, I'm starving,' Indigo said.

'No need to apologise,' Alex said, tucking a stray strand of her hair under her hat. 'Nothing I like more than watching people eat the food I make.'

'Everyone, this is Indigo,' River said. 'She'll be starting work on the reception tomorrow.'

Everyone looked at Indigo with interest and he suddenly felt a surge of protectiveness. Her eyes made her unique but he could see she could easily be a target for unkind comments. He glanced around, wondering if anyone would say anything and he could almost feel Indigo bracing herself for it too. But he considered these people his family and he suddenly felt guilty for even thinking they might. They came from all walks of life; Lucien from France, Greta from the Netherlands, Alex was from South Africa, Felix came from Denmark. They always welcomed new members to the family with open arms. Indigo would be no different.

'Come, take a seat,' Felix said, pushing a chair back. 'I'm Felix. Me and Greta are in charge of the grounds, we look after the gardens, take care of maintenance, repairs, that kind of thing. Lucien here is part of the housekeeping crew. Alex is the best chef in the whole of Wales, if not the UK.'

Alex laughed.

'Tell us about yourself,' Felix said as Indigo sat next to them.

'I know you,' Greta suddenly said. 'You worked at that fancy hotel in Bristol, the Crystal Orb.'

Everyone 'ooohed' to show they were impressed.

Indigo glanced over at Greta. 'I remember you. You were in charge of the flowers and plants in the hotel. Greta always did the most elaborate flower displays for our reception. That must have been three years ago, just before Infinity Hotels took over. You didn't work there long though.'

'No, six months I think, then my mum got sick and I had to go back to Rotterdam to look after her.'

'Oh, I'm sorry to hear that,' Indigo said.

'Oh, she's fine now. But I remember you because you were always kind. Some of those front-facing staff were always a bit snooty with us invisibles. They saw themselves as being above the rest of us, the ones that actually kept the place ticking like clockwork. But you were always kind and friendly. I liked that.'

River liked that too. This wasn't the kind of place where there was a hierarchy.

'I did keep in touch with a few others who worked there,' Greta went on. 'I was sorry to hear about your... car accident.'

Indigo busied herself with her turnover. 'Thank you.'

There was something in the way Greta said that which made River think it was so much more than a car accident.

Felix waded into the awkward silence. 'How are the new treehouses coming along?'

'Good,' River said. 'We're running a bit behind right now but we have twelve pretty much done apart from the painting.'

'I could help with the painting,' Lucien said. 'Cleaning the treehouses in between guests takes a lot of my time but I'm normally done by the afternoon.'

'I could help too, now and again,' Felix volunteered.

'We could all help,' Indigo said. 'We could have a painting party, get as many people involved as possible. Maybe we can offer a prize for the most houses painted over a period of say three or four hours – or the best painting job, because we want quality not quantity.'

Lucien perked up. 'What kind of prize?'

'What kind of prize would you like?' Indigo said.

'How about a meal for two at Pandora's?' Lucien immediately suggested and River noticed he gave a brief glance in Alex's direction.

'That's posh,' Greta said, whistling. 'But hell, I'm in if that's the prize. Me and my husband never eat out anywhere that fancy.'

'I'm in,' Alex said. 'I think a lot of people would join in for that prize.'

'Perfect,' Indigo said, excitedly. 'Maybe we can do it tomorrow, put the word out to all the rest of the staff.'

River smirked that she had decided this was a done deal, without even checking it was OK with him. And he would be the one to stump up the cash for the meal voucher. Although a painting party *was* a good idea. With the building of all the other treehouses the painting just wasn't getting done and at least he could tick them off as finished once the painting was completed.

'OK, four till six tomorrow, we'll obviously provide all the paint,' River said. 'I'd be very grateful for any help anyone can give us.'

'Grateful enough for a meal for two for the winners?' Felix asked.

'Yes, that can be the prize. Now, we'll leave you guys to it before hanging around here costs me any more money. Indigo…' he gestured for her to come with him and she picked up the remaining turnover and followed him out, leaving excited chatter behind him.

'I'm sorry, I probably should have checked with you first before offering that,' Indigo said when they got outside.

'That would have been a good idea,' River said. He had been about to say that the painting party was a great way to get everyone involved and to help them finish the tree-houses but for the briefest of seconds he thought he saw a smug smile of satisfaction on her face and decided to keep the compliment to himself. Had she done that deliberately? Surely not.

Something was going on here and he planned to find out what.

CHAPTER THREE

Indigo lay staring at the sun setting above her, leaving clouds of flamingo pink across the sky. The day had not gone to plan, not one bit. Not only had she not told River her news but she'd discovered he had a wife and children, which was horribly disappointing. She'd been offered a job in this magical wishing wood and now she was going to have to work alongside him and his lovely wife every day. To top it off she was spending the night in her car because part of the money Violet had given her had gone to pay for petrol and lunch because this baby was making her hungry all the time. There wasn't enough left for even the cheapest of hotels. Her bank, when she had gone to the ATM, had steadfastly refused to cough up any money, so the car had been the only option. Tomorrow she would need to come up with a plan of where she could stay for the next few weeks until she got paid.

She placed a hand on her belly. 'I promise this is only temporary, little one. By the time you come along I'll have money, lots of money to pay for food and toys and nappies.'

She swallowed a lump in her throat because, regardless of what happened, she couldn't expect River and Meadow to pay for maternity leave, so where would the money to pay for her baby come from then? She pushed that thought away and carried on with her bolstering pep talk.

'And we'll have a house with a freshly painted nursery and a mobile hanging over your bed with little dinosaurs and unicorns.'

She smiled at the memory that triggered.

She thought back to the night she'd met River. He'd talked about Wishing Wood and what the treehouses looked like. He'd showed her some designs he'd quickly drawn on napkins and then they'd designed one together, which had been wonderful and inspiring. They'd spent an hour creating their perfect dream treehouse. It had a bathroom with a roll-top bath and a kitchen that would be the heart of the home. There were round windows and doors just like a little hobbit house because she loved *Lord of the Rings*. There was a room upstairs with bunkbeds for the older children and a helter-skelter slide that would take them down to the forest floor. There was a secret room behind a bookshelf for the children to play in too. There was a studio area because River had said he loved to paint, even though he wasn't any good at it, but that he never had the time or a place to do it. There was also a nursery for a baby she'd had no idea she was going to have and a dinosaur and unicorn mobile hanging over the bed.

What would it be like to live here and raise her baby here? She knew that was a ridiculous thought because how could it ever work, her and her baby living in the same place as River's wife and children? But for a rose-tinted moment she allowed herself to imagine what that would look like.

Living in a treehouse was every child's dream. When she, her brother and sister were little they had a treehouse at the bottom of the garden. Nothing as incredible as the ones here, it was very basic, but they had spent many hours playing in it when they had nothing more than their imagination to pass the time. Life was so much easier back then. As a small child she'd imagined living in a big treehouse when she was older, growing her own vegetables, having chickens for eggs; it was a simple, uncomplicated dream. But when she'd grown up that had seemed silly and fanciful. Working in a prestigious hotel had given her a glimpse of the life of the rich and her own dreams had changed. A few years before she'd have told anyone who asked that one day she'd work in some of the most glamorous hotels and cities in the world, the Beverly Hills Hotel being at the top of that list.

But would that really make her happy?

Lying here in her car with nothing and a baby on the way really brought it home to her that her dreams had changed. She just wanted to be able to provide for her baby, for her child to grow up happy.

Raising her child here, letting them play in the woods and the nearby beaches every day, living in a real treehouse with a helter-skelter slide from the bedroom, that would be a dream come true. She didn't need the riches of a glamorous life. As long as there was enough money for bills, food and clothes, she and her child could make their own happiness. They could create collages from autumn leaves and necklaces from acorns. Her child would grow up with nature, surrounded by wildlife rather than big hotels, shopping malls and office blocks.

River had escorted her round the whole resort that afternoon, the restaurant, the beaches. He'd showed her every magical treehouse and she couldn't help falling completely in love with the place. She really wanted to live and work here. She just had the small problem of carrying the married owner's baby to deal with.

Her phone rang and she knew straightaway it would be Violet. She quickly answered it.

'Hey, are you OK?' Violet said. 'How did it go?'

'Well, I got a job,' Indigo said, feebly.

'Oh that's wonderful.'

'Yeah, I start tomorrow.'

'That's fantastic. So he took it well then?'

Indigo swallowed the lump in her throat. 'No. He's married, with kids.'

'Oh shit.'

'I know. I couldn't tell him. His wife gave me the job, she's really nice.'

'Oh god.'

'Vi, he had no clue who I was. Even when we were alone together, it was clear he had no memory of me at all.'

'You're kidding?'

'No, when I introduced myself he didn't even recognise the name. I mean, Indigo is not that common, you'd think he would have remembered that if nothing else.'

Violet was silent for a moment as she thought. 'But did you introduce yourself as Indigo, that night? Sometimes you go by Indy.'

Indigo thought about it. 'It's possible I introduced

myself as Indy. I was drunk, happy, relaxed. A lot of my friends call me Indy.' She thought back to when she and River had been making love and how he'd whispered her name. He *had* said Indy then. In fact it had sounded a bit like Mindy but she'd shrugged it off at the time, too busy enjoying what he was doing with his hands and mouth. But she was sure she must have mentioned her full name at some point in the night.

She pushed that away. 'But you'd think he would have recognised me.'

'I've seen photos of you from that night,' Violet said. 'Dressed as a cat, you looked amazing but you also had that cat eye mask make-up that took up half your face. You had those green cat eye contact lenses. And let's not forget your hair is bright purple now, instead of the beautiful blonde from that night. I imagine you look quite different now than you did then.'

Indigo sighed. Violet was always the voice of reason. And what she was saying was fair but she had been disappointed that she had been so unmemorable to River. She had remembered him vividly.

'Are you OK?' Violet asked, gently.

'Yeah,' Indigo sighed. 'That night, it felt like we shared this incredible connection and now it feels like I'm just one of many women he's slept with behind his wife's back.'

'So what are you going to do?'

'I guess I'll take the job and find the right time to tell him. I don't want to do anything to break up his family, but he still deserves to know, don't you think?'

'I suppose. He sounds like a bit of a dick if you ask me.'

'Yeah, everything I thought I knew about him has changed.'

But Indigo didn't remember River like that. Before he'd got drunk, he had been so lovely. She supposed if she was simply one of many women he was screwing around with behind his wife's back, he was probably used to laying on the charm by now.

Suddenly a huge shadow loomed close to the window and Indigo let out a little shriek. But as River's face peered in through the glass at her, it did nothing to stop her heart racing.

'You OK?' Violet said.

'Yes, sorry, umm, someone's at my hotel room door,' Indigo said. 'I'll speak to you tomorrow.'

She quickly hung up, smoothed down her hair and opened the car door.

'Hello?' she smiled, breezily as if her sleeping in her car was perfectly normal.

'I got a report that some homeless person was sleeping in their car in the car park. What are you doing here?' River asked.

She noticed Tierra was with him, dressed in her pyjamas and fluffy pink dressing gown, but still wearing her sparkly green wellies. The little girl was staring at her with wide eyes.

'I'm, umm…' Indigo tried and failed to come up with a plausible reason why she was lying in the back of her car at nine o'clock at night. 'Well, I didn't want to be late tomorrow so I thought I should spend the night here.'

River scowled. 'Do you not have somewhere to stay?'

Indigo sighed. 'I'm… things are a little tight right now, financially.'

'Right, get your things, come with me.'

He started walking away, Tierra following him, looking over her shoulder at Indigo as she went.

Indigo quickly grabbed her bag, threw her phone inside it and scrabbled out of the car. She locked it behind her and hurried to catch up with River. 'Look, I don't want to inconvenience you.'

'You're not. You can stay with me tonight, tomorrow we'll sort something else out for you.'

Oh god, she couldn't imagine anything more awkward than staying under the same roof as River and Meadow and their two kids, with his third on the way.

'We're over here,' River said, pointing to a beautiful pink magnolia tree that was just starting to bloom with an oversized treehouse emerging out of the branches. Fairy lights hung from the leaves and warm golden lights poured out of the wonky windows. It looked enchanting.

'You live in a treehouse?' Indigo said, in surprise. He hadn't mentioned that when they first met, but to be fair he hadn't mentioned he was married with children either.

'I have a five-year-old daughter and I own a wood filled with treehouses, I don't think there was any way I couldn't live in one. Tierra and Star helped me design this one, so it's a bit kooky.'

Indigo couldn't help but smile. 'Every child's dream.'

She followed him up the wooden stairs and across a small rope bridge which was also lit up with more fairy lights. There was an entrance to a helter-skelter-style slide next to the door, which would take the girls back down to the ground level, and which made Indigo smile – although, unlike the one she and River had designed together, it hadn't come from the bedroom. The doorway was a large, triangular shape which River opened and stepped back to let Indigo go ahead inside. He followed her in and closed the door behind him.

'I'll just put Tierra to bed and then I'll show you around,' River said.

He disappeared up another small spiral staircase with Tierra and Indigo was left standing in the most magical room she had ever seen. The trunk of the tree grew up through the middle of the room, small branches and the odd flower growing round the windows and across the ceiling. There was a large cream leather sectional sofa curved around one part of the room and a kitchen with a white sparkly marble-effect kitchen top and pale pink cupboard doors curved around another, which matched the magnolia flowers perfectly. A large dining room table, simply a large chunk of wood that was wider at one end and shorter at the other, filled the middle of the room. Large wooden chandeliers lit up the room, gleaming off the polished wooden floorboards. The staircase had a banister and railings of twisted wood. Everything had a natural feel to it as if it hadn't been built but was simply growing straight out of the tree. In the corners were large wooden sculptures of squirrels, foxes and rabbits which Indigo presumed were Tierra and Star's influence. She'd seen many of those around the wood too. It was all so beautiful.

On one wall was a large canvas painting of the sun setting over the sea. It was stunning. The way the scarlets and pinks were reflected across the waves was beautiful. In the corner were the initials 'RB' and Indigo wondered if this was one of the paintings River had done. If so, he'd certainly undersold his skills when he'd told her he wasn't very good.

She suddenly realised how quiet it was. She could hear River and Tierra talking softly up above her but there was no other noise. Maybe Star and Meadow were already asleep.

River came running down the stairs. He was dressed in dark jeans and a loose pale blue shirt with the sleeves rolled up, exposing strong, tanned forearms. She tried to ignore the memory of what it felt like to be held in those arms. She didn't want to think of him like that any more.

'Is this yours?' she asked, needing to distract herself.

He glanced at the painting and nodded.

'It's really good.'

He shrugged as if he didn't really believe the compliment. 'Let me just give you a quick tour and then if you don't mind I'll be hitting the sack myself. My day starts very early with Tierra and work here, so I tend to have early nights, at least two or three nights in the week. You're welcome to watch the TV if you're not ready to sleep. Well, this is the lounge, dining area and kitchen. Help yourself to any food and drink in the kitchen. Up here are the bedrooms,' he gestured for her to follow him back up the stairs.

There were three rooms on the next level with a ladder leading up to a mezzanine level and another ladder that possibly led to some kind of loft. He pushed open a small pink door carefully. 'Tierra's room,' River whispered.

Indigo peered inside to see Tierra lying in a pink canopied bed that was lit up with star fairy lights. In fact there was an abundance of pink and sparkles everywhere in here, along with hundreds of cuddly toys of every animal in the world. Indigo couldn't help but smile.

River closed the door softly. 'This is the bathroom.'

Indigo was impressed to see a large tiled wetroom with a huge shower head in the middle of it. There was a toilet and sink up one end. It was stark but looked like something from a high-end spa hotel.

'That is the ladder up to the roof terrace and this ladder goes up to the spare bedroom,' he indicated the mezzanine level above them. 'And this is my bedroom,' he said, opening the door on the last room which was huge and one hundred percent masculine. A large bed built on a wooden frame stood in the middle of the room covered in fake fur blankets. It was very caveman and suited River perfectly. But the most obvious thing was that the bed was completely empty.

'Where are Meadow and Star?' Indigo blurted out.

'Presumably in their own treehouse,' River said with some confusion.

'So you and her are not...'

'God no, I love her, she's my best friend, we grew up together, but it's never been more than that between us. Now ask my brothers that question and that's a whole other complicated story, but me and Meadow are just friends. Not that it's any business of yours.'

Indigo blushed furiously. 'Of course not. I just presumed that you two were together. My mistake.' Relief flooded through her. She paused because she had to know if he was single. If he was then maybe she could share the real reason she had come here, get it out in the open now. She wasn't expecting the news to be met with happiness but she had to tell him and she didn't want to hide it from him. 'So you're not married?'

His scowl deepened. 'Not any more.'

Oh, god, his wife had died. 'I'm so sorry.'

'Don't be. I married Tierra's mum purely because I got her pregnant. We stayed together for six months after Tierra was born before she ran off with another man and never came back. I was glad to see the back of her. But again I fail to see how this is any of your business. When I offered you a place to sleep tonight, I did not mean in my bed with me.'

'Oh my god, of course not, that's not what I meant,' Indigo back-pedalled as fast as she could.

'I only have one woman in my life,' he nodded his head towards Tierra's room. 'I don't have room for anyone else.'

She shook her head. 'I haven't been in a relationship with someone for two years and I didn't come here looking for that. It was just something Meadow said that made me think… I'm sorry, this has been a big misunderstanding. I would never sleep with my boss. Never. My last boss tried to blackmail me into his bed and I was never tempted, not for one second. Even though I think that was the thing that made him fire me in the end. Well, that and my freaky eyes. But please believe me that jumping into bed with you tonight was the very very last thing on my mind.'

He stared at her and then his face softened. 'You would have felt safer sleeping under my roof if there was a wife or girlfriend here.'

Oh god, now he was jumping to conclusions. What a mess.

'You have my word that I would never—' River said.

'River, I'm not scared of you, not one bit. Please, let's just go to bed and forget this whole conversation ever happened.'

He paused, then arched an eyebrow. 'Let's go to bed?'

She burst out laughing. 'Separately.'

His mouth twitched in a small smile. 'Your bed is up there.' He pointed up the ladder. 'Goodnight Indigo.'

He turned to go into his room and she wondered if she should just tell him now, put all this confusion behind them once and for all. 'River.'

He turned to face her again but how could she explain that she was some random woman he'd shagged in a moment of drunkenness over two months before and now she was here, carrying his baby? That was a heavy conversation for so late at night.

She swallowed down the words she wanted to say. 'Thanks for letting me stay.'

'No problem.'

They stared at each other and for the briefest of moments she thought she felt that spark, that force that had pulled them both together that night they'd met. But she'd been a different person then, hiding behind the green cat eye contact lenses and the black eyeliner that had covered both eyes like a large cat eye mask. He'd been attracted to her body, poured into the black catsuit he'd been so desperate to get her out of once they'd got back to his flat. Now she was the real Indigo, purple hair, different-coloured eyes, the tiniest of scars across her temple which she always covered up with her hair, starting to put on a little bit of weight thanks to their baby. He wouldn't be attracted to that package. But he was still staring at her.

Her mouth suddenly dry, she went to move back downstairs so she could get a drink.

'Indigo.'

She turned back to look at him.

'For the record, I don't think your eyes are freaky.'

Her heart leapt in her chest. 'You don't?'

He shook his head. 'Not at all.'

With that he disappeared inside his room and softly closed the door.

River lay in his bed, staring at the ceiling, his mind filled with the beautiful woman lying in bed on the floor above him. There had been many attractive women who'd wanted to help him get over his ex-wife in the last five years and he hadn't been interested in any of them, so why would Indigo be any different? She was beautiful, there was no denying that, but since he had no interest in a relationship with anyone, her looks should not be the thing that was keeping him awake. But he knew it wasn't that.

She was so familiar to him, but he didn't know why. How could he feel like he knew her when they'd never met? Their connection was so deep and strong that he could already imagine what making love to her would be like.

He swore under his breath.

She was his employee, he shouldn't be having thoughts

like that about her. She would be totally creeped out if she knew he was thinking of her in that way after meeting her only a few hours before, but he couldn't deny that need for her.

He shook his head and rolled over onto his side. He was tired and he was seeing things that simply weren't there. Tomorrow he'd find her somewhere else to stay until she could sort herself out with somewhere to live and then he'd avoid her after that. He didn't need that kind of complication in his life.

He closed his eyes and drifted off to sleep, dreaming of a woman with green cat eyes.

Indigo lay on the bed on the mezzanine level, staring at the twisted branches above her that made up her roof. She had to come up with a plan and she didn't know whether it was selfish or crazy but there was a part of her that wanted to hold off from telling River the truth about why she was there, just for a little while.

She had been so relieved to find out he was not only unmarried but single too. She couldn't bear to find out that he'd cheated on his wife or girlfriend with her. She hadn't come here with any hopes for any kind of happy ever after but she couldn't deny the connection between them. Even when she'd been pissed off at him, she'd felt a pull to him. That had been one thing she hadn't expected. And while he had made it clear he wasn't looking for a relationship right now, she wondered if it was worth holding back her secret to see if that spark that had exploded the night they'd met, the spark she'd still felt at meeting him again, was worth pursuing and whether it might unfold into something more.

If she told him now who she was, and that she was pregnant with his baby, then his attitude towards her would revolve around that. He would want to marry her, just like he had with Tierra's mum. Not because he loved her and wanted forever with her, just because marrying her was the proper thing to do. She didn't want that. She didn't want to marry for duty or responsibility. She didn't want to ruin his life with that. Maybe it was old-fashioned but she wanted to marry for love. It was possible that their connection was physical only and that wasn't something to base a marriage on either. If she kept quiet for the next few days, really got to know him, she could see if they had something more than just a sexual attraction.

Watching him with Tierra and Star made her realise he was a wonderful dad and she wanted him in her child's life in that capacity, regardless of whether they had nothing more in common than one amazing night. Even if nothing further happened between them, she wanted him to be a part of her child's life but, more than that, she wanted him to want that too.

She placed a hand over her belly. She wanted this child to be loved even if *she* never had that from him. And while she felt guilty for keeping her secret hidden and not being upfront with River, she had to act in the best interests of her child. He'd said he didn't want anyone else in his life other than Tierra, which meant he didn't want another child to upset the relationship he had with his daughter. If she told him now, he might resent her for ruining his perfect life and resent her child too. If they got to know each other, even on a friendship level, he might be more inclined to want to be part of their baby's life too, not out of duty but out of love.

She would give herself one week of getting to know him, one week to explore that spark, and then, regardless of what happened, she would tell him the truth.

Indigo woke from a restless sleep in the middle of the night. She could hear a noise and it sounded like someone was climbing up the ladder. She sat up but realised it wasn't the ladder to her mezzanine but the ladder up to the roof terrace. She watched as River climbed quietly to the top, lifted the roof hatch and then, just before he stepped outside, he glanced over in her direction.

'Oh sorry, I didn't wake you, did I?' River said, softly when he saw her sitting up.

'No, it's fine,' Indigo whispered back. 'I was having trouble sleeping anyway.'

He nodded. 'Me too.' He paused for a moment. 'You can come and join me if you want.'

She didn't need to be asked twice. This was exactly what she needed, time to get to know him properly. She scrambled out of bed and then tried to slow herself down so she didn't look too eager, but River was already climbing through the hatch and disappearing onto the roof.

She grabbed a hoodie and pulled it on over her pyjamas

and then climbed down one ladder and up the other to get to the roof.

River was waiting at the top and he offered out his hand to help her out onto the terrace. She took it and that familiar jolt shot through her at the feel of his hand against hers and, by the look on his face, he felt it too.

She stepped out and let out a little gasp. They were almost entirely surrounded by an incredible wall of magnolia flowers, large pink blooms twisted and curled around them, cutting them off from the outside world. They were at the very top of the tree here and above them was a canopy of stars, twinkling in the darkness. Nearby she could hear the gentle lapping of the waves on the sand. It was perfect.

'Oh, this is incredible,' Indigo said, softly.

There were two sunloungers in the middle of the wooden decking and a few ottomans dotted around the edge near the railing.

'I come up here to think sometimes, or if I can't sleep. It's peaceful,' River said, pulling a large furry blanket out of one of the ottomans and draping it around her shoulders. He gestured for her to sit down on one of the sunloungers and then went over to the main trunk of the tree and flicked a switch, so that suddenly hundreds of tiny fairy lights lit up the branches and flowers around them.

'River, this is so lovely. I bet Tierra loves it up here.'

'If it's warm enough, this is where I read her bedtime stories. She thinks it's magical.'

'I bet she does.'

Indigo sat down and River sat next to her.

'So I have to ask you something,' River said. Indigo's

heart leapt wondering what it could be. 'You seemed annoyed with me earlier yet now you're quite happy to keep me company.'

She cringed. 'That was a mistake too, I'm sorry.'

'Want to tell me why I was in your bad books when we'd only just met?'

She thought about it for a moment. 'I think that's something I could tell you in a few days when we know each other better.'

'Well now I'm intrigued.'

'I like to maintain an air of mystery.'

'You certainly have that. There's something about you that...' he trailed off.

'That?' she prompted.

He shook his head. 'Maybe I'll tell you in a few days.'

She smiled.

He lay down, stretching out his long legs across the sunbed, putting his arms behind his head and staring up at the stars. Indigo lay down too, getting herself comfortable. Tierra was right, it was magical. The stars stretched out for miles above them, some bright, some faint.

'It's so beautiful,' Indigo said.

'It is. Coming up here helps me to put things into perspective sometimes. Billions of stars, planets from distant galaxies, maybe some of them are inhabited just like here. It makes me feel small in the grand scheme of things, it makes my problems seem small too. There are millions of people all beneath this diamond sky, their lives intertwining, some fleetingly, some connected forever. I imagine most of them have problems bigger than mine.'

She looked at him. 'That's very deep.'

'Sorry.'

'Don't apologise. I like it. And you're right, there is a whole world of people out there with their own complicated and messy lives. But just because your problems, in your opinion, are not as big as other people's problems, doesn't make yours any less valid.'

'Hmm.' He didn't sound convinced.

They were silent for a while contemplating the sparkling vista above them.

'Do you want to talk about it?' Indigo offered gently.

There was a pause as he stared at the stars and Indigo presumed that he didn't. But then he spoke.

'Meadow, who is definitely not my wife,' he gave her a smile. 'Is convinced we all have our one person, The One, which is ridiculous when you think about it. One person who we are connected to in such a way that it's like finding the other half of your heart. Your soul mate. That's stupid, right?'

She thought about it for a moment. She had met thousands of people in her job and throughout her life and it was hard to believe there had only ever been one she had felt so inexplicably tied to. However, one moment in time had changed her life forever and not just because of the baby she carried, but because of the connection she'd felt that night, the connection that still crackled in the air between them now. She glanced across at him. He had to feel that too.

He must have sensed her watching him because he suddenly turned his head to look at her, his eyes locking with hers in a way that made her stomach clench with need. He quickly glanced away, letting out a heavy sigh.

'Have you ever met someone that you feel like you know when you've only just met?'

Her heart leapt, her breath catching in her throat. 'Once.'

He was silent for a moment. 'Twice for me. The first one was a few months ago, the second one was… a lot more recent.'

Oh god, was he talking about her? Were both incidents her?

'It's the weirdest feeling,' River went on. 'Knowing when you meet that person for the first time that they are going to change your life so completely and there is nothing you can do to stop it.'

Her heart sank a little. 'That sounds like a bad thing.'

'Definitely not a bad thing. Change doesn't necessarily mean something bad. Just that life is going to be different. Tierra changed everything in my life but she is the best thing that ever happened to me. I think change can be a good thing, if you're brave enough to follow it.'

Her heart was racing, thundering against her chest.

'What happened to the person you met?' River asked.

Indigo wasn't sure how to answer that question. 'It's… a work in progress.'

He turned to look at her again and for the longest time they didn't speak, a thousand words unspoken. It felt like there was a bridge between them and neither one of them wanted to take that step to cross it.

He let out a heavy sigh. 'Tell me more about yourself.'

They clearly were not going to talk about this connection but Indigo didn't know what to say to him about it either so she decided to let it go for now.

He looked at her. 'Indigo is an unusual name. Do you have other rainbow-coloured siblings?'

She frowned slightly. It had almost seemed like he was talking about that night they'd met a few moments before but yet he couldn't even remember her name.

'I suppose Indigo is quite unusual,' she agreed. 'Ever met anyone with that name before?'

'No, I would definitely remember that.'

She sighed. Maybe Violet was right. She wouldn't normally introduce herself to a stranger as Indy but maybe she'd felt so relaxed around him that it had come naturally.

'I think my parents were embracing their hippy side when they named us. I have an older sister called Violet and a younger brother called Blue. Well I did. He changed his name to Jake as soon as he was old enough.'

He laughed. 'That's amazing, although I bet you're glad that your parents didn't start from the other end of the rainbow.'

'Yes, well I would have been Orange which I'm not sure is as easy to carry off. My brother would have been Yellow and he definitely isn't that. He wasn't even a Blue as it turned out.'

'So your parents didn't have any more rainbow-coloured children?'

'Oh, well Mum had a few miscarriages after Blue and I think she stopped trying. Dad died a few years later. There was no one for my mum after that, so we didn't get to make a full rainbow.'

'I'm sorry.'

'It's OK. I don't really have any memories of him. Although from what I've heard he was a wonderful man.'

'And your mum, how did she cope being on her own – with parenting, I mean?'

'She did an amazing job, we were very close growing up. She moved to Vancouver several years ago, so we don't get to see each other that often any more. What about your family?'

It was funny they hadn't really spoke about their families the night they'd met, they hadn't really talked about anything deep and personal at all, yet she'd still felt like they'd clicked in a way she'd never experienced before.

He was silent for a while. 'My parents divorced when I was eight. Neither of them had any interest in being a parent any more. The arguments before they left were not over who wanted custody of us more, they argued over who should take responsibility of us because neither of them wanted to. I think we reminded them of their ex-spouse and their life together, they didn't want that life any more so they didn't want us any more. We rarely saw them after that. Heath was six and Bear was only three years old so you can imagine what an unattractive package that was for anyone looking after us. Various unwilling relatives and friends came to watch over us in return for a few weeks by the sea; food and accommodation provided. We were raised by a long list of aunts, uncles and cousins. Our mum would turn up for a few days two or three times a year before swanning off again, and we saw our dad even less than that.'

Indigo stared at him, her heart breaking for him.

'And then, weirdly, after several years apart they got back together again and continued to live the life away from us that they had enjoyed for all the time they were divorced. And we couldn't help but feel really crappy about that. It wasn't their differences that drove them apart in the first place, it was us.'

'You can't think like that. I think them divorcing was very much their messed-up issues and had nothing to do with you three. I'm so sorry you grew up feeling unwanted and unloved.'

He tried to shrug it off but then he sighed. 'It wasn't easy, I'm not going to lie. And in a way, it shaped who I am now. My relationships with women, or rather the lack of them. I have never had a serious relationship before. I don't count Danielle; we married for the sake of Tierra, not out of love or even like for each other. But I suppose, in some way, my upbringing had a positive impact too. When Tierra was born I was determined she would never ever feel the way I did as a child, that there would not be a day go by that I didn't tell her how much I love her. I wanted to be the dad that I never had.'

'I think it's very obvious that you're an amazing dad. I was watching you today with the girls and you were incredible with them, so patient and kind. It's clear they absolutely adore you.'

He was quiet again, staring at the crystal-filled sky. But then he spoke. 'Thank you for saying that.'

'It's the truth.'

'You're very easy to talk to. I don't know why I feel the need to spill my darkest innermost secrets when I'm with you. It's not really appropriate since I'm your boss.'

She paused before speaking. 'No, but… maybe we can be friends too.'

He thought about that for the longest time. 'I'd really like that.'

She smiled and they sat there in companionable silence for a while, watching the stars twinkling, the occasional plane or satellite zooming across the sky, and, much closer to them, they were also joined by a few bats.

'I think I better get back to bed,' River said, standing up. 'Tierra will be up in a few hours.'

Indigo stood up too. 'I better go to sleep too, big day tomorrow, or rather today. First day in my new job.'

'I'm sure you'll do amazingly. I'll go down first. Will you be OK to close the hatch?'

'I think so,' Indigo said.

River quickly manoeuvred himself over the ladder and climbed halfway down, then stopped to wait for her, which she thought was sweet.

She carefully climbed down the ladder a bit then reached over to pull the hatch closed. She made her way down the ladder and goosebumps erupted across her skin when River made it to the bottom and put a guiding hand on her back to help her safely down the last few rungs.

She turned round to face him and realised he was standing really close.

'Sorry, I'm used to guiding Tierra down like that.'

'It's OK, but I'm probably big enough to manage the ladder on my own.'

He grinned and she loved the sight of it.

They stared at each other and that connection, that pull to him, crackled in the air between them.

'Goodnight Indigo,' River said quietly, although he didn't make any move away from her.

'River, I... I hope this person brings the kind of change you want.'

'I've got a funny feeling she will.'

He stared at her for a moment or two longer and then, giving her a smile, he went back into his own room and shut the door.

She couldn't help smiling as she climbed the ladder and got back into bed because she suddenly had a tiny glimmer of hope.

CHAPTER FOUR

River was in the restaurant the next day eating his breakfast, Tierra sitting next to him eating her Rice Krispies as she drew a picture of the newt. Meadow and Star were opposite him talking to his youngest brother Bear. There was hardly anyone else in the restaurant as it was still so early, most of the guests didn't come down to breakfast until much later, if they came at all. A lot of them preferred to keep themselves to themselves and the couples liked to enjoy the romance of staying in the treehouse without the need to leave it.

River had barely said a word since he'd walked into the restaurant, his mind filled with Indigo.

She'd been fast asleep when he and Tierra had left for breakfast that morning so he'd gone up to the mezzanine level to leave her a note and been struck by how lovely she looked while she slept. He rubbed his face now, trying to dispel that image of her purple hair splayed out over her pillow, her long eyelashes casting shadows over her pale cheeks. He'd been at the top of the ladder for only a few seconds and that image was already imprinted on his brain.

His gran, who turned up at the park three or four times a week to wreak havoc over her grandsons' lives, insisted she had the gift of foresight and, while he refused to believe in such things, she'd been right more times than she'd been wrong. He wondered sometimes – if such an ability actually existed – whether he had inherited part of it. Because right now he couldn't escape the feeling that his life was about to change, that he was standing at a cross-roads and his life could go one of two ways – that things could continue exactly as they were right now or they could change beyond all recognition – and he knew that Indigo was the catalyst.

His brother Heath strolled into the room looking happy and relaxed. He and Bear were so similar in many ways, even when it came to their taste in women. Heath was definitely the more chilled out of the two, so laid-back he was practically horizontal.

Heath kissed both Meadow and Star on the cheek. 'How are my two favourite girls this morning?'

For two people going through divorce proceedings, River was always surprised how well Heath and Meadow got on. There was never any animosity between them, they were best friends, and River knew they always would be. They just didn't love each other, and apparently never had.

Heath had been nineteen and Meadow only seventeen when she'd fallen pregnant with his child, which had been odd to River at the time. Although Heath had a reputation for sleeping with any woman with a pulse, River never realised he'd turned his attention to Meadow, their childhood best friend. Heath had married her immediately, without question. He'd taken her on a two-week camping holiday to Scotland and they'd come back married and raised Star together.

A few years before they'd decided to separate, still very much there for Star but living their own lives, and now they were ploughing ahead with a divorce, which they both seemed really happy with. Heath and Meadow lived in treehouses next door to each other with a rope bridge between the two houses. There was no schedule, where Heath would have Star every Tuesday and Thursday or at weekends. Star switched between the two houses quite happily, staying with Heath some nights and Meadow other nights, just wherever took her fancy. They'd all have dinner together some nights, breakfast together most days. And, while it was an unconventional way of living, it worked. Star knew she was loved completely by her parents and everyone was happy.

Except Bear.

Bear had secretly been in love with Meadow for pretty much his entire life and had been gutted when Heath had married her when Bear was just sixteen. And while, in the last few years, Meadow had been actively pushing Heath to start dating other women, seeing their marriage for the sham it was, Bear was secretly furious with Heath for treating Meadow with such little respect.

Although Heath was unaware of all this. Bear was a closed book and he'd never told anyone about his feelings for Meadow. But River knew. He was good at reading people, at seeing what was really there.

And that was why he got a feeling about Indigo, that she

was going to change his life completely and he wasn't sure he was happy about that.

'Dad, can I stay at yours tonight?' Star said.

'Of course.'

'I want to finish that book we're reading together.'

'*The Adventurers*, yes I want to see how that one ends myself.'

Heath and Star started talking about the book and Meadow leaned forward slightly to talk to River.

'What's your problem?' Meadow asked. 'You've been like a bear with a sore head all morning.'

'I'm fine,' River said.

'You're clearly not,' Bear said.

'What's up?' Heath said, catching on to what's going on.

'We had a mermaid stay with us last night,' Tierra said loudly, as she coloured in the newt.

'Indigo?' Meadow asked in surprise.

'Yes,' Tierra said, happily. 'Daddy told her he wasn't sharing his bed with her and that he didn't want another woman in his life.'

Heath's smile stretched from ear to ear. 'Well, this just got interesting.'

'Did she make a pass at you?' Meadow said, with a frown.

'No, it was a big misunderstanding, on both of our parts. She thought we were married so she was surprised not to see you in my bed.'

'Why was she in your bedroom in the first place?' Bear said.

'I was showing her around,' River said.

'Why was she in your treehouse?' Meadow asked.

'Because Tom found her sleeping in her car and came and told me. I could hardly leave her there. She had no place to stay.'

'Oh crap, of course. She said she'd lost her job and her flat. I should have realised she wouldn't have anywhere to sleep,' Meadow said.

'Who is this we're talking about?' Bear asked.

'New girl,' Heath said. 'Star told me all about her.'

'She and River were giving each other moony eyes in the woods yesterday,' Star giggled.

Bear snorted into his coffee.

'There were no moony eyes, I can assure you,' River said. 'But I need to find somewhere else for her tonight.'

'Did something happen between you two?' Meadow asked.

'No, nothing.' Apart from a connection so powerfully strong that he knew it was going to change his life.

'But you wanted something to happen,' Heath said, still grinning. 'And that's why you want her out.'

For someone who had no idea that his little brother had been secretly in love with his wife for the past seven years or more, Heath was very perceptive sometimes.

River didn't say anything but Heath gave a triumphant laugh. 'That's exactly it, isn't it? You're scared that if she stays you might try to—'

'Age appropriate,' Meadow quickly reminded her husband.

'You might try to horizontally get to know her better,' Heath quickly amended.

'No, that definitely isn't going to happen,' River said.

'Oh but she's got under your skin, hasn't she?' Heath

said, clearly not willing to let this go. 'I need to meet her if she's rattled you this much.'

'She's beautiful,' Tierra said, adding orange spots to her newt.

'Yes she is,' River said, trying to push away the image of Indigo lying in her bed. He felt like a creep for thinking of her in that way when she'd had no idea he was there. 'But it's more than that I feel like I know her, like we share this instant deep connection. We've only just met, how can I feel this way so quickly?'

'I haven't seen you get bothered by a woman before,' Bear said, and then grinned. 'Well, apart from Mindy.'

'Who's Mindy?' Tierra said as she gave the newt large purple eyes.

'Do you and Star want to go and see if there are any more strawberries?' River said. 'I think Alex might have put some more out.'

Tierra climbed down from the table at supersonic speed, practically running across the restaurant with Star hot on her heels. Alex roasted the strawberries for breakfast and the girls absolutely loved them.

Heath launched into Barry Manilow's song 'Mandy', switching the 'Mandy' lyrics for 'Mindy'.

'I thought it was her,' River said, quietly, when Heath had finished. 'For a moment yesterday when I met Indigo, I thought she was Mindy. They look so similar and Mindy used to work in a hotel too, though I can't remember if we discussed which hotel it was. But although my memories from that night are hazy, I do remember that underneath her cat eye make-up that looked like a black masquerade mask, Mindy had these startling green eyes. She was bold and confident too, whereas Indigo looked almost terrified when we first met. But there's something about Indigo that really reminds me of her.'

'Do you think it *is* her?' Meadow said, with a frown.

'And what, she gave me a fake name that night?' River said with disbelief.

'That's not that implausible,' Bear said. 'The women I've met through online dating, some of them give a fake name to start with as they don't want weirdo men stalking them online.'

'Or maybe she's given a fake name now,' Meadow said.

River shook his head. 'No, she seemed so genuine that night. Besides, Greta knows her, they worked together briefly at the Crystal Orb Hotel. I would think she'd know if Indigo wasn't her real name. But if she *was* Mindy, why wouldn't she tell me?'

'I don't know, the fact she thought we were married might be a good enough reason not to come out with it to start with,' Meadow said.

'But she knows now we're not.'

Although Indigo had only found that out the night before. He shook his head. No, she couldn't be.

'The annoying thing is, for that brief moment, I wanted it to be Mindy. And I know it's sad and pathetic that I'm still hung up on a woman who was clearly a one-night stand from over two months ago, especially when she ran away. I thought I was over it, but meeting Indigo for some reason brings all those memories back. Indigo reminds me of her, I think that's all this is and I'm feeling a connection that isn't really there.'

He felt like he was saying this to convince himself

rather than his brothers and his friend because what he felt for Indigo had no place being there at all. It certainly wasn't something he had any interest in pursuing.

'It's not sad,' Heath said, in a rare moment of seriousness. 'Four months ago if you'd told me I was going to have that connection with a woman, meet someone I could honestly imagine forever with, I'd have laughed you out the door, but now I know what that feels like. I know what it's like to meet someone who can change your life and how hard it is to let them go.'

River knew Heath was talking about Scarlet. He'd fallen for her hard after one incredible weekend. And then she'd found out he was married and wanted nothing more to do with him.

'Do you have to talk like that when you're sitting next to your wife?' Bear muttered.

Meadow laughed. 'Bear, I love you, I love your protectiveness, but I don't need you to fight my battles. Heath and I are friends and it's never been more than that. I would be delighted if he finally met someone he wanted to spend the rest of his life with. He deserves to be with someone wonderful. We should never have got married, and he shouldn't have to live like a monk for the rest of his life because he was kind enough to propose to me and I was silly enough to accept. We all deserve to be loved and I never gave him that, not in that way.'

Heath smiled with affection for her and, slinging an arm around her shoulders, he kissed her forehead. 'I never gave you that either. But I don't regret marrying you, not for one second. You gave me Star and a family and I will always be grateful for that. I want you to find someone amazing too, someone who will love you and Star completely. And then I'll give you away at your next wedding day with a big smile on my face.'

'Because you've finally got rid of the old ball and chain?' Meadow laughed.

'Because I know you'll finally be happy,' Heath said.

Meadow smiled. 'Although I'm not sure where I'll find anyone. Maybe *I* need to try online dating.'

'I don't like the sound of that,' Bear said.

'Why not?' she said.

'Because there are lot of weirdo men out there,' he said.

'You do online dating, you're not weird,' Meadow said.

'That's different. You deserve someone special. You're not going to find that online.'

'Well I'm not having much luck finding it offline either.'

River looked at his two brothers and Meadow. 'God, we're all a mess, aren't we? We're hardly good role models for our children.'

'I don't know about that,' Bear said. 'If you've done one thing right in your life, you three are amazing parents to Star and Tierra.'

'And you are a brilliant uncle to them,' Meadow said, leaning her head on Bear's shoulder.

River watched Bear blush.

'OK, enough of this mushy love fest,' River said. 'Is there anywhere I can stick Indigo? I would prefer not to project my complicated feelings for Mindy onto her and she's not looking for a relationship right now either, so this weird chemistry between us isn't going to go anywhere.'

'If it's not going anywhere then you have nothing to worry about, do you?' Meadow said, smiling sweetly.

'Getting involved with Indigo doesn't need to be a bad thing,' Heath said.

'Oh I think it would be,' River said.

'I don't think it would do any harm to see if you two have something beyond the echoes of your one-night stand with Mindy. Who knows, she could be your One,' Bear said, mischievously. 'And as Meadow said, we all deserve to be loved.'

River shook his head. 'You guys are the worst.' He turned to Meadow. 'Surely you don't want me to get involved with one of your employees?'

Meadow shrugged. 'I like Indigo, I think she'll be a great asset to our team. But in places like this, employees come and go all the time. If she gets involved with you and you break her heart and she leaves, I'll be a bit pissed off, but I can get a new employee the week after. Real love doesn't come around so easily.'

'This isn't love,' River said in exasperation because he knew at the heart of this interfering was not a desire to see him happily married but just a need to wind him up. He had no idea how to describe the feelings that had slammed into his stomach when he'd first laid eyes on Indigo, but he refused to believe it was love. 'What about Tierra? I can't just start a relationship with someone, I have to think about how this will impact on her.'

'We're not suggesting marriage, babies and happy ever after,' Meadow said. 'But apart from Mindy you've not been with a woman since your ex-wife left. Is the plan to stay celibate until Tierra's eighteen so she never gets to see you with a woman? That gives Tierra a wonderful example of how to conduct her own relationships. Why not have some fun, get to know her? I'm sure you can be discreet around Tierra and we are all happy to babysit if you need some alone time.'

Heath and Bear nodded their agreement.

'What is going on here? I'm not interested in having a relationship with Indigo, casual or otherwise.'

'Except you clearly are,' Bear said. 'Why else would you be getting so worked up?'

'I'm getting frustrated at all the weird matchmaking, nothing is going to happen between us.'

'Well, as it happens, there is nowhere else for her to sleep,' Meadow said, obviously enjoying his discomfort. 'Every treehouse is occupied, so it looks like she'll have to stay with you. So regardless of what you do or don't feel for her, be nice. She's been through a rough time lately and she doesn't need you taking your frustration out on her.'

River stared down at the breakfast he'd hardly touched. He couldn't help feeling that his decision at the crossroads was already being made for him. Change was in the air and he didn't like it.

Indigo woke up to another cloudless day and smiled to see the sun pouring through the little windows. She hadn't slept particularly well, so she was feeling tired this morning. But when she had slept, she'd had some wonderful dreams which she'd preferred not to have about her new boss.

She looked out the tiny window next to her bed. Through the branches of the magnolia she could see the bright streak of cobalt-blue sea no more than a few hundred yards away. It looked like a sheet of glass today, reflecting the fluffy white clouds like a mirror. She smiled, what a beautiful place to live. She rolled over and glanced down at the treehouse below her, everything made specifically to fit the walls of this kooky little home. She also noticed how quiet it was. Had she really slept through River and Tierra getting up and going out? She checked her watch, it was only half past seven. They really were early birds if they'd gone out already.

She noticed a piece of paper fluttering on the floor next to her bed and she reached out and grabbed it, reading the note River had left for her.

Indigo, there isn't much food in the house, so please come over to the restaurant and help yourself to breakfast. All staff eat for free so you don't need to worry about paying for it, I'll tell them to expect you. I'm sorry about last night, accusing you of wanting to share my bed. I don't know what you must think of me. And I'm sorry for telling you my life story. Rest assured things will be completely professional between us from now on. River

She frowned. He wasn't apologising, he was redrawing the boundaries between them. And she'd thought lots of things about River since discovering he wasn't married and none of them were bad. In fact, she was back to remembering that amazing, beautiful night with fond memories again.

Indigo got up, grabbed her soap bag and climbed down the ladder. She could clearly see Tierra and River's bedroom doors wide open and no one was inside. She walked into the bathroom and closed the door. A large shower head hung from the top of the room, but there was no cubicle or door partitioning the shower from the rest of the room. She cleaned her teeth and then stepped under the shower. The force of the water was invigorating and definitely woke her up.

She was just lathering her head with River's shampoo when the bathroom door opened and Tierra walked in, completely unfazed by Indigo's presence.

Indigo stood frozen in shock. Should she grab a towel? Although it was a bit too late for that.

The little girl picked up her toothbrush and started brushing her teeth, staring at Indigo with wide eyes.

Indigo cleared her throat. 'Morning.'

Tierra took her toothbrush out of her mouth to speak. 'Hello.'

'Are you supposed to be in here?'

Tierra looked at her as if she was stupid. It was Tierra's bathroom after all.

'Daddy sent me to clean my teeth. I always clean my teeth after breakfast.'

'Right, of course.' Indigo turned away, quickly washing the shampoo out of her hair.

'You have really big boobs,' Tierra said.

Indigo turned round in shock. She didn't think her breasts were particularly big. They weren't small and she supposed they were slightly bigger than average but she'd never had anyone point out her breast size before.

Suddenly she heard a thunder of feet and then River burst into the room with his hand clamped over his eyes.

71

Indigo yelped in shock and tried to cover herself.

'I'm so sorry, I had no idea you were in here when I sent her to clean her teeth.' He opened one eye to find Tierra and scooped her up. 'Let's finish those teeth in the kitchen, shall we. Indigo, I really am very sorry.'

He kept his eyes on the floor as he hurried out and Indigo heard them talking.

'Daddy! I can't clean my teeth in the kitchen, that's silly.'

'Well we can't clean them in there. Indigo is our guest and I'm sure she doesn't want people staring at her and talking about her boobs while she's having a shower.'

'Well she does have big boobs.'

'I know, but that kind of thing isn't appropriate to talk about.'

Their voices faded away and Indigo couldn't help but laugh. So much for complete professionalism.

She quickly finished her shower, went up to the mezzanine to get dressed, then moved down to the kitchen to join River and Tierra.

'Indigo, I'm so sorry. I thought you were still in bed. It was only when I heard you two talking that I realised what had happened. I'm sorry.'

'It's OK.'

'I'm sorry too,' Tierra said. 'I'm sorry for talking about your big boobs.'

Indigo suppressed a smile. 'It's OK.'

'Daddy says that you probably know they are big so don't need to be told they are big and that you might feel sad because I said they were big.'

Indigo turned a snort of laughter into a cough.

'Are you sad that you have big boobs?' Tierra went on.

'Tierra, this isn't helping,' River said and Indigo couldn't help noticing how red his cheeks had gone.

'No, I'm not sad,' she said. 'I suppose they are quite big.'

River deliberately looked away.

'And they bounce around when you move,' Tierra said.

'Tierra!' River said. 'I said we shouldn't talk about Indigo's boobs.'

'You said we shouldn't talk about it because it might make her sad but she's not sad so we can talk about it. And they do bounce, don't they, Indigo.'

Indigo fought back a bubble of laughter. 'Yes they do.'

'I'm sorry,' River said to Indigo. 'She's obsessed with bodies lately and how they are all different. She wanted to know all about my... ummm... body the other day.'

'Daddy has a willy,' Tierra said. 'Girls don't have willies.'

'No we don't,' Indigo said, trying her best not to laugh. River looked so uncomfortable, which was almost as amusing as the conversation.

'Meadow has small boobs,' Tierra went on.

'I think we should let Indigo go for breakfast,' River said.

'Yes I suppose she does,' Indigo said, deciding this conversation was way too amusing to miss it by going to breakfast. She could sit here and listen to Tierra inappropriately talk about breasts all day, especially as River clearly found it so excruciating.

'I like the big boobs better as they look more fun and bouncy,' Tierra said. 'Which kind of boobs do you like, Daddy?'

River made a strangled noise as he inspected the counter, focussing his attention on an imaginary stain. 'I think… all women are beautiful no matter what size their boobs are,' he said, awkwardly.

'Good answer,' Indigo said.

For the first time since this weird conversation started he looked at her and he suddenly couldn't help smiling himself.

'Are you OK with this?' River said.

'I'm more than OK with this. This is probably the funniest conversation I've ever had. I might actually be a little bit in love with your daughter.'

River's face lit up into a huge smile. 'I'm rather partial to her myself.'

Tierra suddenly threw herself at Indigo's legs, wrapping her arms around her and hugging her tight. 'I love you too.'

Indigo smiled and knelt down to return the hug. Life was so simple as a five year old, they gave their hugs and love away freely, they made an observation about someone's breasts and then they said it out loud because why the hell not.

'Your boobs are squishy too,' Tierra said.

Indigo nodded. 'Is that a good thing or bad thing?'

'Good I think, it's nice when I hug you. When I hug Daddy he's very hard.'

'Yes he is,' Indigo said, remembering the feel of River's rock-hard body against hers before suddenly realising that in her guise of Indigo, the employee, she wouldn't actually know what it would feel like to have his hard body pin her to the bed. She glanced up at River who was looking at her in confusion. 'I mean, I imagine that he is.'

'You imagine that I'm hard?' River asked.

'I meant that you don't have squishy boobs like me, so you're probably the opposite of squishy.'

God this had suddenly got awkward.

'Come and feel his chest, then you'll see,' Tierra said, grabbing Indigo's hand and almost dragging her over to River. She was surprisingly strong for a little girl.

'No, no, that's OK, I don't need to feel it.'

'Yes you do, then you'll see how hard it is,' Tierra explained in exasperation.

To Indigo's frustration, River was clearly finding the whole thing hilarious, watching Indigo with a big grin on his face. He was obviously not going to do anything to help her out.

'I don't think it would be appropriate to touch your daddy,' Indigo tried.

'I'm not sure what appro-priate means,' Tierra said, sounding it out carefully. 'Daddy said it when I was in the bathroom with you but it doesn't sound like fun.'

'It means that I shouldn't touch him, he's my boss and it isn't OK to touch my boss.'

'Daddy, you don't mind if Indigo touches your chest, do you?'

He grinned. 'Not at all.'

Indigo watched him; he was almost challenging her. Oh to hell with it, it wasn't like she hadn't touched him before.

She cocked an eyebrow to accept his challenge and placed a hand over his chest. A punch of desire slammed into her gut unexpectedly and she was surprised to see the smile slip from his face as his eyes darkened.

Shit. This wasn't supposed to happen. She wanted to see if she and River had something beyond lust and passion

75

but, within twenty-four hours of meeting him again, she had practically propositioned him the night before, well he had thought so, he'd seen her naked and now she was touching his chest and wanting to touch a hell of a lot more.

She took a definite step back.

'Well?' Tierra demanded.

Indigo cleared her throat. 'Yes, very hard.' Her voice came out rough and ragged.

'Now Daddy, you touch Indigo's boobs and see how squishy they are.'

'Absolutely not.' River said. 'And I've got work to do and so does Indigo, so let's leave her to get ready.'

With that, River scooped up a protesting Tierra and marched out the treehouse.

Indigo stared after them. It was only eight o'clock in the morning on her first day and already it was going swimmingly.

CHAPTER FIVE

Over breakfast, Indigo decided to send a few messages to keep her friends and family in the loop. She sent a brief explanation to her sister first, telling her that River wasn't married. She knew Violet would be at the bakery by now so would probably reply tonight or at lunch. Then she opened up the group chat with her friends and sent them a message too.

So, I haven't exactly told River yet about the baby. He didn't recognise me when I arrived, probably because I was dressed as a cat that night we met. He did however offer me a job, which I'm very grateful for and I'm going to spend the next few days getting to know him before I break the news.

'Morning.'

Indigo looked up to see Felix standing next to her table. Christ, had he seen her text about the baby? She quickly put the phone face down just in case. He was eating a piece of toast from a paper bag, a big smile on his face.

'Hi, do you want to join me?' Indigo asked.

He shook his head. 'No I have a ton of work to do this morning, so I'm going to eat on the go. You're here nice and early.'

'Oh… I… had heard all about Alex's wonderful breakfast, didn't want to miss that,' Indigo said, not wanting to share that she had spent the night in River's house, despite that it was completely innocent. A place like this with such a small number of staff, gossip would spread like wildfire.

'Ah that explains it,' Felix said, smiling as if he knew a big secret. 'That and I'm pretty sure I saw you coming out of River's treehouse this morning.'

She cursed under her breath.

'It wasn't like that. I didn't have anywhere to stay last night. River let me sleep in his spare room,' Indigo explained.

'Oh it's not my place to judge,' Felix said, giving her a wink. He walked off chuckling to himself.

Indigo sighed. Still, once her secret came out, the staff would have much juicier gossip to talk about.

She picked up her phone to see her friends had already responded to her text.

Joey had got in first. **Is lying to him such a good idea?**

Indigo replied, **It's not lying, it's just not revealing all the facts.**

Vicky was next to join the conversation. **What do you have to gain from not telling him the truth? Please don't tell me you have some silly rose-tinted idea that you're going to get a happy ending out of this?**

Indigo sighed. Vicky was one of those people who was painfully blunt to the point of being rude and hurtful. She was also the type of person Indigo would never have chosen as a friend. The year before she had slept with her engaged boss and then promptly married him at the ceremony where he was supposed to marry his former fiancée. It was all very underhand. Indigo had lost a lot of respect for her after that. Vicky also clearly hated married life, she was not a fan of the happy ever after. Joey had added her to the text group a few years before because she saw the good in everyone and because *poor* Vicky didn't have many friends at work. It was little wonder why.

We have a connection, I want to explore it, Indigo wrote.

Oh yes, I remember, love at first sight wasn't it? Indigo could practically hear the sarcasm through Vicky's message.

Why shouldn't Indy go after her happy ending? Etta wrote.

Perhaps she shouldn't get her hopes up for that, Tilly added. **Get to know him but don't skip ahead to the fairytale ending just yet.**

I hate to be the realist here, but he will hit the roof if you keep this from him. It's hardly going to endear you to him, Vicky typed. **And fairytale endings never happen. If you're lucky he might agree to pay child maintenance but in reality he probably won't want anything to do with you or your child.**

That's a bit harsh, Etta wrote.

But true, Vicky continued. **Having a baby will change his world. Why do you think he will welcome that change with open arms? He's going to resent you for it and the sooner you realise that and get rid of these Disney-style fantasies the better.**

Indigo chewed on a piece of toast. Her little bubble of excitement about how things could develop between her and River had well and truly popped.

I do think you should probably tell him sooner rather than later, Tilly agreed.

Well, thanks for the encouragement, Indigo wrote.

We can blow smoke up your arse if you want or we can tell you the truth. This is not going to end up how you want it to end, Vicky typed.

Only you know what you and River shared, Joey wrote. **If you think he could be your happy ever after, then go for it**.

Indigo put her phone face down on the table and let out a heavy breath. Now she had so many more doubts running through her head. Maybe she should come clean with River. But him not knowing who she was added a complication to her problem that she hadn't even thought about before. She couldn't just blurt out that she was pregnant and he was the father, he'd think she'd lost the plot.

She looked at her watch. It would be time to start work soon. She would have to make a decision later.

'So this is our reservation system,' Meadow said, clicking an icon on the computer. 'Bear designed it so if there are ever any technical difficulties, he'll be able to fix it. If someone rings up to book a treehouse, you can click on the date they want and it will come up with which treehouses are available. The treehouses are all varying prices and we also have different prices at various times of the year, and sale prices too, so by clicking into that treehouse on that date it will tell you how much it is for that specific date. Also, here you can find out more information for each treehouse so if people haven't seen it online you can talk through with them what we offer. Our online booking system is synced with this too so as soon as someone books it online it will show as sold on here. You can also check someone in through here too. For example, today we're expecting Mr and Mrs Andrews, you can see that they are staying in Oak Tree Cottage, so you click on that booking to see all their details and at the bottom there is a check-in button. Once you click that you'll also be given a check-out option for when they leave. It's all very straightforward, but I'll be here to help you for the first few days.'

'It looks very similar to the system we used at the hotel,' Indigo said. 'Only better, more streamlined.'

Meadow smiled proudly. 'Bear is a bit of a genius when it comes to stuff like this. He created our website, our reservation system. He has done so many courses and training over the years, although a lot of it is self-taught. He has studied robotics, electrics, website design, social media marketing, computer game design, mobile phone app design. He loves tinkering and playing with anything like that. He actually helped a lot with all the electrics in the treehouses and the lighting around the resort, but his passion is creating websites and computer programs and apps. He's a bit of a geek when it comes to stuff like that but I love him for it.'

'Is he your husband?' Indigo said, noting the affection in her voice as Meadow spoke about him.

'Oh no, Heath is my husband, soon to be my ex-husband. I love him too, although not like that. We were never in love, we got married because Star was on the way. It was silly really, but I was so young and scared and Heath really was my knight in shining armour. In hindsight, I would never have married him, not because he isn't the loveliest bloke in the world but because it wasn't fair on him or me.'

'Would you have raised Star on your own?' Indigo asked. She wondered what that would be like. Raising her baby would be hard and infinitely better if she had a partner to share the load but she had to agree with Meadow, being in a loveless marriage was not something she wanted to be a part of. It sounded like Meadow had got lucky with Heath, and they'd made a good team raising Star together, but, even if he offered, Indigo didn't want to get married to River purely so she'd have someone to help her with her baby.

'Heath is my best friend and an amazing dad to Star, I wouldn't want to deprive Star of having him in her life, but yes I would have,' Meadow said. 'Love is an important part of marriage.'

'I agree.'

Meadow stared at her and then gave a little shake of the head. 'Sorry, I'm not sure why I went off on that tangent. You have a way about you that makes you very easy to talk to.'

Indigo smiled. River had said the same thing.

'I think that's going to be a great thing for our customers,' Meadow went on.

Indigo felt her face fall. 'Are you sure you don't want me

in a less customer-facing role? I might scare the children away.'

Meadow frowned. 'Your boss really did a number on you, didn't he? He shattered your confidence.'

Indigo scrolled through the different reservations so she wouldn't have to look at Meadow. 'I guess he was the main contributing factor to how I feel about myself, but my fiancé, ex-fiancé, probably started the ball rolling after the accident when he couldn't bear to even look at me. I didn't even have the eye thing then, that came later, but I had the scars. Six months after the accident, he broke up with me. Later, my eye started to change. My old boss wasn't the only one to make a comment on them, although his comments were the worst.'

'Arseholes,' Meadow said. 'You always get them no matter what you do, there will always be arseholes, bullies and bitches. The people who laugh at others for being overweight or underweight, or for not wearing the right clothes or shoes. The kids at school who tease the super smart kids, poor Bear got a ton of that growing up. You could be the most beautiful woman in the world and people would still hate on you for being too beautiful. It's jealousy, small-mindedness, or an egocentric immaturity whereby anything different from them is fair game for abuse. Life is filled with arseholes. Fortunately, at least in my experience, the good people far outweigh the bad, but the bad ones are the ones who always stick in our minds. My friend is an author and she says she could have a thousand five-star reviews on one of her books but the review she will take to heart will be the only one-star review. Why do we give these people power over us, power to ruin our day or our lives?'

Indigo stared at her, but Meadow was clearly not finished.

'I think sometimes we are bad at giving compliments, especially to strangers. The amount of times I've seen a woman wearing a fabulous dress and I've wanted to tell her how great she looks but I haven't because it's weird right to go up to a stranger and say they look amazing. But imagine how that stranger would feel to get that compliment, how that small act could change their day for the better. So let me tell you now, you are very beautiful, and I'm not just saying that, you are. Your eyes don't make you ugly, they make you unique and that doesn't detract from your beauty, it adds to it.'

Indigo swallowed. 'Umm, thank you.'

'And I'm not the only one who thinks it,' Meadow said.

Indigo couldn't help but hope it was River who thought she was beautiful.

'Anyway I have to pop down to one of the treehouses,' Meadow said. 'So I'm going to leave you for a few minutes. If you get a call you can't handle or one of the guests comes in with a question you can't answer, you can call me on the walkie-talkie. Or Bear will be here shortly, you can ask him.'

'OK, sure.'

Meadow left and after a moment Indigo got up and wandered over to a painting on the wall and she smiled to see the initials 'RB' on this one too. The painting showed another sea scene, this time with heavy grey storm clouds and the white horses of the huge waves rolling in onto the shore. He definitely had a talent for this.

Suddenly a fabulous display of flowers walked into reception. It was so big she couldn't see the face of the person carrying it but, judging by how spectacular it was, she assumed it must be Greta.

She rushed forward to help her guide it down onto the table in the corner and then Greta emerged from the foliage.

'Greta, this is wonderful,' Indigo said, admiring the spring blooms of every colour.

'Thank you. All grown here in the wood so no carbon footprint on these.'

'No, I don't suppose there is.' Indigo stepped forward to sniff them, they smelt divine. 'That's certainly going to cheer up the place.'

Greta touched her on the arm. 'I'm so sorry about yesterday, mentioning the accident in front of everyone. I certainly didn't mean to make it awkward for you. I just wanted to offer my condolences but I could have done that at a more appropriate time.'

'It's fine,' Indigo said. 'I don't really talk about it often, people never really know how to act when you spill the whole sad story and it inevitably makes them feel awkward.'

'That's their problem not yours. Grief is horrible and it's not something you should lock away for the benefit of other people. Talking about it helps a little. I know it's been two years or more since it happened but it will always be with you. If you ever want to talk about it, I'm more than happy to listen.'

Indigo smiled at that genuine sign of compassion. 'Thank you.'

'Right, I better go, I need to put some flowers in one of the treehouses. Honeymooners arriving today so we need to make the place look extra special for them.'

Greta gave her a wave and disappeared out the door.

Indigo had been on her own for only a few minutes when a man walked in who looked like a younger, more carefree version of River.

'Hello, you must be Bear,' Indigo said, standing up to offer out her hand.

'I am,' Bear said, a big smile on his face as he took her hand and gave it a firm shake. 'And you must be Indigo, I've heard a lot about you.'

'Oh, that's… worrying.'

'All good, I assure you.' He glanced around. 'No Meadow?'

'She's just popped down to one of the treehouses.'

'Oh cool.' He sat down at one of the computers at the far end of the desk but swivelled his chair to face her. 'So tell me all about yourself, the good, the bad, the ugly.'

Indigo smiled. There was so much she could say, but leading with *I had a one-night stand with your brother two months before and now I'm pregnant with his baby* was probably not the kind of thing Bear wanted to hear.

'Well, I've worked in hotels all my life, I love to surf, paddleboard and swim in the sea so being here this close to the coast is a dream come true. I like to paint, I especially love pimping old furniture into something beautiful and colourful.'

'Ah, that's where the idea for the painting party came

from. You want to win this prize for yourself with your painting skills.'

Indigo laughed. 'I hadn't even thought of that. But I probably should take part, it was my idea after all. What else would you like to know about me?'

Bear studied her for a moment. 'Dogs or cats?'

'Oh, dogs.'

'Coffee or tea?'

'Tea, can't stand coffee.'

'Chocolate or crisps?'

'Oh there's a time and place for both.'

'Single or in a relationship?'

She smirked. 'Single.'

'Happily single or looking for love?'

She laughed. 'Bear, is this your way of asking me out?'

He laughed too. 'No, I'm not looking for a relationship right now. I've kind of had a run of bad dates. I'm just… getting the lie of the land. You know, just in case anyone asks about you, romantically, I can tell them you're not interested or you're open to suggestions.'

'You could have just asked me that rather than the whole interrogation thing.'

'Ah but it's interesting,' Bear said. 'I'm a cat man myself and I love coffee so I'm afraid we can never be together.'

She grinned. 'I will cry myself to sleep over a nice cup of tea.'

He dug a pager out of his pocket and put it on the desk next to him.

'What's the pager for?'

'I'm on call today, lifeboat crew. A lot of us volunteer round here, so I'm not actually on call that often, maybe twice a month. Nice day today though, so I'm unlikely to be needed.'

'Oh that's interesting.'

He smirked. 'Does that make me more attractive? Will you cry harder now over your cup of tea?'

'Sorry, no. It's the cat–dog divide, I'm afraid. It would never work.'

'Bugger. So? Happily single or…?' Bear said, clearly not letting this topic go.

Indigo wondered how to answer that question. In seven months' time she was going to be a mum to a baby who would need twenty-four-hour care. That hardly left a lot of room for a relationship with anyone else. But she was definitely open to seeing how things developed with River and she didn't want to close that door with Bear in case he told his brother she wasn't interested in a relationship.

'I… haven't been with someone for two years and my life is pretty complicated right now so a relationship wouldn't be easy, but if there was someone special who could… embrace those complications, I would definitely be open to that. But it would have to be someone really amazing.'

River would have to be pretty amazing to want to embrace her and her baby, to not just accept that life out of duty but *want* that life. As Vicky quite rightly said, an unexpected baby would upend his world. It was a big ask.

'I can understand that,' Bear said. 'You're not looking for something casual.'

'There is nothing casual about my… complications. But what about you?' Indigo quickly deflected before Bear started asking about her complications. 'You shouldn't give up on love just because you haven't had much luck finding it so far. I'm sure the perfect woman is out there for you.'

'I don't know. The kind of women I meet in bars, the ones only interested in one-night stands, are not interested in marriage, babies and forever.'

'Is that what you want?'

'With the right person, yes.'

'A lot of people find love online now,' Indigo said.

Bear pulled a face. 'I've tried that. I find a lot of women's profiles are less than truthful.' He studied her for a moment. 'Some even give fake names.'

'But I get that,' Indigo said. 'With Facebook, Twitter, Instagram, even Google, the whole of our lives are online now in a way that they weren't twenty years ago. You don't want to chat with someone online, find out he's some weirdo and then have him stalk you across social media for the rest of your life.'

'That's what I said to Meadow, too many weirdos out there.'

'Exactly.'

'So have you done the fake name thing?'

'I've never done online dating so no, but if I did I wouldn't pretend my name was Jenny, I'd just go by Painter Girl or Surfer Chick, something like that. So I'm not revealing all of my details but not lying about my name either.'

'Never given a fake name to someone you've met in a pub?' Bear said.

She shook her head. 'No, meeting someone face to face is different, you can't pretend you're a six-foot supermodel when you look like this. Besides, I think honesty is the best policy. There's no point pretending I like hiking up mountains to impress the other person because if they love hiking up mountains too I'm going to get found out pretty quickly, probably halfway up a mountain when I'm gasping for breath. And what's the point? If the man is looking for someone to hike up mountains with, and I pretend I like it but secretly I hate it, then I'm not really ticking that box for him. It's dishonest and it's not the best way to start a relationship.'

Except she wasn't being honest with River right now, about who she was or why she was really here. If they ever did have a relationship her lack of honesty was obviously going to be a problem.

'I think honesty is one of the most important things in any relationship,' Bear said and she knew he was right.

Just then a young man came into the reception and she leapt up to deal with him, glad of the distraction.

'Hello, can I help you?' Indigo said.

'Hi, I'm Kit Lewis. I'm staying in Lilac Cottage with my girlfriend Zoey and our dog Moonstone. We're here for the week and on the last night I'd like to propose and I was wondering if there was somewhere special or romantic nearby that I could take her.'

A proposal was right up Indigo's street, something romantic and incredible to help organise.

'I would love to help you with that but I'm new to the area myself. If you can come back and see me tomorrow, I promise I'll have a list of different options for you.'

'OK, sounds great,' Kit said.

'And if there is anything that Wishing Wood can do to

help the proposal run smoothly, we're happy to pull out all the stops for you.'

'Thank you. This place is incredible. You're very lucky to be working here.'

She smiled. 'I feel very lucky.'

~

River snatched his hand back in pain as he smacked his finger with the hammer instead of the nail he'd been aiming for. He swore and shook his hand to try to make the pain go away.

'Bloody hell,' Heath said. 'You're a liability today. Get your mind on the job before you cause yourself or someone else a serious injury.'

'I know, I just can't get my mind off Indigo, it's driving me mad.'

'The old River would just shag her and move on,' Heath said, hopping down from the roof of the new treehouse they were building.

'The old River is long gone. I'm trying to lead a respectable life, someone Tierra can look up to.'

'But I agree with Meadow, you can still be a good role model and not be celibate for the rest of your life. Give her a positive example of what a proper relationship should look like.'

'I don't think I can show her a good example of a relationship, I can't do that kind of thing. And I really need to find Indigo somewhere else to stay. Tierra walked in on her in the shower this morning. I had to go in there and get her out.'

Heath let out a bark of a laugh. 'I bet you did.'

'It wasn't like that.' Christ, he hoped Indigo didn't think he'd gone into the bathroom just so he could see her naked. 'I don't want her to be uncomfortable working here or around me. She needs her own space.'

'Why not put her in one of these?' Heath said, gesturing to the building site around them filled with half-finished treehouses. Then he smirked. 'Blossom Cottage is done.'

'No,' River said, firmly, which he knew was ridiculous.

The night he'd met Mindy they had chatted about lots of silly things but eventually he'd talked to her about the treehouse resort. She'd seemed genuinely interested in how it was done, the plans, the electrics, the plumbing. He'd started sketching out a few of the treehouses on napkins to show her the kind of thing they had here and then somehow they had ended up designing a treehouse together. They'd discussed what they would have where and how many levels it would have and he had come up with a detailed design that had taken several napkins. He'd drunkenly promised her he would build it for her. After she'd run away and he'd never seen her again he'd had no inclination to build it, but when he'd looked at the design a few weeks later, it had actually been really good. Blossom Cottage was Mindy's treehouse. And although he hadn't built it for her, it felt somewhat strange to let the woman he had some weird crush on stay in the treehouse Mindy had helped to design.

Heath smiled, clearly deliberately goading him and River had walked straight into it.

'Any reason why you don't want her to have that treehouse?' Heath asked innocently.

River cleared his throat. 'It's a family treehouse, it's too big for her.'

Heath nodded, clearly not believing that excuse for a second and River wondered if his brother was going to mock him any more but he obviously relented.

'Willow Cottage is nearly done,' Heath said. 'We need to fit the kitchen but she can eat in the main restaurant so she won't need to cook for herself. We have a bed and sofa in storage, we could put them in there this afternoon. All the electrics and plumbing are done. It's definitely liveable.'

'That's a brilliant idea,' River said, in relief. 'She can move in today or tomorrow.'

'Or you could just take Indigo on a date, what harm could it do?'

'Her old boss tried to blackmail her into having sex with him.'

'Christ.'

'Exactly. I want her to feel safe here. And you know what I'm like with women, I don't have a great track record in the relationship department. I don't want to do anything to hurt her.'

'I think... you have a kind heart, even though I'm sure you don't want anyone to know that, but I also think, from what I've heard from Meadow, that Indigo can probably take care of herself. You ask her out and she says no, it doesn't need to be a big deal.'

'Apart from how awkward things would be after that.'

'Is there something else going on here, apart from not wanting to be the creepy boss who hits on his employees? Is there another reason you don't want to take a chance with her?'

River sighed, taking a big drink of water as he looked out to sea. Tierra was a big part of it – not wanting her to see him with a string of different women – and the creepy boss thing was part of it too, but in his heart he knew it was more than that. He just didn't feel he had anything to give a relationship. His parents had left the first chance they got, shipping him and his brothers between family and friends who would quickly move them on to the next unwilling guardian after a few weeks. Their uncle Michael was the only one who looked after them for any length of time but even he largely kept himself to himself, letting the boys do their own thing. It was hard for River to believe he had any endearing qualities, certainly not enough to make someone fall in love with him. He had spent most of his life avoiding any kind of relationship because what was the point in falling in love with someone if they could never fall in love with him? But of course he was never going to say these things to Heath.

'You know, as far as dating advice goes, you wouldn't be my go-to guru,' River said. 'You don't have a long track record of successful relationships either.'

'I have a seven-year relationship under my belt, that has to stand for something,' Heath said, grabbing a few more roof tiles.

'I don't think living with your best friend can really count as any kind of real relationship.'

'Probably not,' Heath sighed, sadly.

River watched him. 'How is the divorce going?'

'Very smoothly, as you would imagine. It's not going to change us, Meadow will still be my best friend, Star will always be a big part of my life, they both will. It just means

I'll be officially allowed to date again without people being so judgy about it.'

'That's true. I certainly don't think Star will be any worse off for it.'

'I hope not. I think she knows I will always love her. I also have a responsibility to Star that she sees a proper relationship,' Heath said, meaningfully. 'Not this weird, separate-bedroom, separate-house arrangement and have her think that's what a real marriage is. I hope, one day, I can show her what real love is.'

'You've done that by showering her in love for the last seven years,' River said, deliberately not taking the hint. 'She will never grow up feeling unloved and unwanted like we did.'

'No, I made sure of that,' Heath said.

River turned his attention to the wooden frame he was building but he knew Heath was right. In reality he had been hiding behind his obligations to his daughter as a reason for not ever getting involved with a woman but he knew Tierra would be OK if she did. He would make sure of it.

CHAPTER SIX

Indigo was trawling through the website for Wishing Wood, trying to find her way around it while surreptitiously watching Meadow and Bear flirt with each other. There was definite chemistry there and she wondered why, if Heath and Meadow were divorcing, she and Bear didn't get together.

Just then Alex came in brandishing neatly wrapped foil parcels.

'Here's lunch,' she said, handing out the different parcels.

'Thank you so much,' Meadow said, eagerly. 'Alex makes the best sandwiches.'

Bear smelt his and groaned with appreciation.

Alex passed one to Indigo.

'Thank you, I was just thinking how hungry I am.'

'Can you take Heath and River's down to them too?' Alex said, handing over two more parcels.

'Oh sure,' Indigo said. She turned to Meadow. 'I'll be right back.'

'No rush, eat yours down there if you want, the woods are a lovely place to be this time of day.'

Indigo nodded and walked off into the woods, the green canopy of leaves swallowing her as she entered. It really was a beautiful place. Bristol was such a busy city with everyone rushing to get everywhere, faces she'd pass in the street and never see ever again. And for a while, probably since the accident, it had felt like she didn't belong there any more. But she'd had no idea where she did belong, either. She didn't know if Wishing Wood would become her new home, that largely depended on what happened with River, but she could see herself here. It was a different way of life, living among the trees, right next to the beach, it was slower, more peaceful, and she felt like she really needed some peace in her life right now.

She walked down to the area where the new treehouses were being built and stopped dead when she saw River at the bottom of one of the trees, sawing several pieces of wood, completely topless. He had the most incredible body, strong arms, muscular back and shoulder blades. He was smooth and tanned and had that wonderful tattoo of leaves that climbed up one of his arms like a vine. She had enjoyed tracing that when they'd made love. He had a smattering of hair under his belly button that disappeared into his jeans. She couldn't take her eyes off him.

Suddenly she realised she was being watched and she looked up to see another man, presumably Heath, grinning hugely at her reaction to his brother.

She blushed and quickly looked away.

'Lunch is up,' Heath said.

River turned around and smiled when he saw her. Her

heart leapt at that tiny thing, which was silly because he was probably just smiling about his lunch arriving.

'Hey Heath, this is Indigo Bloom, our new girl. Indigo, this is my brother Heath.'

'Hi Indy,' Heath said.

Indigo waved then turned her attention back to River who was suddenly frowning. He shook his head and then came over to her, taking two of the parcels. He turned and lobbed one up to Heath's waiting hands before turning back to her.

'Is that yours?' he gestured to the final parcel.

'Yes, I thought I might eat it in the woods, I saw picnic tables back there so…'

'You can eat it here if you want,' River pointed out a fallen tree. 'I could… join you. If you want?'

She smiled at him repeating himself. 'I'd like that.'

'Don't mind me,' Heath shouted down from the tree-house. 'I'll just sit up here and eat all by myself.'

Indigo laughed. 'You can join us if you want.'

'Nah, I'm only joking. Besides, I have work to do, unlike some people.'

Indigo watched River roll his eyes. Heath disappeared inside the treehouse and she could hear banging noises as he continued with his work.

She sat down next to River and felt the warmth of his body next to hers. He smelt amazing, all woody and manly and divine.

He opened the parcel. This was the perfect time to get to know him better but, after chatting with Bear earlier, there was only one thing she really wanted to say and that was to tell him the truth about who she was. Although it wasn't something she could really blurt out.

She opened her sandwich parcel, playing for time.

'This place is wonderful, I'm so excited I get to work here.'

'Thank you, it's been many years of hard work so I'm proud of how it's turned out.'

'Tell me, how did it all start?'

'Well that's a story,' River said, taking a bite of his sandwich and chewing thoughtfully for a moment.

She wondered what kind of story it was and whether he would tell it. There was so much she wanted to know about him. That night they'd met they'd talked about a lot of things: places in the world they'd been or would like to go, favourite TV shows or books. They'd talked a great deal about Wishing Wood too, spending time designing their dream treehouse. And while that had been fun to create they hadn't delved deep into any personal stuff and that was the kind of thing she wanted more of now.

River cleared his throat. 'When I was fifteen, Heath was thirteen and Bear was ten, our parents were killed in a car accident.'

'Oh my god, I'm so sorry,' Indigo said, immediately placing a hand on his arm. She hadn't expected that. 'You don't have to tell me any more if it's difficult.'

He stared down at her fingers on his skin. She quickly snatched her hand away, her cheeks turning a crimson red. 'Sorry, that was inappropriate.'

'It's OK and I don't mind telling you.'

'I know you weren't that close to your parents but I guess it still hurt when they were taken from you.'

'It's hard to miss what we never had. They were never there even when they were alive. But life did change for us after that. We lived in the nearby town and would spend a lot of time up here at my uncle Michael's place, playing in the woods and on the beaches over there before my parents died. When we were little, he built us a treehouse which was the most wonderful thing in the world. It was right on the clifftops, overlooking the sea, and we used to pretend we were pirates on a big boat, sailing the seven seas. We spent so many hours of fun up there.

'So when my parents died it seemed only natural that Michael would take us on so we could stay at the same school and our lives wouldn't be disrupted. Back then, he had a one-bedroom cottage and a huge field he let out for camping. There was a toilet and shower block and that was it. For two months, me and my brothers lived in a tent outside his house. It was funny really. Our parents left us quite a bit of money too and we ended up living in a tent. We'd have all our meals with him but other than that we were left to our own devices. It was the summer holidays so we spent our days playing in the woods and our nights under the stars. We loved it. I know it sounds callous that we were having so much fun after our parents died but they were people we didn't know; Michael went to more parents' evenings and school events than our parents did. And suddenly we had all this freedom to do what the hell we wanted rather than having some distant relative telling us what we could and couldn't do.'

Indigo smiled. 'I bet that was a very different lifestyle.'

'It was. Michael decided to build us a wooden lodge to live in, he was always good with his hands and had spent years being a carpenter. And we were able to help him. Me and Heath loved it, we were building our own home. Bear was always too busy tinkering with robots and his computer to have any interest in building stuff out of wood, but for me and Heath it gave us a lifelong passion for carpentry. Our house had a bathroom, kitchen, small lounge area and three very small separate bedrooms. Building that house taught us so much.'

He smiled as if he had such fond memories of that time.

'Well, once it was finished and we moved in, some of the campers expressed interest in staying in it too. It wasn't conventional-looking. Michael had never built a house before so it had this quirky charm that people liked. So me and Heath helped Michael build a second one which my uncle rented out throughout the year, and it was so popular we built a third lodge too. All three of them had that quirky, wonky look to them which made them unique, the guests loved them. Then my uncle had a bad fall and he couldn't build any more after that. But I had a dream that when I was old enough I was going to build a whole field full of little wooden huts for people to stay in. I'd spend hours drawing and designing them. I never thought Michael was using his land to its full potential and it could be so much more. Michael would listen to all my ideas but he never wanted to implement any of them, he was too stuck in his ways.'

Indigo took a bite of her sandwich while she listened.

'One day, I came across our old treehouse that we'd played in when we were small. It hadn't really survived the years but it sparked in me this wonderful idea. I started designing treehouses too, the wilder and wackier the better. I had no idea back then how we would go about fixing them to the trees, or the complications of adding plumbing and electrics to houses in the middle of the woods, but it was something I just couldn't let go. Michael would spend hours talking to me about how we could make it work and I could see it was something he was excited about too.'

Indigo watched River as he talked; it was obvious this was something he was passionate about.

'My uncle died when I was seventeen, left the park to me and my brothers. My grandparents moved over from Australia to look after us. We were three big lads by this point, practically falling over each other in our little lodge, so we each moved into one of the lodges Michael had built and just continued renting out the field as a campsite. But we'd get so many phone calls about renting out the lodges so it was always something I wanted to start doing again. Heath and I did carpentry courses at college and I went to university to study architecture too. Heath was as passionate about making this place work as I was and he loved the idea of turning this place into a treehouse resort, it was something we talked about all the time.'

He took another bite of his sandwich.

'When Star was born we decided we were going to build her a treehouse. This was the first time we'd built our own house from scratch. We made tons of mistakes but we learned quickly. This wasn't a house to live in though, we just wanted somewhere she could play. But immediately we started getting enquiries to stay in it. So with lots more trial and error we added a bathroom and bedrooms, plumbing and electrics and started hiring it out. Star was still only a baby by then so she had no idea we'd stolen her treehouse. Within weeks of sharing it on Facebook, we were fully booked for the whole year. So we built a second and a third and a fourth, each one bigger and better than the one before. We added luxuries like hot tubs, barbeques, slides and rope bridges and swings and we kept that wonky quirky charm that had appealed to so many people when my uncle built the lodges.'

'You fulfilled your dream,' Indigo said. 'There's a lot to be said for that.'

He nodded. 'I know it's silly, other people have far bigger and more sensible dreams. I wanted to make a wood filled with treehouses.'

'Why is it silly? It makes you happy, the girls clearly love growing up here. It makes the people who stay here happy too. And obviously it's profitable, or you wouldn't be pouring your time and money into making twenty more.'

'It is. We make our money back in a month of renting it out.'

'You should be very proud of what you've achieved here.'

'I am. That old expression of when life gives you lemons you make lemonade couldn't be more true. I never wanted children, I grew up without any parental role in my life and I doubted I had anything to offer a child. My life was a mess. I'd go out and get drunk every night and wake up most mornings with a random woman in my bed. I was not father material, at all. And then Tierra came along and she changed my life. Overnight I had to be this responsible adult. I wanted to be a better person, a role model. I took being a dad very seriously. I stopped going out to get drunk, I read all the parenting books, tried to be someone she could look up to. Making this place work for the girls was a priority. It wasn't just us three boys, eating Pot Noodles and living off toast any more. We had a family to support, we had to make it work for them. The girls have been firmly in our minds when designing these treehouses, we wanted to make the place magical for them. We added fairy lights everywhere, we made it look like fairy houses in the trees, not just wooden lodges. People love it.'

'I do too. And I might have only known you for a short time but I can tell you're an amazing dad.'

River looked away, awkwardly, and they ate in silence for a short while. He clearly didn't take compliments well.

'What about your dreams? What was the big plan for you?' he asked.

'I always wanted to own my own hotel,' Indigo said. 'My nan had one when I was little, not a huge one, it was probably more of a guest house, twelve bedrooms, only some of them were en-suite. I used to stay with her in the summer holidays and I loved it. People would come and go, some would be there for work, some would come on holiday. I loved getting these little glimpses into people's lives. I found it all so fascinating. I've worked in a hotel all my life, ever since I was fifteen, and, apart from the last few years when the hotel went under new management, I have loved every second of it. I've never quite had enough money to open up my own but dreams change. I think I could be very happy working here. It's so beautiful and I love working with people, new customers arriving every day, regulars coming back time and time again until they are like family. This place ticks all of those boxes for me.'

He smiled. 'All of our staff are like family here. If you stay you'll be part of our family too.'

She smiled. 'I like the sound of that.'

Except, if she really wanted to be part of his family, she had to be honest with him.

Just then a squirrel came running up, jumped up onto the log next to River and put one paw on his leg.

'Ah, this is Hope. I rescued her when she was only a day or so old. I found her on the ground not far from here and she was still blind, completely bald and fitted perfectly in the palm of my hand. I didn't think she would make it but she did. I raised her until she was old enough to fend for herself and then released her back into the wild. She comes to say hello most days. Last year she brought her babies along to meet me too.'

'Oh my god, River, that's incredible,' Indigo said.

He shrugged as if it wasn't a big deal.

'That must have been a lot of hard work.'

'It was a lot of research on what to do, what to feed her, when. She needed feeding every two hours to begin with. I even needed to help her go to the loo.'

She smiled, her heart filling for him. 'You're a wonderful man. Most people wouldn't have the patience to do something like that.'

River fished out a packet of nuts from his pocket and Hope moved gently onto his lap. He pulled a nut out and handed one to her and she sat on his lap and munched it. Indigo couldn't help but smile at that.

'Do you want to try and feed her? She might not come to you but she might,' River offered out the packet.

Indigo took the packet and pulled out a nut.

'Put it in your open palm for now,' River said.

Indigo leaned over towards River and Hope, holding out her nut.

Hope regarded her carefully for the longest time and River gently pushed Indigo's hand down so it was resting on his leg with the nut in the middle of her palm. His leg was solid muscle and she was very aware of how close she was to other parts of his body.

After a moment, Hope moved slowly forward and took the nut.

'Animals can tell when people are trustworthy and kind,' River said, watching her. 'I think people are rubbish at making those judgements but animals know instinctively. She trusts you.' He paused. 'I feel like I can trust you too.'

Indigo stared at River, his eyes locked on hers.

'River, you don't know me, you don't know who I am.'

'I feel like I know you. I know that sounds weird.'

She swallowed. 'It doesn't sound weird at all.'

He studied her face. 'Maybe we met in a former life.'

'Or this one and you just don't remember.'

His face clouded with confusion.

'I need to tell you something,' Indigo said, trying to find the right words to explain who she was when he clearly had no memory of her and maybe didn't even remember that night.

Just then there was a shout and a crash from the treehouse that Heath and River had been working at. Hope darted off into the bushes at the noise and River leapt up and ran towards the treehouse. Indigo quickly followed him, climbing up the wooden staircase to the decking on the upper level. They ran into one of the rooms where Heath was lying on his back groaning, evidently having fallen off a ladder.

'You stupid twat,' River said, running to his side. 'Why the hell are you going up a ladder when I'm not there to hold it for you?'

'You're not good at the tea and sympathy, are you?' Heath wheezed. 'I'm fine by the way.' He tried to get up.

'Don't move,' River said, holding him down. 'Where does it hurt?'

Heath groaned. 'Everywhere.'

Indigo knelt next to him. 'Shall I call an ambulance?'

'Thank you for the concern, Indigo.' Heath gave River a meaningful look. 'But I'm fine, a bit winded perhaps but I'm fine,' he said, rubbing his shoulder.

'You could have broken something,' River said. 'Like the floor or the shelf or the wall.'

Heath laughed, which turned into a cough and a groan. 'You're an ass.'

'OK, sit up, carefully,' River said and Indigo could see the concern for his brother in his eyes.

Heath sat up, gingerly, wincing as he did.

'I think we better get you checked out,' River said.

'I'm fine, we haven't got time to mess around going to doctors.'

'And as site manager and foreman, I'm not letting you go back to work until you've been seen by a doctor.'

'I'm not sure you have those credentials,' Heath grumbled as River helped him to his feet.

'Can I help?' Indigo said.

River put one arm around Heath and guided him to the stairs. 'No, it's fine, I've got it,' River said.

Indigo stared after them as they hobbled down the steps and disappeared into the trees with Heath bitching and moaning with every step.

CHAPTER SEVEN

Indigo was sitting at the reception desk, the door open letting the warm spring air drift in. Outside the sea was sparkling in the afternoon sun which she could look at all day and never get bored of it. River had returned with Heath an hour before and apparently Heath had only bruising to worry about but River had insisted he take the rest of the afternoon off. She felt a bit guilty. If River hadn't been having lunch with her, he would have been helping Heath and the accident wouldn't have happened. Although Heath wasn't too bothered by his injuries so she didn't feel too bad.

Bear was now helping River, and Meadow had left Indigo alone to go and collect the girls from school but, as everyone due to check in already had, she wasn't too worried. Meadow had said that if someone phoned with questions she couldn't answer, she was to take a message and Meadow would call them back. Indigo was using the time to make sure that wouldn't happen, reading up on every treehouse and getting used to the different prices so she would be ready to handle any call that came in.

She heard the roar before she saw what it was and she ventured from her spot behind the desk to watch a bright orange Lamborghini skid to a halt outside the reception. Indigo stared at it in surprise. The car didn't seem to fit inside this quiet little haven.

But her eyebrows shot up when the switchblade doors pointed up in the air and from the driver's seat a lady, probably in her seventies or eighties, emerged wearing leather trousers and a bright red satin blouse. Indigo also noticed the diamante six-inch heels too. Her silvery hair was long, almost to her bum. As entrances went, this was pretty dramatic.

But what was this lady doing here? Surely she had taken a wrong turn. Indigo couldn't imagine her staying in one of the treehouses, no matter how wonderful they were.

'Hello, can I help you?' Indigo said, trying to rearrange her shocked face into one of welcome and professionalism. She had dealt with many surprising customers in her time working in a hotel, this was no different. She stepped outside.

The lady fixed her with an astute gaze. 'Do you work here?'

'Yes.'

The lady stared at her some more, until it started to get a little uncomfortable. 'Well, that is interesting.' She offered out her hand. 'Amelia Morgan, and you are?'

Indigo could see this was a woman who didn't take any nonsense. 'Indigo Bloom.'

'Indigo.' Amelia rolled the name around on her tongue. 'Indigo Brookfield.'

'Bloom,' Indigo corrected. 'I'm not part of the Brookfield family.'

'Hmm, why do I get the impression you will be? Now, let's see who you're here for?' Amelia studied her face. 'Bear? Heath? River? Oh, it's River, now that is interesting.'

Christ, Indigo thought she'd remained completely impassive when Amelia had reeled off the names of the brothers, but clearly not. This woman would be hell to play poker with.

Indigo decided to try and divert her. She obviously knew River's family, she might even be a part of it herself.

'Are you here to see them? I can call them on the walkie-talkie if you want?' Indigo said.

'No need. They would have heard me arrive. And if you're someone important, River certainly won't want me speaking to you, filling your head with my nonsense, scaring you away. I'll give him one minute before he turns up. Oh, will you look at that. You must be someone *very* important.'

Indigo turned to see what Amelia was looking at and, sure enough, River was striding out of the woods like a giant yeti.

'We better be quick, he'll tell me off if he catches me. Have you slept with him yet?'

Indigo's eyes bulged out of her head. 'I, erm…'

'Oh, you have, this is very exciting. He doesn't do relationships, the only serious relationship he's ever had was that awful woman he was forced to marry because she'd got herself pregnant.'

'I think you'll find it takes two people to make someone pregnant,' Indigo said. 'You can't lay the blame purely on the woman's shoulders. Both parents have to take responsibility.'

'Oh, I wouldn't put it past Danielle to have got pregnant deliberately, she knew River and she also would have known that when he inherited this place there was quite a lot of money from his parents. She had nothing when she showed up here with a bun in the oven, expecting River to take care of her and then leaving him to raise Tierra alone. That woman knew nothing of responsibility.'

This conversation was depressing. Was that how everyone would look at Indigo when the truth came out, that she was some kind of gold digger looking for a free meal ticket? Would people think that she had got pregnant deliberately to trap River and ruin his life?

'Amelia, how lovely of you to drop by,' River said dryly, dropping a kiss on the lady's cheek.

'River, you're looking well. Some might even say happy, if that's even possible when it comes to you.'

River gave a small smile.

'Aren't you going to introduce me?' Amelia gestured to Indigo.

'I would have thought you'd have done that yourself since you've been talking to her for the last five minutes, but Indigo, this is my gran, Amelia, and this is Indigo, our new receptionist.'

'That's a very formal introduction for someone you're sleeping with,' Amelia said.

River's eyebrows shot up into his hair. 'I can assure you, nothing could be further from the truth.'

'That's not what Indigo said when I asked her.'

'I didn't say anything when you asked me if we'd slept together,' Indigo said. 'You came to your own conclusion.'

'The truth was in your eyes, dear.'

'I think what you saw in my eyes was shock at being asked that question by a complete stranger.'

'No, there was desire there, a memory of incredible sex.'

Indigo blushed as those amazing memories flooded her mind. She wondered if there would come a time when those recollections weren't so vividly wonderful.

'Look, there it is again,' Amelia said, triumphantly.

River was watching her with some confusion.

'There is nothing in my eyes,' Indigo said. 'I'm just embarrassed we're talking about this. River is my boss, there is nothing more to it than that.'

'Hmm.' Amelia was clearly not convinced. 'There is something going on here. If you haven't slept together yet, you will soon, it's obvious you're both crazy about each other. River, you want her, don't you?'

Indigo saw it. He could deny it all he wanted but the flash of desire and need that crashed into his eyes was clear as day. It made her feel warm inside. It didn't matter if nothing was going to happen between them, it didn't matter if River was actively avoiding relationships because of Tierra, and whether he would simply be their baby's father from a distance, he wanted her, and that knowledge gave rise to the most wonderful feeling in the world. It had been two years since anyone had looked at her like River was looking at her right now. He'd craved her that night they'd slept together, but he had been drunk and she had been hiding behind her cat make-up and green contact lenses. But it was very clear River wanted her just as she was, right now, and that made her heart soar.

'Amelia, this really isn't appropriate. Indigo is my employee and she has a right to come to work and not be sexually harassed by me or my meddling granny.'

'You silly boy, she would clearly be over the moon if you took her into the back office right now and made love to her on the desk.'

Holy shit. This conversation was uncomfortable, wonderful, awkward and hot as hell all at the same time. The thought of that was utterly delicious. God, what was wrong with her? Indigo had wanted to get to know River, see beyond that sexual attraction, but her horny baby hormones were taking over.

'Enough. I've got work to do and so has Indigo,' River said, sternly. 'Are you here to see the girls or just to make my staff feel really really uncomfortable?'

'Well, the girls were the main point of the visit, closely followed by seeing my favourite grandsons, but I certainly couldn't pass up an opportunity to interrogate your new girlfriend.'

'Employee,' River quickly corrected.

'Oh come on, I haven't seen you interested in a woman for… well forever.'

'Amelia, can I have a word?' River said, cocking his head away from Indigo.

Amelia followed him a short distance away and Indigo watched as they talked quietly, then to her surprise they shook hands as if striking some kind of deal. Amelia then came back over to Indigo.

'Indigo, my dear, you have my fullest and most sincere

apologies for interfering in what is clearly none of my business. You have my word that I will not mention this ever again.'

Indigo stared at her. Where the hell had this complete U-turn come from?

Amelia went back to her car, whipped off her leather trousers to reveal a pair of tight, gold sparkly hot pants and legs to die for and then pulled out a pair of red diamante wellies, which she quickly changed into. With a wave of her hand and a flick of her silvery mane, she disappeared into the woods.

Indigo turned back to River.

He suddenly placed a hand on her shoulder, burning her skin with his touch. 'I'm so sorry about her. She's reached that age in her life when she has no boundaries. She says what she wants and to hell with the consequences. Normally, her inappropriateness is directed at us, but for some reason you've fallen under her cross-hairs. Christ, my daughter walks in on you while you're in the shower, we end up having a whole conversation about your breasts and now you've been subjected to my gran in the worst possible way. This is not the kind of first day I would want for you.'

She stared at him. He was so lovely and gentle. She had an overwhelming desire to step up to him, lean her head against his chest and just hug him, because there would be no greater feeling than being held by him. Well, apart from being pinned to the bed by him.

No, she had to stop thinking like that.

'What kind of first day would you have wanted for me?' Indigo said.

He frowned slightly and suddenly realised where his hand was. He quickly removed it, making her shoulder feel cold without his touch.

He cleared his throat. 'I'd want the kind of day that would make you want to stay.'

She swallowed. 'I'm not going anywhere.'

He nodded. 'Good.'

'What did you say to Amelia to make her stop her interrogation?'

'I made her a deal. I told her if she left you alone and stopped asking you all the inappropriate questions, and if she apologised to you for her behaviour, I promised that, if something did happen between us, I'd give her a very detailed blow-by-blow.'

Indigo felt her eyes widen. 'You promised her you'd tell her all the sordid details about our sex life?'

He cocked his head in confusion. 'But it's not going to happen, is it, me and you? I'm not going to pin you to the desk and make love to you like she wants. There will never be anything to tell. It's like promising her a slice of the moon, if I ever fly there. That's not actually going to happen either.'

Disappointment crashed through her. 'Of course not.' She forced a laugh. 'Good idea. I can't believe she fell for that, because of course nothing is going to happen between us.'

He was watching her, his frown deepening.

Of course he wouldn't want anything to happen between them, regardless of how much he wanted her. He had his daughter to think about and he was her boss, that could lead to a whole load of awkwardness between them.

'Well, I have work to do so I better get back to it,' Indigo said, breezily. 'Thanks for getting her off my back.'

She turned away and he snagged her arm. A thousand emotions crossed his face, indecision fighting with need.

Just then Meadow came running over and River quickly released her arm.

'Oh my god, I'm so sorry,' Meadow said, gesturing to the orange Lamborghini. 'Did she collar you?'

'Yes but it's OK, River took care of it,' Indigo said, turning to walk back into the reception.

'Indigo,' River stopped her.

She turned back to face him.

'What did you want to tell me earlier, before Heath threw himself off a ladder?'

She glanced at Meadow. Would everyone hate her when the truth came out? Would they believe, like Amelia did about Danielle, that she was only here for money or to trap River into marriage? Would Meadow be angry that she hadn't been entirely truthful with her about who she was?

'I... it was nothing,'

Meadow smiled and went inside the reception, obviously sensing there was something going on here or that Indigo wanted to say something in private, but her absence didn't make it any easier.

River gave her an encouraging nod.

'I...' she quickly changed her mind. 'I wanted to know, if you were going to propose to someone round here, where would you do it?'

He frowned. 'What?'

'One of the guests wants to propose to his girlfriend at

the end of the week and asked me for ideas for somewhere special he could do it. I said I'd research it for him.'

'Right, umm… I'm not really the romantic type. You're probably better off asking Meadow that question.'

'Come on, you love someone, you want to spend the rest of your life with that person, where would you pop the big question?'

He brushed his hand through his hair, looking around for inspiration.

'I live in one of the most beautiful places in the world and there are lots of places round here that would be considered romantic,' River said. 'Lilac Cove right over there is quiet and secluded. Tenby isn't far from here and the beaches there are wonderful and interesting because of the old walls that surround the town. We also have the beaches of Manorbier and Skrinkle Haven nearby which are lovely, and a bit further down the coast is Barafundle Bay which is just beautiful. It's a bit of a walk over the cliffs to get to it, but because of that not many people go there and the colours of the sea will make you think you're in the Mediterranean. You always find sea gooseberries there, washed up on the sand, these tiny balls of jelly that are iridescent like small rainbow crystals. I remember collecting loads of them in my little red bucket when I played there as a child, they were like these tiny seeds of magic on the beach.'

She couldn't help but smile as he talked with so much fondness for the place he lived.

'Church Door Cove is a spectacular and fascinating place to visit,' River went on. 'And there are lots of great restaurants if you wanted somewhere classy. There are many places here in the woods you could dress up with fairy lights or candles. We can certainly help with that. But, honestly, I don't think it's the place that's important as much as the words. If I was asking the woman I loved with all my heart to marry me, I'd be more worried about getting that right than anything else.'

She stared at him, a lump in her throat. 'What would you say?'

He looked surprised. 'If I was going to propose?'

'For research purposes, if you were going to propose to me, what would you say?'

His eyebrows shot up. 'You want me to propose to you?'

'Hypothetically of course.'

He cleared his throat. 'Well, I'd probably start by saying, "I know we haven't known each other for long."'

Indigo smiled, she loved him for going along with this. Just like when they'd created their dream treehouse together, it was a silly hypothetical treehouse but she'd loved that he'd gone along with it then too.

River stepped closer. 'But sometimes you just know, when you meet someone for the first time, that this is the person you're meant to be with for the rest of your life. I'd say, I know I haven't got a lot to offer—'

'And then I'd say you have plenty to offer, being a kind and wonderful man is just the tip of the iceberg.'

He stared at her for the longest time then looked down. 'I'd probably take your hand.' He reached out and took her hand, cradling it in his, rubbing his thumb over her wedding finger. The second his fingers wrapped round hers, she felt a jolt of something between them, an attraction so strong it felt like she could touch it. A hundred memories of that amazing night played through her mind, him pinning her to the wall as he made love to her, the way he'd touched her, the way he'd craved her. The best night of her entire life. A quick glance at his face showed he was experiencing that connection too. He might not remember that night in vivid technicolour like she did, but he'd certainly felt that spark. He was simply holding her hand and every nerve in her body was now standing to attention, finely attuned to him, his scent, his proximity, his warmth. Her heart was racing, goosebumps exploding all over her body.

He stared at her hand and he frowned slightly. She glanced down as he traced his thumb over a tiny scar on the side of her wrist. She'd got that in the car accident when her hand had gone through the window. It had healed a lot over the years and it now looked like a star. The night they'd met he'd kissed it and muttered something about making a wish on it.

He looked up at her and she could see the question in his eyes.

'And then I might tell you all the reasons I love you and say something like you'd make me the happiest man in the world if you'd be my wife,' River said, dropping her hand and taking a step back.

Did he know?

She cleared her throat. 'Well that's rather lovely.'

'And not a candle in sight.'

'I do think there should be a little bit of effort involved,' Indigo said.

'You'd want the bells and whistles?'

'I'd want a few candles at least.'

He nodded. 'I can stretch to that. Look, I better go, I have to sort out all the paints and brushes for this painting party that someone coerced me into.'

She grinned. 'Well, I'm going to paint as well. I thought it only fair.'

'Good, I'll see you then.'

He gave her a smile and a wave and headed back into the woods. She stared after him and he kept looking over his shoulder at her until he disappeared from view. It was then that she realised that Meadow was watching her from the reception doorway. Being subtle was definitely not one of Indigo's strongpoints.

River watched Bear climb up the steps to the treehouse where River was working. He'd been sorting out the electrics in one of the other treehouses for the last hour but now he'd come to give River a hand.

'What needs doing?' Bear said, looking around.

Bear wasn't the most natural carpenter, he had no real idea about building a treehouse as he was always doing stuff with computers, but he took direction really well. He also knew that they were behind on the all-important deadline. They had to have the treehouses finished in three months as that was when many guests had already booked to come and stay. It wasn't just the treehouses either but the area surrounding them, the paths, lights, and a whole load of rubbish to get rid of. With Heath off this afternoon and possibly for a few days, Bear would know that meant they'd be even more behind.

'You can cut those planks of wood in half.'

Bear picked up the tape measure and started measuring and marking the wood. 'I met your girl.'

'She's not my girl.'

'Well, either way, she seems lovely, fun, kind, I can see why you're taken with her. I asked her whether she'd ever given a fake name to someone in a pub and she said no. I believe her.'

'How did that come up in conversation?'

'I was subtle.'

River sighed at the meddling but he had to say out loud what had been playing on his mind for most of the day. A least with Bear, he wouldn't take the piss as much as Heath would.

'I don't think she did give a fake name. I think she gave the name Indy and I misheard.'

Bear stopped what he was doing. 'What?'

'It's her, I know it is. I know it's been two months and I know I was ridiculously drunk by the end of the night and I know she was dressed like a cat with a face half full of make-up but I know it's her. I can feel it.'

'You can feel it?' Bear said in disbelief.

'It's little things, her smile, her infectious laughter, her scent, and it would explain this irrational need for her. I remember how incredible we were together and how it was way more than just sex, and when I look at Indigo I get this feeling of wanting more. How can I want more if I've not had her in the first place? My body, my heart recognises her even if my mind is refusing to catch up. We have this affection for each other, this closeness that would only be there because of our past. I feel like I know her.'

'Are you sure?'

River sighed because he wasn't totally convinced he was right, but that was largely because Indigo hadn't said anything. 'Ninety percent sure, yeah. She has this scar on her wrist. I remember the scar from that night. I remember kissing it.'

'Lots of people have scars. It might look similar to Mindy's.'

'I know you're right.' River brushed his hand through his hair. 'Amelia asked her if we'd slept together.'

'Christ.'

'But she didn't deny it. Her instinct wasn't to say no as soon as she was asked.'

'What did she say?'

'She didn't say anything. If I asked you if you've slept with Meadow what would you say?'

Bear shrugged. 'No, obviously.'

'So why wouldn't Indigo deny it unless we had?'

'I think in a court of law, all of this would be circumstantial at best.'

'Yeah sadly, I don't have any DNA,' River said. 'I just have my gut and my gut says Indigo is the woman I met that night. As soon as I saw her here, I thought it was her but the purple hair, her eyes and the fact her name was Indigo threw me off, but I know it's her. What I don't know is why she is pretending we've never met and why she is here.'

'What are you going to do?'

'I don't know, get to know her, talk to her, gather the evidence and then strike.'

Bear frowned. 'What does strike involve? Do you mean

taking her back to bed and rekindling that spark? Because I don't think I can get on board for some revenge attack on her for running away.'

'Christ no, I don't want revenge. I want to know why she ran when we shared this incredible connection. And yes, there is a huge part of me that wants to make love to her again, to build on what we shared that night, to grab hold of this second chance and see if we have a future together.'

'If it is her.'

'Yes, if it is. But I also want to confront her about why she isn't being honest about who she is. That feels underhand to me, like she has some kind of agenda.'

'I like her,' Bear said.

River sighed. 'I do too. The woman I've been chatting to today and last night, I really like her, which makes it all the more confusing.' He checked his watch and glanced across to the wood where people were starting to gather near the most finished treehouses. 'I better go and kick off this painting party she's organised. Once you've finished that, can you go up to the loading area and bring down ten planks of the dark wood ready for tomorrow. Then we might as well call it quits for the night. And for god's sake don't climb any bloody ladders while I'm not here.'

Bear grinned. 'You got it.'

CHAPTER EIGHT

Indigo had been painting for about an hour. She'd painted the interior all cream and was now adding details like stars above the beds and flowers climbing up the walls in the main living areas.

There was a knock on the door and she turned round to see River standing there with his toolbox. 'Thought I'd come and give you a hand as all the other treehouses have teams of two or three painting them and you're in here on your own.'

'Is that so if we win you won't have to fork out on a meal voucher?'

He looked around. 'Oh you'll be getting the meal voucher if you win, this place looks fantastic.'

'Thank you.'

'Seriously, these flowers are wonderful. I'm not sure what I can contribute to this.'

'Are you not arty?'

'Not really.'

'But I've seen your paintings, they're wonderful.'

'That's nice of you to say, but they're just landscapes, that's quite easy to do. Just sea and clouds, nothing special. I couldn't paint an elephant or a tiger with any degree of accuracy. I certainly couldn't paint any flowers.'

Indigo thought he was playing down his skills but decided to let it go.

'You can paint the door frames.'

'Good idea.' River cracked open a tin of white gloss paint, dipped a brush in and got to work. 'I wanted to apologise again for Amelia's behaviour earlier.'

'It's OK.'

'It isn't. I'm actually horrified for you. We've all long got used to her meddling ways, but for her to turn her attention to you is not on. It won't happen again.'

Indigo focussed her attention on finishing a deep blue and purple rose.

'I think she has a way of seeing things, reading people,' Indigo said. 'I think sometimes we don't say the things that need to be said, too afraid of the reaction or the outcome, so we do nothing and then it's too late. A woman of her age and experience, I'm sure she has a few regrets, things she never said or did, and I guess she doesn't want her grandsons to make the same mistakes she has.'

There was silence from River but eventually he cleared his throat. 'I think you are giving her more grace than she deserves.'

They were silent for a while as they painted.

'Oh by the way, I have somewhere for you to stay. One of the new treehouses will be ready tonight. It just needs furniture now. You can move in there for however long you need so you can save some money for a deposit or for rent. The opening of the new treehouses isn't until the end of July, so you have three months before we start filling them with tourists.'

She turned to face him working next to her. He was giving her a house, for three months. And he'd just offered that to her as if offering her the last slice of pizza when it was a really big deal.

'You're offering me a treehouse?'

He nodded. 'It's not ideal, I know. The treehouse I have in mind, Willow Cottage, is quite small, perfect for a romantic weekend away, not great for living in full time, but it's the best I can do. Maybe when—'

'River, that's… that's incredibly generous. But I can't take that. If the treehouse is finished you could start renting it out straightaway, make some money on it. I can't give you any money for it, you'd be losing out massively by giving it to me.'

He shook his head. 'We can't rent it out until all the others are finished. No one wants to come here to this magical wood and stay in a building site. We'd need to finish all the pathways between the treehouses, add lights so people can get to the treehouses safely, clear away all the rubbish. Plus the noise down there during the day is not great for the tourists, there's banging and drilling, but you won't be in there during the day as you'll be working, so you'll only be sleeping in there. And I wouldn't want to take money from you in any case. You work for us. I'm not in the business of taking money from my staff.'

She stared at him. He was such a wonderful man. Christ, she could fall for him so easily.

'Thank you, that's so kind.'

He shrugged and turned his attention back to the door frame he was painting.

'You just have no idea what that means to me. I haven't had a job in six months, I had to leave my beloved little flat and move in with my sister because I had no money coming in. And now Meadow has offered me a job and you've offered me a home, which I know is temporary, but it feels like…'

She wanted to say that since meeting him her life had changed. That wonderful night she had felt desired and wanted for the first time in two years. He had given her her life back. Now there was a baby on the way, a baby she had wanted for so long. And to top it off she now had a job and a home. She couldn't help smiling about the way her life was turning out, all because of him. Admittedly, she might not have a job once the baby was born. She hadn't told Meadow she was pregnant and that might not go down well later, but right now things were looking good.

'You've taken a huge weight off my shoulders, thank you.'

'It's not a problem. You can't stay with me and be subjected to conversations about your boobs from my daughter every morning.'

She laughed. 'Tierra is amazing, I think I could talk to her every day and never get bored of it.'

He smiled. 'Thank you. She likes you too.' He stared at her for a few moments and then quickly turned his attention back to the door frame again. 'By the way, I bought a bottle of wine for you, for everyone, I mean. I figured everyone should get something for helping to paint even if they don't win.'

'Oh thanks,' she bit her lip. 'But I can't actually drink anything right now.'

At least she wouldn't for the next seven months and probably beyond that if she was breastfeeding.

He frowned. 'Oh?'

'I'm on medication,' Indigo quickly lied. 'But I'll take the wine for when I've come off it.'

'What kind of medication?'

What a tangled web we weave, Indigo thought. 'It's stuff for back pain.'

He seemed to accept this. 'I don't drink either.'

She knew this from the night they met but she wanted to push him on it. 'You don't drink at all?'

'No, I gave up alcohol five years ago when Tierra was born. It's funny how one tiny moment, when I held her in my arms for the first time, changed the rest of my life completely. The way she looked at me, I knew I could never ever let her down.'

'And you've never been tempted?'

'No, never. Before Tierra I'd be drunk in a pub or club every night, wake up with a different random woman every morning, feeling like crap. I wasn't a nice person when I was drunk. I didn't want her to be exposed to that kind of life.'

'So you've never touched a drop since?' She wondered if he would be honest about what happened just over two months before.

His face darkened. 'Not willingly. A few months ago I went to Bristol for a friend's birthday. I used to live there when I was doing my architectural studies and I still have a flat there. My friend, Ben, lives there and it was his thirtieth. I had no problem in going out for a few drinks with him. I'm not one of those people who can't be around alcohol. I'm not remotely tempted to drink ever again so I can go to pubs – I can drink lemonade or Coke and still have a good time with friends without the need for alcohol. One of Ben's friends saw things differently though. He spiked my drink without me knowing. Because I hadn't drunk anything for five years, I had next-to-zero tolerance for it. I got very drunk very quickly. One thing led to another and…' he trailed off, clearly embarrassed.

'You slept with another random woman.'

He looked at her. 'No. Well, I did sleep with her but Mindy wasn't just some random woman.'

Indigo felt the penny drop. He *had* misheard her. He thought her name was Mindy.

'She was incredible,' River said, his face filling with affection as he remembered her. 'We had this instant connection that I've never felt before.'

He did remember her, not what she looked like but he remembered that night. Indigo had thought she was just another face in the crowd for him but it was clear he'd felt that connection too. Unless it was just a physical attraction.

'You found her attractive?'

'No. Yes, she was very attractive. She was dressed like a cat, I remember that, and yes she looked amazing but that wasn't what attracted me to her. We just clicked, we talked so easily. It's ridiculous to say but as we sat there chatting for hours, for the first time in my life I felt like I had found someone I wanted forever with.'

Indigo swallowed a lump in her throat because she'd felt that too, this bond, this link between them that was almost a tangible thing you could reach out and touch, something solid and strong. Something that was way more than just a sexual attraction. It was deeper than that. Like suddenly realising you'd spent your entire life with a piece missing and turning around and finding it.

Then he'd got drunk, she'd taken him home, he'd kissed her and they'd ended up in bed together and she'd been left wondering if all they really had was a drunken night of passion with no longevity at all. She'd doubted what she'd felt. The next morning she'd convinced herself it had just been lust and great sex and nothing more. She'd told herself that River wouldn't want her when he saw who she really was. Love at first sight didn't really exist and she'd talked herself out of believing in that. It was better to run away with those wonderful memories than to wait around to be disappointed, and now it seemed she'd got it all wrong.

'What happened?' Indigo said quietly.

'I woke up the next morning and she was gone,' he looked gutted.

Christ, in all of this she hadn't once thought about how he would feel the next day. She had presumed it was a drunken one-night stand for him and he would quickly try to distance himself from it the next day. But it now seemed he had thought about her as much as she had about him in the last few months.

What the hell had she done? She should have stuck around, given them a chance, but instead she had panicked and ran. She could have missed out on something wonderful... No, he wouldn't have wanted that, not when Tierra was his whole world.

'What would you have done if you'd woken up and she was still there? You've already said you don't want another woman in your life because of Tierra.'

River let out a heavy breath. 'I've asked myself that a hundred times. Danielle, Tierra's mum, was a vile person and certainly not someone I wanted around Tierra. It was a huge relief when she left. I vowed then that I didn't want anyone else in my life. I wanted to protect Tierra from unsuitable women and believe me, I've been with a lot of unsuitable women. But Mindy was different. I don't know if it would have worked out between us or if she would even have wanted a relationship with a single father but, for the first time in five years, I had found someone I was willing to give it a go with.'

Indigo's mouth was bone dry, her heart was racing.

'The funny thing was, I thought she wanted that too. You know when you connect with someone so strongly that you just know they feel the same way too? That's how it was when we met but the next day she was gone and I can't help wondering why.'

She wanted to cry at the missed opportunity.

'You remind me of her,' River said, suddenly. 'I was so completely drunk that night and I only have snatched memories of her, and mostly it was the cat costume I remember and these vivid green eyes, but there's something about you that reminds me of her.'

Indigo suddenly felt like she was going to pass out, the room seemed like it was spinning, she felt dizzy, sick, weak. She'd had this a few weeks ago, before she'd known she was pregnant and again when she'd found out she was. Googling it suggested it was fairly common in pregnant women, although that didn't help when it happened.

'I don't feel so good,' Indigo muttered.

'Jesus, you've gone as white as a sheet,' River said, grabbing her by the shoulders and forcing her to sit down. He crouched in front of her, taking her hand. 'You're all clammy.' He wrapped his other hand round her wrist, taking her pulse. 'Your heart is racing.'

'I'm fine, probably just hungry.'

He grabbed his toolbox and fished out a Mars bar. 'I always carry snacks around with me. Mainly because Heath is always complaining he's hungry. Here, take this.'

She was already starting to feel better. But she took a bite of the Mars bar anyway.

'Was it something I said?' River asked.

She shook her head. 'No, it's just... I didn't sleep that well last night.'

'Neither did I.' His eyes locked with hers and she wondered if he'd been thinking of her in the same way she had of him. 'Your colour is coming back. Are you OK?'

'I'm feeling better now, thank you,' Indigo said, quietly.

He was still holding her hand and didn't seem in any rush to let it go. She couldn't believe he had such amazing memories of their time together. She'd thought she was one of many women he'd slept with, one he didn't even remember. She had such vivid memories of that night, not just the incredible sex they'd shared but that wonderful time they'd spent talking before he'd got so drunk he didn't know what he was doing. But as far as he was concerned that amazing night was with someone else. There was a huge part of her that wanted to explain everything, but if he knew who she was and that she was carrying his child it would change everything between them. She had wanted a few more days while he saw her as just Indigo, not the mother of his child who was going to ruin his life. She didn't want him to taint her with the same brush as Danielle.

'I'm sorry if it made you feel uncomfortable telling you about the best night of my entire life,' he said.

She stared at him. 'The best night of your life?'

'Well, yes, but it doesn't matter now. It's in the past. I'm never going to see her again.'

She swallowed, her heart racing. 'And if you did?'

'I'd want to know why she ran after what we shared. If it was something I could forgive, then I'd probably take her back to bed and make her forget about running away ever again.' He frowned. 'Christ, your pulse is skyrocketing.'

She cursed her treacherous body for betraying her. 'I'm OK. What would be forgivable for you?'

'I don't know. Maybe if she had to rush off to donate a kidney to a friend or relative in some life-saving surgery.'

'Right, of course,' Indigo said, swallowing down the disappointment. 'And what happens if it isn't forgivable?'

He let out a heavy breath. 'I honestly don't know. I'd like to say it doesn't matter but of course it does. I need someone reliable around Tierra, not someone who is going to run away at the first sign of trouble.'

'No, of course not.'

All hopes of a happy ending for her vanished in an instant. River would never forgive her. There was no point in holding out for a few more days, she wasn't going to get what she wanted out of this. She needed to stop hiding and tell him who she was.

'River, that night—'

Just then Tierra burst into the room followed by Meadow. Meadow stopped when she saw River crouching in front of Indigo, his hands still wrapped around hers.

'Everything OK in here?' Meadow said, looking between them in confusion.

'Indigo felt a bit faint,' River explained, standing up.

'What does faint mean?' Tierra said as he scooped her up.

'It means she didn't feel very well.'

'I'm OK,' Indigo said. 'Probably just a bit tired and hungry.'

She gestured feebly to the Mars bar and took another bite. What would Meadow think of her? She'd only been here a day and she was seemingly making a move on the boss already.

'Well, we've just been round the treehouses to choose the winner,' Meadow said, recovering herself quickly. 'Everyone has worked very hard. This place looks great, I love the flowers. But Tierra gets to choose the winner. Which one was your favourite?'

'This one,' Tierra said, beaming a big toothy grin at her dad.

Indigo smiled at her loyalty.

'Where's Star?' River said. 'I thought she was going to help choose the winner too, which might have given a bit more of a balanced view.'

'Looking after Heath. She's wearing her nurse costume and when I left them she was taking his temperature and looking in his ears. Are you sure this is your favourite?' Meadow asked Tierra. 'I thought you liked the sea that Felix had painted.'

'I did but I like the flowers and the stars more.'

'OK then,' Meadow nodded. 'Looks like the winners of the romantic meal for two are River and Indigo.'

'Oh no, this is all Indigo, I can't take any credit for this,' River said. 'I'm sure she can find someone else to take.'

Indigo shook her head. 'Honestly, I've enjoyed doing this, I didn't do it for the prize. Give it to someone else.'

'No, you have to have it.' Tierra looked most affronted.

'OK, thanks,' Indigo said, awkwardly. She glanced at River who looked away. 'And I don't mind eating alone. I can take a good book. Right, I think I might get my stuff and move into Willow Cottage.'

'It's not ready yet. I just need to get some of the boys to move the furniture. It will be ready tonight,' River said.

'OK then, I'm going to go back to Magnolia Cottage and have a lie-down.'

Meadow and River were exchanging looks which Indigo couldn't interpret as she made a move to walk out. She wanted to be away from him right now, if only so she could gather her thoughts and maybe have a little cry by herself.

But River snagged her arm. 'Sleep in my bed, I don't want you climbing ladders while you're not feeling well.'

She chanced a look at Meadow because there was something hugely intimate about her sleeping in his bed. Judging by the expression on her face, Meadow clearly thought so too.

'I'm fine.'

'Please. Enough people have fallen off ladders today.'

She nodded and he let her go and she stepped outside into the warm spring evening.

It was ridiculous to feel disappointed that nothing was going to happen between them, she hadn't come here hoping for that, but seeing him again had brought all those feelings back to the surface. They shared a connection and after that silly hypothetical proposal earlier that day, she'd already imagined what it would be like to have a rose-tinted happy ending with him. But that was never going to happen now. He wasn't going to forgive her for running away and he probably wasn't going to be too happy when she came clean about who she was.

She climbed the steps up to Magnolia Cottage.

She had hurt him. That was the worst thing about all of this and she hated herself for that. He was a wonderful man and he deserved so much better than that.

She knew she finally had to tell him the truth about who she was. If that went well, she'd tell him about the baby too. If it didn't she'd hold off on that a bit longer.

She slipped off her shoes and climbed the stairs that led up to the bedrooms, letting herself into River's room. It felt strange being here without him. She pulled back the covers and climbed into bed. It smelt of him and that gave her a pang of desire and regret.

She closed her eyes and, surrounded by his scent, she immediately drifted off to sleep.

River watched Tierra splashing in puddles as they made their way back through the woods.

'What the hell is going on?' Meadow said when Tierra was suitably far enough away.

'It's her,' River said.

'Who?'

'Mindy. Or should I say Indy. I clearly misheard her name that night. Indigo is the woman I met that night. Indigo is the woman I shared a connection with like I've never felt before. She is the woman I took back to my flat and made love to three times. It's her.'

'Seriously? Are you sure?'

'One hundred percent. I wasn't sure before and I've spent the whole day today second-guessing myself, convincing myself she is, convincing myself she isn't. Now I know. You should have seen her face when I started talking about that night and how incredible it was.'

'If she has a crush on you, then you talking about how amazing another woman is would certainly provoke a strong reaction.'

'No, it wasn't that. She knew I was talking about her.'

'Are you playing games with her?'

'No, I genuinely didn't realise when we first met yesterday. I thought it was her but then disregarded it. But as I've spent time with her today I started to think I might have been right. And I thought, let's talk about the elephant in the room. I knew if I started talking about that night, it would become clear very quickly if I was wrong and it wasn't her. Fortunately, it became very obvious I was right. I just don't know why she's not said anything. Even if she only came here for a job and not for me, you'd think she'd go, *Hey, not sure if you remember but we slept together two months ago.'*

'Not if she didn't think you remembered her. If she came here because she regretted running away and wanted to see if you were prepared to give things another go and you clearly didn't recognise her, if I was in her shoes, I wouldn't humiliate myself by going, *Hey, remember me*, to then have you go, *No, not really.'*

River sighed. Meadow was right. Indigo had been shocked to hear he had remembered that night. She clearly thought he didn't and she hadn't realised he would have such amazing memories of it. She'd obviously thought it was a one-night stand, at least for him. He wasn't sure about her feelings about the night but she had been visibly upset when he'd said he wasn't sure he could forgive her.

'What are you going to do?' Meadow said.

'I don't know. I've never stopped thinking about her. I built Blossom Cottage for her, for crying out loud. I've thought so often about what would happen if I saw her again and here she is. It feels like I've been given this wonderful second chance. But I'm frustrated and confused about why we aren't talking about that night, why she's pretending it didn't happen when there's still clearly an attraction between us. And I'm still upset that she ran away without talking to me or explaining why, that she threw away what we had when it was so special – at least it was for me – and I don't know if I can get past that.'

He picked up a sweet wrapper lying on the path and put it in his pocket.

'So I'm going to go home, make her some dinner and

maybe when Tierra has gone to bed we can finally talk about all of this.'

'I think that's probably best,' Meadow said. 'I'm sure she's not trying to deceive you. I'm sure, with you waiting for her to say something, and her maybe waiting for you to say something, it's probably been a big old misunderstanding.'

'You're probably right.'

'Look, this is important. Why don't I take Tierra tonight so you two can get this out in the open once and for all?'

'That would be great.'

'I'm probably going to have Star anyway, even though she was supposed to be at Heath's tonight, but I think Heath will probably be grateful for a bit of quiet so he can rest and recover.'

'Thank you, that would be a massive help.'

River looked up at Magnolia Cottage as he drew near. Now all he had to do was figure out what to say to Indigo.

CHAPTER NINE

'What are you doing, Dad?' Tierra asked, appearing behind him carrying her favourite cuddly dinosaur.

'I'm preparing a nice meal for Indigo,' River said, lifting her onto the counter next to him.

'Why?'

He sliced a potato as he thought. He had always tried to be honest with Tierra, as much as he possibly could.

'Because... I want to talk to her about something important.'

'Is it a date?'

He paused in his chopping. 'What makes you say that?'

'Because Star says you fancy her and when I came to see the painted treehouses this afternoon you were holding her hand and Emily at school has a boyfriend and they hold hands sometimes and he lets her use his favourite pencil. Is that what you and Indigo will do if you become boyfriend and girlfriend?'

He tried to divert her because now the conversation

had gone from talking to Indigo to suddenly being boyfriend and girlfriend.

'I don't think we're going to be boyfriend and girlfriend. Well, not yet,' River said and immediately regretted adding that last part.

'When will you be?'

'We have to talk about that first to see if that's what we want,' River said. He and Indigo had to discuss whether they had any kind of future together. Although she had run away, she had come here for a reason and he couldn't help hoping she had come here for him.

'Do *you* want her to be your girlfriend?' Tierra asked.

Of course he did, but it wasn't as simple as that.

'I like Indigo very much but there's a lot of things we need to talk about before we get that far.'

'If you're boyfriend and girlfriend will you give her your favourite pencil?'

'I don't have a favourite pencil. I guess having a girlfriend or boyfriend means different things to different people.'

'What does it mean to you?' Tierra asked.

He smiled at the weight of that question, which had come from a place of such innocence. But he supposed if his talk with Indigo went well they might start dating at some point and he should probably lay the groundwork for that with Tierra and prepare her for what that would look like.

'If we become boyfriend and girlfriend we will spend a lot of our time together, with you of course, and she might sleep here more often.'

He chewed his lip as he thought about that. He had

never brought a woman into his world with Tierra. How would Indigo or any woman fit into his life? How would Tierra feel if Indigo was here all the time, sleeping in his bed?

'Will she sleep here tonight?' Tierra asked eagerly. Clearly his daughter was OK with it. Or at least the idea of it.

'She's going to stay in one of the other treehouses tonight.'

'Why?'

'Because she needs her own space.'

'But she doesn't need that space if you're boyfriend and girlfriend?'

'Well, she probably does need some space, but if she was my girlfriend, she also might like to stay here some nights too.'

'Why?'

This was a slippery slope to go down.

'Because when you're older and you have a boyfriend or girlfriend, instead of giving them your favourite pencil, you give them lots of kisses and cuddles. I can't give Indigo cuddles if she is staying in another treehouse.'

How on earth had Tierra got him talking about having a relationship with Indigo as if it was a done deal?

Tierra clearly thought about this. 'I'd like to give her cuddles too.'

'Well you can if she stays here sometimes.'

'But if she is sleeping in the bed at the top of the ladder I can't go up there without you to help me so I can't cuddle her in the morning in bed like I cuddle you in bed.'

'If she stays here she will probably sleep in my bed.'

143

'Where will you sleep?'

'No, I'll be in my bed too.'

Tierra stared at him with wide eyes.

'Why will you be in bed together?'

This conversation wasn't just teetering at the top of the slippery slope, it was already avalanching down it with great speed.

'So we can cuddle,' River said. He half wished Indigo was here to listen to this conversation – she would get such a big kick out of it.

'You'll cuddle in bed all night? Won't you be tired?'

He smirked. 'We'll sleep too. We won't be cuddling all night.'

'So then she'll go back to her own bed once you've finished cuddling?'

'She'll probably stay in my bed in case we want to cuddle some more when we wake up.'

'Is that what happens when you have a boyfriend or girlfriend? I'm not sure I want a boyfriend or girlfriend.'

'But you like cuddling?' River asked in confusion.

'I do, but if I was in my boyfriend or girlfriend's bed all night then who would look after all my toys?'

'Oh I see, yes that is a problem.'

'Matilda would get very lonely,' she held up her dinosaur, which always looked a bit sad with its large doleful eyes.

'Well I'm sure when you have a boyfriend or girlfriend they might want to cuddle with you and Matilda.'

'What about the others?'

'Maybe they could take it in turns,' River said.

'Do you think Indigo would want to cuddle with me and Matilda?'

'I'm sure she would.'

He hoped she would. For Indigo, being with Tierra was cute and funny now, but would she love his daughter as much as he did if they got involved?

'I like the idea of cuddling in bed with you and Indigo,' Tierra said.

'And Matilda. And Bert and George and Sally. I'm sure Indigo would like to meet them all.'

Tierra grinned. 'I hope she becomes your girlfriend.'

'Well tonight, we will chat and decide if we both want to do that. And you are going to spend the night with Meadow and Star.'

'Yay! I love sleeping over with Star. And Meadow always lets me do baking. She's very good at making cakes.'

'She is, yes. But if you make some cakes, maybe don't eat them all, maybe save some for Heath, Bear, me and Indigo. Eating ten cakes before bed is probably not the best idea.'

Tierra giggled. 'OK and then tomorrow you and Indigo will be boyfriend and girlfriend?'

'I don't think it will be tomorrow but maybe sometime in the future. I'm going to go and wake her for dinner. You should go and get ready to spend the night with Star and Meadow.'

Tierra hopped down and ran up the stairs and River followed her. He could hear her banging around in her room as he let himself into his bedroom and closed the door behind him. Indigo was fast asleep in his bed and he had an overwhelming feeling that she belonged there.

He wiped his hand down his jeans and gently shook her awake.

Her eyes fluttered open and she looked at him blearily, her face lighting up in a big smile when she saw him. 'Are you coming to join me?' she said, sleepily.

His heart missed a beat, then another because there was nothing he wanted more right then.

Her eyes suddenly widened in horror as she became more awake. 'Oh my god, I'm so sorry, I was half asleep.'

'It's OK.'

'Is Willow Cottage ready? I'll get my stuff and get out of your hair.'

He sat down on the bed next to her. 'I thought we could have dinner first then I'll take you down there after.'

'Oh OK.'

'There's something I'd really like to talk to you about.'

She sat up. 'I need to talk to you too.'

He nodded. His hand was next to hers and he was desperate to reach out and hold it. But he had so many questions, so many things he needed to get straight in his own head. If she'd come here and told him straightaway who she was, all he'd have to deal with was why she'd run. But now he had that and why she was keeping her identity a secret. He had such mixed feelings about her right now and he had to resolve that too.

He stood up. 'You probably have a half hour until it's ready, I thought you might want to have a shower or freshen up a bit before you eat. Are you feeling better?'

'Yes, thank you. I slept like a log.'

'It's the bed, it's super comfy.' He cleared his throat

because he still had an overwhelming desire to join her in it. 'I'll leave you to get ready.'

He turned and walked out. He had to talk to her, they couldn't move forward until they'd dealt with the past. Tonight it was going to come to a head, whether she liked it or not.

Indigo had just climbed down the ladder from the mezzanine after her shower when Tierra poked her head out of her bedroom door and frantically gestured for Indigo to come inside. She quickly stepped inside the bedroom and Tierra shut the door.

'You and Daddy are having a date tonight,' Tierra said excitedly.

'No honey, we're just having dinner.'

Tierra stubbornly shook her head. 'No, he wants to talk to you about being boyfriend and girlfriend.'

That threw Indigo. 'He said that?'

'Yes. He says he likes you very much and that when you're boyfriend and girlfriend you will sleep in his bed so he can cuddle you and give you his favourite pencil.'

'What?'

Tierra nodded. 'And then I can cuddle you in bed too.'

Indigo smiled, her heart melting for the little girl. 'We can always cuddle even if me and your daddy are not boyfriend and girlfriend.'

'I'd like you to be boyfriend and girlfriend.'

'Well, I'd like that too but I think we probably need to talk about it.'

'You need to wear a pretty dress.'

'What?'

'For your date. You need to look nice.'

'I... don't think it's a date, your daddy didn't say anything about it being a date, he just said he wanted to talk.'

'Yes, about you two kissing and cuddling and holding hands. Do you have a dress?' Tierra said.

'I do but...' As it was getting warmer Indigo had packed a few summer dresses but nothing she'd normally wear to a date.

'Go and put it on quick.'

Indigo hesitated.

'Please.'

'OK, sure, why not,' Indigo said.

She went back up the ladder to get changed and then looked at herself in the mirror, hoping it didn't look like she was trying too hard.

She was just about to go back downstairs when her phone beeped with a message.

She picked it up and smiled when she saw it was Joey.

How's it all going, have you told him yet?

Indigo sent her reply. **No not yet. We've been getting on really well today and I'm just about to have dinner with him. He wants to talk. His daughter thinks we're going on a date. Apparently he told her he wants to talk to me about us being in a relationship.**

Joey was quick to reply. **Oh my god, how exciting.**

Tilly typed her message. **Wow, that's a bit unexpected. And fast. I'm happy for you though. You deserve to have some fun.**

148

Vicky was next to join in. **What the hell. Are you kidding me? The man has no idea who you are and you're going on a date? Is he that desperate that he'd ask out the first woman who crosses his path?**

Indigo felt herself go cold. Desperate? She felt the pain of that casual throwaway comment like she'd been slapped round the face. She knew River hadn't been with a woman for five years, but she refused to believe he was that desperate he'd go out with anyone. She knew what they had and it was something special, something huge and life-changing. Her friends didn't understand that. But was that what Vicky really thought of her, that any man would have to be desperate to go out with her? She knew her eyes looked disturbing, but surely she had more to offer than just her looks or the lack of them. She didn't need this kind of negativity in her life. She had spent two years hiding away, her confidence shattered, and she was just starting to come out of her shell again. It was hard enough navigating her future with a baby, without Vicky dragging her down at every available opportunity.

She smiled slightly to see Etta's message. **Vicky, don't be such a bitch.**

Without giving it any more thought, she went to the menu at the top of the screen and left the group chat. She still had Etta, Joey and Tilly's numbers. She could always message them privately, but maybe until she had figured out what she was going to do with her life, she didn't need any more input from them to cast doubt on her decisions. Just as she was about to put her phone back in her bag, it rang in her hand.

She smiled when she saw it was Violet. So much had

changed since they'd spoken the night before. She didn't really have time to give her sister a detailed rundown, and being on the mezzanine there was always the chance she could be overheard, but she could give her the bullet points. She went to the furthest corner and answered the phone in a whisper.

'Hey Violet.'

'Indy, what is going on? River isn't married?'

'No, he's single,' Indigo whispered. 'He is a dad though. One of the little girls is his.'

'OK,' Violet said slowly. 'So have you told him yet?'

'No, I thought the fact that he didn't know who I was would give me a chance to get to know him better without any memories of that night getting in the way but that was stupid. He at least deserves to know who I am even if I don't tell him about the baby yet. I'm going to tell him who I am tonight. He's cooking dinner for me and apparently he wants to talk to me about… us. So I'll tell him then.'

Violet let out a little squeal of joy. 'Is it a date?'

Indigo smiled with love for her sister. This was the kind of excitement and encouragement she needed from her friends too.

'I don't know. What we shared that night, that chemistry, that link, is still there, for both of us. It's so easy between us and I think we both want to get to know each other better.'

'I'm so excited for you.'

'Well don't get too excited. Tonight I plan to tell him who I am. It might go very downhill from there.'

'And it might not. He might be overjoyed to see you again.'

Indigo doubted that. 'Look, I better go, dinner will be ready soon. I'll let you know what happens tomorrow.'

'OK, love you,' Violet said.

'Love you too.'

She climbed down the ladder and then the stairs leading to the kitchen, her heart suddenly thundering in her chest. She wanted tonight to go well, she wanted River to fall for her so much he wouldn't care when she revealed herself as Mindy. He'd laugh it off and then take her to bed. She smiled at that thought and shook her head. Her baby hormones were making her horny as hell, especially around River. And while she wanted to find out if they had something beyond sex, she couldn't deny she'd thought a lot about that wonderful night and there was a huge part of her that was desperate to relive it.

She had decided that, unless things went spectacularly well, she wanted to keep the baby a secret just for a while longer. She didn't want the baby and River's responsibilities to it to impact on any decision he made about being with her. She wanted to see if they stood a chance first.

River turned round from preparing the dinner and smiled when he saw her.

'Indigo, you look lovely.'

'Thank you. I was kind of coerced into wearing a dress. Tierra thinks tonight is a date.'

He sighed and put down the spatula. 'God, I'm sorry. Once that girl gets an idea in her head, it's pretty hard to dislodge.'

'She said you were going to give me your favourite pencil. I wasn't sure if that was a euphemism.'

He stared at her and then burst out laughing. 'No, it wasn't. I… do want to talk… about us. But it's not a date.'

She smiled. 'I thought as much.'

'Meadow will be here in a moment to collect Tierra and then we can sit down and eat.'

She nodded. 'Dinner smells amazing. Thank you for going to so much trouble.'

River opened the oven a crack to check on the food.

'I enjoy cooking. When I was young, we lived next door to a young Italian man called Stefano and his wife Guilia. He *loved* to cook. He would spend hours cooking these amazing meals and me, Heath and Bear would spend hours watching him. It started with the three of us, pressing our faces against his kitchen window, the smells were amazing and we all loved to watch these meals come together. After a few days, he invited us in and he'd get us to taste the food and give him feedback. Soon enough we were helping him to cook the meals too. Guilia was big on cakes and she would create these towering mountains of cream and fruit piled between the most moist and soft sponges. She taught us how to do that too. It instilled a lifetime passion for food and cooking in all of us. I don't get to do it half as much as I'd like now. We tend to eat in the on-site restaurant now for most of our meals as it's easier than cooking after a long day building treehouses, plus it's nice to sit down together as a family. Though I would like to spend more time cooking with Tierra and teaching her about food. Do you like to cook?'

'When time allows. I used to work long shifts at the hotel and I'd come home and eat something quick for convenience. But on days off I used to like experimenting in the kitchen. Mum was an awful cook so I didn't have any good role models like you did, at least in the kitchen, so everything I know is self-taught. I'm not sure if my experiments with food are that great, but I do make a mean meatball Bolognese. I love making the meatballs from scratch. I bet Tierra would love to make meatballs, it involves a lot of getting your hands dirty.'

'She'd definitely love that,' River said. 'Oh, here she comes.'

Indigo turned round to see Tierra running downstairs in a lovely gold dress that sparkled as she moved. Tierra ran straight up to her and Indigo quickly knelt down to give the little girl a hug.

'Hello you, you look beautiful,' Indigo said.

'So do you.' Tierra gave her an over-the-top wink that involved cocking her head and blinking both eyes alternately but Indigo got the gist.

'Tierra, why are you wearing your best dress?' River said.

'For our date,' Tierra said, giving a little twirl.

Indigo couldn't help but smile.

River frowned in confusion. 'But you're staying over with Meadow and Star, I told you that.'

Tierra looked at him as if he was stupid. 'Yes, after our date.'

Indigo's heart filled with love for her and her complete misunderstanding that of course she would be part of the date, even though there wasn't one.

Just then there was a knock on the door.

'That will be Meadow come to collect you,' River said.

Indigo watched Tierra's face fall.

'But we've not had our date yet.'

There was no way Indigo was going to disappoint her, not when she'd got herself dressed up for the occasion.

Indigo moved towards the door. 'Silly Meadow, she must have got the wrong time. I'll tell her that we'll drop you by later, after our date.'

Tierra clapped her hands together. 'Oh good, I thought I was going to miss our date then.'

Indigo opened the door and spoke quietly to Meadow. 'Hey, change of plan, can we drop Tierra round in an hour or so? She's going to eat with us first.'

Meadow frowned in confusion. 'OK, I thought River wanted to talk to you.'

'He does but Tierra has got it in her head that we're having a date that of course she's part of. We can talk after, it's no big deal.'

Meadow smiled. 'That's… very kind. I can get her out if you want? If I tell her we're making chocolate brownies, she'd be over at my house in a heartbeat.'

'No, it's totally fine. We'll bring her round in an hour.'

Meadow nodded and gave her a wave as she went back across the rope bridge. Indigo turned and returned inside.

River was staring at her in a way she couldn't read. She smiled at him.

'Tierra, we're going to be having dinner in a moment, can you go and wash your hands upstairs.'

Tierra ran back up the stairs with a big grin on her face.

'I'm sorry,' River said. 'I did explain to her that she would be sleeping over with Meadow and Star.'

Indigo stepped closer to him. 'River, this is totally fine.

154

We can pretend we're on a date to keep her happy and then we can talk by ourselves after dinner.'

He studied her for a moment. 'What does pretending we're on a date involve?'

'I don't think she really knows what a date is, other than it somehow involves a pencil, so we can just talk, eat and, if you feel it's appropriate, you can always give me a pencil.'

He smiled. 'OK. I can do that.'

'I'm ready!' Tierra announced as she came storming down the stairs again.

'I get the feeling you might regret being so gracious,' River said, quietly.

'I get the feeling our first *date* is going to be a fun one.'

CHAPTER TEN

River sat watching Indigo finish off her dessert while chatting to Tierra about a science experiment they'd done at school. They'd talked, nothing too heavy because of Tierra and he knew that when his daughter was gone they'd be free to talk about more serious topics. They'd laughed a lot and Tierra had sung along to the music because, despite his best efforts to play nice background music on his iPhone, it kept playing children's songs, probably because Tierra knew his iPhone better than he did.

But as he'd seen Indigo engage with his daughter so easily, when he'd watched her make Tierra laugh and take so much time for her, something had unfurled inside of him, something strong and powerful, something he had never felt before in his life. He knew he was falling for her.

Suddenly Whigfield started singing her famous song, 'Saturday Night', completing the romantic tone for the evening.

'Oh, I remember this one,' Indigo said, getting up. 'Tierra, do you know the dance routine?'

'Yes, Daddy taught me,' Tierra said, ruining any credibility he had left.

Indigo laughed. 'Is that right? Well maybe we should all dance together.'

She launched into the dance with the complete confidence of someone who had done this routine many times before. There was no hesitation as she tried to remember the steps, she knew every move perfectly. The only problem being it was a completely different dance to the famous Whigfield dance. She was putting her hands behind her head then crossing them over her waist. Even Tierra knew this was wrong and started giggling uncontrollably. River couldn't help the huge smile spreading across his face as he watched her.

Indigo got to the jumping bit where she turned to face the other direction and to his amusement Tierra was almost crying with laughter now.

'What are you laughing at, this was very cool back in the day,' Indigo said in mock indignation and carried on dancing with the absolute certainty that she was doing it right.

'That's not the routine,' Tierra said, laughing so hard she was struggling to breathe.

'Yes it is,' Indigo said.

'Daddy, show her,' Tierra said.

'I'm not sure what dance you're doing but it's not the "Saturday Night" dance,' River said.

'Yes it is,' Indigo said.

He stood up. 'Trust me, I had to do extensive research to be able to impart my dance skills to Tierra. You wave your arms to the left like this and then to the right. Then you do the plate-spinning fingers like this…' He showed her the rest of the dance, which was completely different to what she had been doing, and Indigo looked like she'd just been told Santa didn't exist.

'My whole life has been a lie. How have I been doing it wrong all these years?'

'I don't know.'

'Show me again.'

He started playing the song again from the beginning and then went through the steps, which were very easy, and soon they were all dancing together and laughing over their moves. They got to the jumping bit where they turned direction and she jumped to face the left at the same time he jumped to face the right so they ended up bumping into each other. He put his hands on her shoulders to steady her and she looked up at him.

'Hey,' he said softly, as Tierra continued dancing around them.

'Hi.'

'I've had the best time with you tonight,' River said.

'I have too.'

His eyes cast down to her lips, a need to kiss her exploding through him.

He stepped back from her, clearing his throat. 'Tierra, I think it's probably time you went to see Meadow and Star.'

Tierra's face fell a little. 'Is the date over?'

'It is, yes.'

'But we haven't talked about whether you want to be boyfriend and girlfriend.'

'We'll probably talk about that later, but Meadow has

promised Star you two will be making cakes tonight. Poor Star will be looking forward to that.'

Her face lit up. 'Oh yes, Star said we're going to make chocolate ones. So do you want to be Indigo's boyfriend?'

He smirked and looked at Indigo. 'I don't think it's as simple as that, we have things to talk about.'

Tierra rolled her eyes and let out a groan of frustration. 'Adults. Why do you need to make things so hard? When Emily and Benji became boyfriend and girlfriend she just told him he was her boyfriend and now he is. So just tell her.'

'Adults tend to be a bit more respectful than that,' River said.

Tierra wrinkled her little nose in confusion.

'Do you like her?' she asked.

He wished that was the only thing that mattered. He glanced over at Indigo to see what she was making of all of this. 'Very much.'

'Indigo, do you like Daddy?'

'I think he's wonderful but—'

'No buts. I now per-nounce you boyfriend and girl-friend,' Tierra giggled.

'Come on, trouble. Let's go and see Star,' River said, picking her up and slinging her over his shoulder.

'Wait,' Tierra said. 'Indigo, will you come to movie night tomorrow, here? We're watching *Frozen*, it's my favourite.'

'I'd love to, thank you,' Indigo said.

'Promise,' Tierra said.

'I promise.'

River grabbed Tierra's overnight bag and turned back

to face Indigo. 'I'll be back in two minutes and then we can… talk.'

She nodded and he walked out the treehouse. He had to cool his head before he got back because all he wanted to do right now was grab her and kiss her. But they needed to talk first, they had to get everything out in the open. They didn't stand any chance of a future if they couldn't be honest about their past.

Maybe kissing could come later.

Indigo paced around the lounge and the kitchen waiting for River to come back. Tonight had been wonderful, laughing and talking with River and Tierra and there was a huge part of her that wanted this life with him, that could easily picture herself here. But was it fair to get involved with him when he had no idea what he was letting himself in for? She'd wanted an opportunity to see if they still had that connection and it was very clear they did. She'd wanted a chance to get to know him to see if they had something more, but the more time they spent together, the deeper the feelings she had for him and she got the impression he felt the same. And just as he was thinking about how she could fit into his life with Tierra, she was going to throw a baby into that equation, too. He had to move forward with all the facts. He had to decide whether he wanted a relationship with her, knowing she was pregnant. She'd been going about this all wrong. It was deceitful and unfair to let him fall for her without him knowing the whole truth.

Suddenly, she heard footsteps approaching the door. It was time to face the music.

River opened the door and he smiled at her.

'Why don't you grab your stuff and I'll take you over to your new treehouse?' he said.

'Oh, I thought we were going to talk.'

'We are, but I want to show you the treehouse first while it's still relatively light outside.'

'Oh, sure, OK.'

She went upstairs and gathered everything into a bag. She was a bit thrown by this. She would have thought talking to each other was the most important thing now. Of course she was grateful that she had somewhere to stay for the next few months and she was obviously curious to see it but was now really the right time?

She went back downstairs and he was waiting for her near the door.

'Before we go, I thought I should give you this.' He handed her a pencil and she couldn't help the huge smile spreading across her face. 'It seemed appropriate.'

'Thank you, I shall treasure it.' She tucked it into her bag.

They walked down the steps into the wood. The sun was just starting to set, painting the trees and leaves with a rose gold glow.

'How are the new treehouses going?' Indigo asked.

'We're a little behind right now,' River said. 'We've already started taking bookings for the summer holiday for some of them so they have to be finished by then, all of it does: the lights, the paths, everything. We'll probably end up getting some local help to get things finished off. I'm not too worried about it at the moment as we have three months but we're not as far along as I'd like to be.'

'Can I help?' Indigo asked, although she wasn't sure what she could do.

'Depends, what are your carpentry skills like?'

'Not great.'

'Then probably not but I loved what you did with the painted flowers this afternoon. I'd definitely like to see more of that in the finished treehouses.'

'I can do that.'

'As long as I'm not taking you away from where you're needed?'

'Reception is not that busy. I can divert phone calls to my mobile and I'm sure I can ask Bear to add the booking program to my tablet. That way I can be painting the treehouses and still be around to answer calls and take bookings at the same time. I can make sure I'm at reception in the mornings for any check-outs or enquiries and then give you a few hours before any check-ins in the afternoon.'

He clearly thought about it before nodding. 'Sounds good.'

'I was thinking about the official opening of the new treehouses. Maybe we could hold a big event. Meadow said you weren't doing anything special for it but we should do something. We could invite travel journalists, bloggers, that kind of thing, maybe some of them could even stay in the treehouses on the opening weekend. We could do nibbles and drinks and have a party, maybe do a barbeque and have fireworks. Really make a thing of it. I could help organise it all if you want.'

'That's a really good idea. Thank you.'

'I really want this expansion to go well for you, you've worked so hard to get it all finished. And I think we should celebrate that.'

'It's nice that you care. A lot of people would just turn up to work, do their job and go home, they wouldn't go above and beyond what was required of them.'

She thought about that as they walked through the trees. 'I don't think that's true. Not here anyway. Your staff love this place. Look at how many turned up to do the painting today. I know there was a great prize on offer but they came because they believe in Wishing Wood, because they want it to be a success as much as you do. They want to support you.'

'I hadn't really thought about it like that, but I suppose they do. They're a great team. But it's important to me that *you* care about this place. Danielle, my ex-wife, hated living here. She wanted so much more than I could ever give her. She always had dreams of being a big actress in Hollywood, living in one of those huge mansions with a massive pool. When Tierra was born there were only two treehouses here. We were in the middle of building more but it certainly wasn't the successful business it is now. I was still living in one of the old lodges which had seen better days. She wanted us to leave, sell the woods, get a big house in London so she could audition for more acting gigs. But this is my home and it always will be. I love living here and raising Tierra surrounded by this beauty. And I have to think about my family as well and keeping the business running for them too. So there will never be more than this. If something ever did happen between us, you need to know that.'

'River, I love it here. I can understand dreaming about a lavish life but does that really make you happy? Right now, I have nothing and there's nothing like a bit of poverty to really make you take stock of your life and think about the things you really need and want. Believe it or not, when I was a child, my parents built us a treehouse at the bottom of the garden. It was very basic, nothing like these wonderful homes. And I imagined a life where I would live in one, where I would grow my own vegetables and have a few chickens for eggs. Those dreams changed when I grew up, but, right now, I would take that simple life over anything. These treehouses are incredible and I want the world to see how amazing they are. I would be very very happy living here.'

She left out saying she would be happy living here with him.

'Well, let's see how you like your new home.'

He gestured to a blossom tree with a large treehouse poking out the top with a wonky turret perched on the roof. It appeared to have three floors and the tree's flowers entwined around all the windows and walls.

'This is Blossom Cottage and your home for the next three months.'

'Oh,' Indigo let out a little gasp. 'It's beautiful. But I thought I was in Willow Cottage.'

'This one was more suitable for you,' River said. 'Come on, I'll take you up.'

He went up a small spiral staircase and she followed

him up to the large circular door, which made it look a little bit like a hobbit house.

'This is so cute, I love it,' Indigo said.

'You should probably hold back that assessment until you see the inside,' River said.

He unlocked the door and pushed it open, letting her go ahead of him. She stepped inside and immediately got a sense she'd been there before. It looked somehow familiar. There was a large soft silvery-grey corner sofa at one end and a big chunky table over by one of the large round windows. It had such a natural feel to it, with bare wood panelled walls and floor and tiny subtle lights dotted everywhere. The kitchen took up the majority of the space, which she loved. It had a huge breakfast bar in the middle of the room with bar stools around it so people could sit and chat while others made dinner. It was perfect and the kind of place she would definitely choose for herself.

And suddenly she knew why the place looked so familiar. This was the treehouse she had designed with River, she was sure of it.

'Let me show you upstairs,' he said, as if he had no idea of the significance of this place.

He walked up a spiral staircase and she followed him up past the first floor to the second floor.

'This is the kids' room,' River said.

It had bunkbeds just like they'd planned. Shelves for toys, although currently empty. River walked to a bookcase and moved one of the books to reveal a doorknob, then turned it and the bookshelf swung open to reveal a small secret playroom for the children. It was a bit sparse right now, it needed fairy lights and beanbags, but it was just like they'd talked about the night they'd met.

Indigo's breath caught in her throat.

'Over here is something special,' River said, walking to a small round door in the wall, but she already knew what was behind it.

He opened the door to show the entrance to a helter-skelter slide that she knew would take the children down to the forest floor.

'I put a door over it,' River said.

'So the kids don't go sliding down it in the middle of the night,' Indigo said, quietly. They'd talked about that too.

'Exactly.' River looked at her and in that instant she knew he knew who she was. That was why he'd brought her here. Had he known all this time? Or had it been her reaction to his description of the night they met this afternoon, had that been the thing that had confirmed it for him? This was what he'd wanted to talk about. The fact she had lied to him since she'd arrived.

Her heart was racing in her chest.

'Let's go back downstairs, I'll show you the bathroom and the other bedrooms.'

She couldn't find the words to say that she didn't need to see them. She followed him back down to the first floor.

'This is the bathroom.'

Sure enough a roll-top bath stood at the side of the room, right next to another round window. She swallowed down the lump of emotion in her throat.

Next to the bathroom was a large landing area that had a huge circular window up one end, affording amazing sea views. There was a room divider, pushed to one side so the landing area could be used as another room if needed.

'Not sure what we'll use this area for,' River said, catching her looking at it. 'Maybe it could be used as a studio.'

She swallowed the lump in her throat.

'In here we have the nursery,' he said, opening the door on a pale yellow room with pictures of baby animals hanging on the walls. She walked in. In the middle of the room was a white crib and hanging above the bed was a dinosaur and unicorn mobile.

Tears pricked her eyes as she stared at it. It was utterly perfect in every way.

She turned round to see River watching her carefully, probably wondering if she was still going to deny who she was.

'You built this for me,' she said, her voice choked.

'Yes I did,' he said, softly.

Tears spilled over onto her cheeks and she walked straight up to him and kissed him. He immediately wrapped his arms around her and kissed her back.

Oh god, his kiss was everything. He was so gentle, kissing her with so much affection, her heart melted with love for him. She wound her arms around his neck, relishing in the feel of his warm body against hers. He stroked the tears gently from her cheeks and that made more spill over.

'Indy,' River whispered against her lips. 'I can't believe you're here.' Then he kissed her again. He moved his mouth to her throat and then her shoulder.

She couldn't stop the tears from falling now. 'River, I'm so sorry. I should have told you who I was when I arrived.'

He sighed against her skin almost as if he didn't want to talk about this but then he took a definite step back from her and, pushing his hands through his hair, he paced across the room.

'Yes you should have. You've played me for a fool. I thought I was going mad with my feelings for you when I'd only just met you. Why didn't you say something?'

'You didn't recognise me when I arrived, not even a glimmer of recognition. I presumed I was just another notch on your bedpost, and not a very memorable one. And then I thought you were married to Meadow with two beautiful children and I didn't want to turn up here and be the homewrecker.'

'But when you realised that wasn't true, why didn't you tell me then?'

'Because... well, for lots of reasons. I was scared you'd be pissed off at me for running away the morning after we met. I was worried you wouldn't remember me at all, and part of me wanted to keep those wonderful memories of that night and not have them tainted by you not thinking they were wonderful. And I suppose, most importantly, I wanted to see if what we shared was real. The night we met, before you got drunk, we shared an incredible connection, I felt what you felt, and I wanted to see if we still had that. That night, I found myself believing in love at first sight, but you were blind drunk and I was quite drunk too and I woke up the next morning and wondered if it was all just a drunken night of passion and lust and maybe love had very little to do with it. I thought if we could start over, would we share that same connection again?'

'You... were testing me?'

'No, that wasn't... I thought if that connection was real we would feel it again and we did.'

He shook his head. 'I did recognise you when you first arrived. But I thought your name was Mindy so when you were introduced to me as Indigo, and with the purple hair and the lack of green eyes, I presumed I'd got it wrong. But I felt this link with you, this tangible bond, and I had no idea why I was feeling this and you let me carry on thinking it without explaining why.'

'I was going to tell you, last night when I realised you weren't married to Meadow and today when we were having lunch before Heath hurt himself and after I met Amelia when I got you to propose to me.'

'That's when I almost knew for sure. There had been little clues all day but I kept convincing myself I was wrong, mainly because I just couldn't understand why you wouldn't bring it up. But then I recognised that scar, I'd kissed that scar. Bear said lots of people have scars but I knew. Then when I spoke about that night and saw your reaction... I knew then.'

'I was going to tell you then.'

'But you didn't. I poured my heart out to you about Mindy and that wonderful night and you never said a word. I kept waiting for you to say something but you didn't.'

'I felt faint and you said you wouldn't be able to forgive me and I realised how much I'd hurt you and... I was scared because we were getting close, enjoying spending time together, and I didn't want to lose you when you found out who I was. I decided I was going to tell you tonight, after dinner.'

He paced away from her. 'You lied to me.'

'I didn't lie, I just didn't tell the truth,' she said quietly, but she knew he was right.

He shook his head and she didn't know how they were going to get past this.

'That night was incredible,' Indigo said. 'When you kissed me as soon as we walked through the door of your flat, god, I have never been kissed like that before. It was the hottest kiss I've ever had, which culminated in the most amazing sex of my entire life. It had been a long time since anyone had looked at me the way you did when we were making love. You were passionate, your touches fuelled by desire and need for me, and that made me feel wanted and adored. Things I hadn't felt in a very long time. You craved me and that turned me on so much. You made me feel alive again. I know it's ridiculous to say but I felt loved.'

He stared at her. 'And then you left. You felt this incredible connection, you had the best sex of your entire life, you felt loved and adored – and you left?'

'I panicked. In my rose-tinted view I'd built it up in my head as love at first sight and a beautiful happy ever after but in the cold light of day I doubted everything. I've never believed in love at first sight before I met you – that kind of thing is ridiculous, isn't it? Who falls in love with someone they've just met and then goes on to live a happy life together? That kind of thing doesn't really happen. And then I started to think it might just have been another one-night stand for you. You had a whole drawer filled with condoms and I wondered if I was just one of many. I didn't want to be there when you awkwardly tried to distance yourself from me. I wanted to remember the night for what it was, the best night of my life, and not have it ruined by you chucking me out of there the next morning.'

'You never even gave me a chance,' River said. 'I was gutted when I woke up and you were gone and I couldn't fathom it after the night we had shared. Not just the incredible sex but how we clicked together so perfectly. And then afterwards, for the last two months, all I could think of was that it must have been me, that there must be something wrong with me. And believe me, when my opinion of myself is already pretty low, that was a hard pill to swallow.'

'I'm so sorry, I never meant to hurt you. I never realised you'd think those things and I wish, with everything I have, that I'd never reacted in that way.'

He studied her for a moment. 'So do I. It's getting late and I have to get up early tomorrow so it's probably best if I go before I say something I'm going to regret.'

Oh god, she had lost him. She moved towards him. 'I'm sorry you have a low opinion of yourself, which I don't understand because I think you're incredible. And I hate that I made you think for one second that you are anything less than wonderful.'

'You must have a low opinion of yourself too. You didn't trust that what we had was enough, you didn't believe you were enough.'

She shook her head. 'Sadly, that's the truth of all of this. I let my shattered self-esteem ruin something beautiful and amazing. I let my past come back to haunt me, I got scared and I ran.'

He didn't say anything for a while, just watching her as if she was a puzzle he was trying to understand. Eventually he spoke. 'What happened?'

She hesitated. Would reliving all those horrible memories really make a difference to their situation? Maybe if he knew where her pain had come from he might understand her actions.

'Two and a half years ago I was in a car accident with my fiancé.' She swallowed. 'I was pregnant with a baby we had tried for years to conceive. He was drunk and I had no idea. I lost everything that night, my baby, him.'

He took a sharp intake of breath. 'They both died.'

'My baby did. Luke couldn't even bear to look at me after the accident, he didn't even want to be in the same room as me. Violet, my sister, says it was because he felt so guilty, it was his fault our baby died. But the scars on my body were horrible. Most of them have faded away now but after the accident they were bad. He wouldn't touch me, he wouldn't make love to me, and I started to feel hideous. Luke left me six months after the accident when my confidence was at an all-time low. Then my eye started changing colour, a side effect from the accident, so the doctors say. I'd hit the side of my head pretty bad.' She lifted her hair from the side of her face to show the faint scar next to her eye. 'My boss was horrified. Staff at his precious Infinity Hotel had to look presentable and beautiful at all times and my weird eyes didn't fit in with that. He said I was hideous and I started to believe it. Sometimes people would pass comments in the street when I walked past, saying I was a freak or a witch or a dog.'

'Jesus Christ,' muttered River.

Indigo felt the tears form in her eyes. 'Yeah, it was fair to say my self-worth was barely there at all. My boss wanted to fire me just because of my eyes, as if I wasn't worth employing if I didn't look good, never mind the many years I'd worked in that job. I did start to believe I was utterly worthless. And then I met you and...' the words caught in her throat, 'you made me feel alive again. You wanted me and that made me feel powerful and desired. It was like stepping into the sun again after two years in the dark. But I was wearing green cat eye contact lenses and was dressed in that cat costume and when I woke up the next morning I convinced myself you wouldn't be interested in the real me, with the freaky eyes. I started to think that the night before had been lust, not love – and drunken lust at that. My self-preservation kicked in because I couldn't bear to see the look of revulsion in your eyes when you realised who you'd slept with.'

River stepped forward and gently wiped the tears from her cheeks. He let out a heavy sigh. 'Indigo, I hate that you've spent two years feeling this way and I hate that your self-worth is wrapped up in how you look, not what is in here,' he pointed to her heart. 'You are beautiful but what attracted me to you was what was on the inside, not the wrapper. If you'd known me, you'd have known I would never be so shallow to have rejected you because of the colour of your eyes, especially not after the night we shared. So I don't think we can call it love when we really didn't know each other at all. That kind of forever love you talked about, it takes time. We didn't fall in love that night, we shared a physical attraction. So I think you're right, it was one amazing night of lust and passion, so we draw a line under it and put it behind us once and for all.'

Her heart dropped into her stomach and tears welled up in her eyes again. 'Don't you think we deserve a second chance? We could date, start over. See if that lust could be something more?'

He paused before he spoke. 'I don't think we have that. If you cared for me at all, you wouldn't have run. You wouldn't have turned up here and lied about it. We both needed each other that night and we fulfilled that need. I don't think we need to drag it out and pretend it's something it wasn't. I think it's best if we just move on from that.'

Tears fell down her cheeks as she nodded. 'I am sorry.'

'I am too. But please don't cry. This is for the best. If you'd stayed and really got to know me, you'd have found out I'm actually a complete twat. And actually not very lovable at all.'

'I don't believe that for one second.'

'Well that's the truth. I hope you're comfortable in Blossom Cottage tonight. I think I'll make the most of having a child-free house and get an early night.'

He moved back towards the stairs and just like that it was all over.

She walked across to the door, watching him go, and then he turned back.

'Why did you come here?' River asked.

It would have been so easy to say she had regretted her actions and had come back for him but that would be a lie and she'd already told enough of them. Yes, there had been a huge part of her that had imagined the fantasy that he would take one look at her and declare his undying love but she'd known it wasn't really going to happen. And she couldn't tell him about the baby, not yet. Right now he hated her and she didn't want that to make him hate her baby too. But she could at least partly tell him the truth.

'You promised me a job, that night we met. You talked about this place so much and you offered me a job working here.'

He nodded. 'Right. So you didn't come back for me?'

'I didn't think that would be an option. I didn't think you'd want me. Turns out I was right.'

He stared at her a moment longer and then walked down the stairs and out the door.

CHAPTER ELEVEN

River walked into the restaurant the next day and immediately Tierra came running over and threw herself into his arms. He held her tight. He loved this little girl so much and he never wanted anything to get in the way of that. But she looked happy enough; clearly she'd enjoyed her night with Meadow and Star.

'Morning beautiful.'

'Daddy, me and Meadow and Star made chocolate brownies last night and they are the best brownies in the world and we put glittery sprinkles on the top and then she let us stick our fingers in the bowl and lick the cake batter and this morning we each had two before breakfast and she told me not to tell you but they were so good and I wish we could have brownies for breakfast every day,' Tierra rattled off without drawing breath.

'These brownies sound amazing, did you save me one?' River said as he walked over to the counter to collect his breakfast.

'We saved you three,' Tierra said. 'And I saved one for Indigo too. Is she going to be your girlfriend now?'

River let out a heavy sigh. Frustratingly, he still wanted Indigo, her deceit hadn't changed that. And now he knew she was Mindy and he'd been given this second chance he'd so desperately wanted, there was a big part of him that knew he had to take it or he'd always regret it. But she hadn't been honest with him and she'd run from him. He wasn't sure he could get past that.

'It's too early to tell yet. Have you had your breakfast, apart from those brownies?'

'Yes, I had strawberries and Cheerios and toast.'

'Strawberries and Cheerios *on* toast, that's a weird combination.'

Tierra laughed. 'No, not together, silly. I had three breakfasts.'

'Four if you count the brownies.'

'Meadow said they don't count.'

'I bet she did.'

He picked up the tray in one hand and, still holding Tierra on his hip, he walked over to join his family.

He sat down opposite Heath. 'How are you feeling today?'

'Better, bit sore, but I'm OK,' Heath said. 'I'll just take it easy when I'm working today, maybe leave all the heavy lifting to you.'

River smirked. 'You always do. Today will be no different, apart from I'll have to put up with you whinging about your back all day.'

'Yup, I'm going to milk this one to get all the sympathy I can get. The girls have been taking good care of me. I even got first dibs on some amazing sparkly brownies last night,' Heath said.

'How was the big hot date?' Meadow said, clearly wanting to hear more about that than her husband's back.

'It wasn't a date.'

'Did she… stay over with you or stay in Willow Cottage as planned?' Heath asked diplomatically.

'She stayed in Blossom Cottage,' River said, taking a bite of his waffles. He watched as Tierra stole a slice of banana from his plate, then slid down from his lap to go and sit with Star again, who was playing some complicated-looking board game.

'Blossom Cottage?' Heath said in surprise. 'But that's—'

'It's her. Indigo is Mindy, or rather Indy. It was actually you calling her Indy yesterday when you first met that made me think I'd misheard. And I thought showing her the house we'd designed together would be a good way to get it all out in the open, find out once and for all if it was her, and it was.'

'Oh crap, I felt sure you had it wrong,' Bear said.

'Yeah, me too,' Meadow said.

'What?' Heath said. 'Indigo is the woman you fell in love with two months ago?'

'Yes… no. I don't think I can really call it love but she was the woman I spent the night with.'

He wanted to distance himself from labelling it as love because if it wasn't then he couldn't get hurt.

'Why didn't she say anything when she first came?' Bear said.

'I didn't recognise her. Well I did but because I thought the woman I spent the night with was called

Mindy I just disregarded it. Last time I saw her she was wearing this catsuit costume, had green contact lenses in and had cat eye make-up. Plus I was...' he glanced at Tierra who was now happily drawing a picture of an elephant '...very very inebriated so I didn't have a clear picture of what she looked like in my head. Because I didn't recognise her, she thought that she was one of many women, and she also initially thought I was married to Meadow.'

He took a bite of his food as he thought.

'She says she thought it was a good opportunity to get to know me without that night impacting how I see her to find out if we really have something. And to be honest, in the cold light of day, I can kind of understand it. What we shared that night was so unexpected, so powerful, that I can relate to her wanting to find out if it was real. If I'd known she was Mindy I probably would have whisked her straight off to my treehouse as soon as she arrived and, umm... showed her my bedroom. We would never have got the chance to start over again. But I knew it was her. I could feel it. My feelings for her were so out of the blue that I knew something was going on so I don't think I really entered into this relationship with a clean slate. I feel like my emotions surrounding her were subconsciously tied to that night anyway. And she knew who I was, so she never looked at me with fresh eyes either.'

'What a complete mess,' Meadow said.

'I don't think she came here with any intention to deceive me, she just didn't know how to explain who she was when she thought I didn't have any idea.'

'Why did she come here?' Bear said.

'I promised her a job that night and I guess she was desperate enough to see if the offer was still open.'

'So what happened when it all came out?' Heath said.

River couldn't help but smile at the memory of kissing Indigo in their treehouse. That had definitely not been his intention for last night. He'd just wanted to talk to her about why she hadn't been truthful and most importantly why she'd run. But his feelings for her from that night had never gone away, in fact they had probably intensified since she'd arrived. Aside from the fact she hadn't been completely honest with him, she was a wonderful woman and he knew he could very easily fall in love with her. That kiss had reignited his need for her, and showed she had real feelings for him too.

'It all came out. She has had a horrible few years and her confidence is shattered. That's why she ran the next morning, because she thought I would reject her, that it was just a one-night stand for me. I'm annoyed that she didn't give me a chance, that she never spoke to me about her worries, but knowing what she's been through I can kind of understand it. As someone who has a low opinion of themselves I can totally relate to not feeling good enough.'

'She should have told you when she got here,' Bear said.

'I agree, but I don't think it's as black and white as all that. She feels awful about deceiving me. I told her all about Mindy yesterday and I'm annoyed that she didn't come clean then, but she wasn't feeling well and then Meadow and Tierra arrived to judge the painting and maybe it just wasn't the right time. She says she was scared of losing me when we were getting on so well.'

'I guess you should feel flattered by that,' Heath said.

'Yeah, I guess I do. She also says she was determined to tell me last night even before I showed her Blossom Cottage, and when I think back to yesterday there were a few times she tried to bring it up, so I think she would have told me soon anyway. And it has only been a day,' River said, feeling a need to defend and protect her. 'Honestly, I'm more bothered by the fact that she ran away after what we shared than her not talking about that night as soon as she got here.'

'So what are you going to do now?' Bear said.

'Isn't it going to be weird having her work here?' Heath asked.

'I don't think we should sack her,' Meadow said, quickly. 'She's had such a crappy few years with her accident and her awful boss, she needs this job, she needs this place. I understand if you don't want to be with her, but I'm sure you can be adult enough to work alongside her or, if not, avoid her like the plague. This place is big enough.'

River nodded. 'I agree. I have no idea if we have any kind of future together, but I don't want to hurt her. I want to help her if I can.'

They all nodded.

'And I don't want any of you to give her a hard time about this either,' said he added, looking at his brothers. 'She made a mistake but there was nothing malicious about her intentions.'

'You won't hear a peep from me. I like her and it's clear she's crazy about you,' Heath said.

River looked at Bear.

'I don't agree with what she did,' Bear said. 'But if you're prepared to forgive and forget then I can too. I like her as well. You two clearly have some issues to work through, but you obviously seem to think she's worth that.'

River turned his attention to his waffles. He wasn't sure about that. Getting involved with Indigo would be very complicated and messy and he wasn't sure he wanted that.

Indigo got up early the next day after lying awake for most of the night. She showered, got dressed and made her way to the restaurant for breakfast. It was almost empty when she walked in, apart from River, his brothers, the girls and Meadow, who were sitting down and having breakfast together in one corner of the room. They all stopped talking and turned to look at her as soon as she entered the room. Talk about awkward.

She went up to the counter and helped herself to a stack of pancakes and some fruit.

'Hello my dear,' Alex said, appearing from the kitchen to top up the containers with some more waffles and fruit. 'How are you settling in?'

Indigo smiled, weakly. The answer to that was long and complicated. 'Good thanks.' She tried to appear positive. 'I do love it here, it's such a pretty, magical place.'

'It is. It almost feels like it's a place where anything could happen. I hear you and River are getting on well.'

Indigo stared at her; how could she possibly know that?

'Amelia was in here with the girls yesterday,' Alex explained. 'She's far from discreet. She wanted to know all the gossip about you two and for once I didn't have any to give.'

'I don't really have any either, I'm afraid,' Indigo said. 'River is my boss and I don't think it will ever be more than that.'

'That's a shame, he could do with a good woman to look after him,' Alex said.

Suddenly a timer went off in the kitchen and she rushed off to deal with whatever was cooked.

'Good answer,' came a voice behind her.

She turned to see Heath standing there, a big grin on his face.

She looked at him warily as he came to stand at her side. 'Are you here to give me a hard time?'

He grabbed a plate and began to fill it with fruit and yoghurt. 'Absolutely not. It's not really any of my business. I care about my brother and of course I want him to make good decisions, especially when it comes to the women he dates, but at the end of the day he has to make those decisions. It's not down to me to try to influence him one way or the other. And this lot,' he waved in the direction of the kitchen, 'as well as my dear old gran, would love to share their pennies' worth and River doesn't need that.'

'I'm not going to say anything to anyone.'

Heath nodded and finished filling up his plate.

She glanced over at the family table. River was watching them avidly.

'Is he mad?'

'Yeah, but probably a lot calmer than he was last night. He's fighting your corner over there.'

That didn't sound like she was Miss Popular with his family.

'Just give him some time,' Heath said.

He went to move away.

'Heath.'

He turned back to face her.

'If River was to ask for your penny's worth. Would I be a good decision or a bad decision?'

He came back to her. 'You have got under his skin like no other woman ever has. I'm pretty sure my brother is falling in love with you. If you make him feel like that, then he shouldn't give up on you in a hurry.' He shrugged. 'That's what I would say if he asked. Not that he ever would. We all have baggage, Indy, and River has a ton of his own. Maybe you can help each other unpack.'

With that he walked back over to his table.

She stood staring after him, holding her tray, and was only disturbed from her reverie when Mr and Mrs Andrews, the couple who had checked in the day before, walked towards her on their way to get their breakfast.

'Hello,' Indigo snapped back into professional mode. 'You two are up early, are you off somewhere interesting?'

'Yes, we thought we'd check out Church Door Cove,' Mr Andrews said.

'Oh yes, I've heard great things about that,' Indigo said. 'You'll have to let me know what you think. One of our other guests wants to propose this week and that was one of the locations I was going to suggest to him. Maybe you can tell me if you think it's romantic enough.'

'Oh we will,' Mrs Andrews said. 'I love a good proposal story.'

Indigo smiled. 'How did your husband propose to you?'

Mr Andrews groaned.

'He didn't. I asked him,' Mrs Andrews said.

'And I've never heard the end of it.' Mr Andrews smiled at his wife.

'He was apparently waiting for the right time. I could have been waiting years for him to get his act together. I told him we were going to get married in the summer and he agreed. It's hardly the romantic story of the century but we've been together forty-eight years now and I still love him as much now as I did then.'

'Romance isn't everything. I think as long as the man I loved proposed by telling me he loved me, I'd be happy with that,' Indigo said.

'Or you could propose to him,' Mrs Andrews said.

She smiled. 'I could. Well, have fun today.'

'We will, we wanted to get out early to avoid the big storm that's coming in later tonight,' Mr Andrews said.

'Oh no, is it going to rain?' Indigo said.

'Thunder, lightning, gusts of up to fifty-five miles an hour according to the weather forecast. But you know what these forecasts are like, it could be glorious sunshine all day.'

Indigo smiled. 'Let's hope so.'

She left the food counter and went to sit down as far away from River as she possibly could. No doubt she would be the hot topic of conversation at breakfast this morning, they could carry on talking about her and the lies she'd told if she wasn't near them to hear it.

It was such a mess and she had no idea how to fix it or

even if she could. The worst thing was she still hadn't told him about the baby.

She took a big mouthful of pancakes and checked her phone. She hadn't bothered to look at her phone last night, and there were quite a few messages from her friends wanting to know if she was OK because she'd left the chat group. Even Vicky had sent her some messages, thinly veiled messages of concern with a whole load of nastiness thrown into the mix too, mainly about how Indigo wasn't being realistic. She should have cut her out of her life long ago.

She decided to reply to Joey because she always saw the light where there was dark. And Indigo needed something to cheer her up right now.

Hey Joey, I'm OK, thank you. I'm sorry I left the group, Vicky is full of so much negativity and I honestly don't need that right now. River finally knows who I am. Turned out he guessed sometime yesterday and it all came out last night. He wasn't happy, understandably. I'm not sure what will happen now. I don't know if he will want me to stay. He doesn't know about the baby yet.

The reply was almost instant.

Oh Indy, don't give up hope. From what you've told me about him and that night, I think you were meant to be together. There will always be hiccups at the start of any relationship but hiccups can normally be cured by holding your breath.

Indigo smiled at that weird analogy.

Joey went on, **There are some pearls of wisdom buried deep inside that analogy.**

Indigo replied, **I'm sure there are.**

Just be patient. Rome wasn't built in a day, Joey wrote.

I'll keep you posted.

She scrolled through some of the other messages from her friends but she couldn't find the words to explain what was going on, nor was she in the mood for any negativity – she had enough of that swirling around her own head.

She saw Violet's message and clicked into it.

How did it go, are you now happily engaged to Mr Man Mountain?

She giggled and replied, **That's rather optimistic and sadly not likely to happen. He was pretty pissed off when he found out who I was.**

To her surprise, given the time of day, Violet texted straight back. **I would have thought he'd be delighted to see you again. So there was no sexy reunion?**

Indigo smiled. **We did kiss. Briefly. But I think we both just got caught up in the moment. The night we met, we designed a treehouse together – well he only went and built it for me. It was a bit emotional when he showed it to me last night. It's the perfect family home.**

It sounds to me like he has it bad for you.

She was just about to reply when River came over to her table.

'You can come and join us if you want,' he said.

She couldn't think of anything worse. 'Probably not a good idea.'

'Got to be better than sitting over here on your own,' River said.

'So you can all sit in awkward silence and avoid talking

187

about the elephant in the room? I'd rather not inflict that on you and your family.'

'Did Heath say something to you?'

'Heath was very kind,' Indigo said. 'But he also said that you were fighting my corner. Which is lovely but doesn't fill me with hope that I'd be that welcome over there.'

River sighed. 'I'll join you then.' He sat down, not waiting to be invited. 'I've been thinking—'

'I have too, do you want me to leave?'

And if that's what he wanted she would tell him about the baby just before she left. She knew it was cowardly but, as he'd been so mad about her not telling him she was Mindy, she knew he'd be furious to find out she hadn't told him she was pregnant with his child either. She'd tell him about the baby and that he didn't need to be involved if he didn't want to be and then leave.

He watched her carefully. She was beginning to realise this was what he did when he was thinking: not saying anything, just taking it all in.

'So running away is your thing. When things get tough, you run.'

'That's a bit unfair. You don't want me here. I thought I'd save you the drama of having to fire me and kick me out if I left myself.'

'See, this is where you went wrong last time, you didn't talk to me.'

'Do you want me to stay?'

'Why would I want you to leave? Meadow and Bear say you're a quick learner and great with the customers. And you promised me you'd organise the opening ceremony, so you should probably stay for that.'

Indigo couldn't help feeling disheartened by that wonderful rundown of her professional capabilities rather than him wanting her to stay out of love.

'What happened between us should not come between you and your job. I offered you a position here and I stand by that,' River said.

She had not been expecting that and there still was no mention of their relationship, if there was one to salvage. She felt desperately sad about all of this. She hadn't come here expecting anything to happen between them but it had and now it was over before it had begun.

She tried to push away the disappointment and focus on the positive. She still had her job.

'Is that not going to be awkward for us after that night? We've seen each other naked, you made love to me three times, won't that always be hanging in the air between us?'

He shrugged. 'I'm sure we can be grown-up about it.'

'And Meadow is OK with this?'

'Yes, of course, she likes you.'

'Well that makes one of you.'

He smiled sadly and then stood up. 'Annoyingly, I like you as well, too bloody much.'

With that he walked back to the other side of the room and joined his family, leaving Indigo with the faintest glimmer of hope.

River was returning to his treehouse with Tierra when Meadow fell in at his side. He looked at her in surprise. Her treehouse was in the opposite direction.

'Tierra, can you go and pick me a bunch of flowers for the reception area?' Meadow said.

Tierra ran off ahead of them, clearly delighting in her mission, as she started picking different flowers from around the wood.

River sighed. 'What do you want?'

He knew very well that she wanted to talk about Indigo and he'd really rather not. He needed to figure that out for himself.

'I kind of expected that if it did turn out to be Mindy last night, which it obviously did, you'd be declaring your undying love to her, not picking a fight with her. So I have to wonder if you're pushing her away because you're scared of getting hurt.'

He felt his eyebrows shoot up. 'That's not what this is.'

'Except I think it is. You love her. I can hear it when you talk about her, I can see it when you look at her. She's here when you thought you'd never see her again and it's very clear she has feelings for you. Why are you not grabbing her and making the most out of this second chance?'

'I'm just not sure where we go from here. I don't know if I can get over the fact that she ran after we shared the most incredible night together.'

'But doesn't she deserve a second chance? She's here, she came back for you.'

'She came back for a job, not for me.'

'I don't believe that for one minute. She adores you.'

'But how do we build on that past?'

'You learn from it, you foster a relationship where next time she gets scared she can talk to you. You show her she can trust you and give her a chance to gain your trust too.'

'You make it sound so simple. I'm not great at relationships.'

'Because you're always too scared to let people in.'

'Because I'm not...' River trailed off.

'Not what?'

Tierra came bounding up to them holding a bunch of flowers. 'Is this enough?'

'Could you try to get more blue ones?' Meadow said.

Tierra scampered off.

'Not what?' Meadow repeated.

River held off from saying that he wasn't lovable. 'I'm not the kind of person people want to be with long term. Mum and Dad left, none of our family wanted us long term.'

'Your mum and dad left because they had issues of their own to deal with, you know that. I think it had very little to do with you and your brothers. And raising three large boys who were... let's say mischievous because they lacked any kind of discipline or love in their lives, was a big ask for anyone else. Most people will have tales to tell of what little shits they were when they were growing up. That's not a reflection on the person you are now.'

'Even Danielle left.'

'You hated Danielle.'

'She was an awful woman, of course I didn't really want a relationship with her but... it still hurt that she left me for another man. We were only married for a year and she wanted out. Even in the beginning when I was always polite to her and I thought that at least we could be friends even if we didn't love each other, she used to laugh about me with her friends behind my back. Her friends were all married to doctors, accountants, lawyers, they were all highly successful, wealthy husbands. Her friends went on big, expensive, exotic holidays, while I'd taken Danielle for a weekend to Scotland for our honeymoon. When I told her my dream was to have a whole wood filled with tree-houses, she laughed and said I needed bigger and better dreams.'

'And again that's her that's the problem, she was shallow, two-faced, and she also left behind the most amazing little girl – what kind of person does that? Her leaving reflects badly on her not you. You two weren't remotely compatible but that's not your fault. I can see nothing wrong with a man making a hugely successful business for himself and his family, giving lots of people jobs. And your guests love this place, the reviews are outstanding, I'm so proud to be a part of it. Indigo loves it too. She spent a long time yesterday writing out little revision cards on all the treehouses so she could learn each one off by heart.'

'She did?'

Meadow nodded. 'I asked her why she was doing that when all that information is on our system, she can access it with a few clicks of a button, but she said she wanted to know everything there was to know about this place and if she ever got asked when she wasn't near the computer, she would be able to answer the question. She doesn't just want to work here, she wants to live and breathe it just like you.'

He remembered Indigo asking him so many questions about Wishing Wood the night they'd met. It wasn't just polite chit-chat, she'd been genuinely interested and enthralled by it all.

He shook his head. 'I just don't know if I have anything to offer her. I don't know if the life I lead is enough for her, whether I'm enough.'

'Shouldn't she be the judge of that? She seems pretty keen.'

'She doesn't know me.'

'But you're not giving her a chance to find out what a wonderful person you are. That's what dating someone is all about, getting to know each other better to find out if you want something more. You have to put the past behind you, and by that I mean your past too. She's here now and she wants to be a part of your life, and if she leaves because she feels unwanted I think you would regret not taking that chance with her.'

The thought of losing Indigo again now he had her back caused him physical pain. He rubbed his chest. He'd thought he'd have time to get his head round having her back but she'd already talked about leaving over breakfast.

'Just take her to dinner tonight,' Meadow said. 'Talk to her.'

'I'm on call tonight and, besides, it's movie night for me and Tierra.'

'Lunch then.'

'I'll see.'

River hated being coerced into anything but he knew Meadow was right. If they stood any chance at all, he had to fight for her.

Indigo hovered outside the reception door, wondering if Meadow was going to be mad at her. She wouldn't blame her if she was.

Meadow looked up and smiled when she saw her. 'Come on in. I told you, this isn't a place where you can hide.'

Indigo walked in. 'I'm sorry, it was never my intention to deceive anyone. It was only when River didn't realise who I was that I thought I could see if we really did have something beyond a drunken night of passion. I never meant to hurt anyone.'

Meadow nodded. 'River understands that. He doesn't like it but he understands it.'

'He does?'

'Yes.'

Indigo sighed. 'I feel like I've ruined everything between us. I tried to tell him who I was but things kept getting in the way, my own selfishness being one of those things.'

'I don't think it's that you weren't upfront with him when you arrived that bothers him the most,' Meadow said. 'He understands that he didn't make it easy for you when he didn't talk about that night either.'

'It's the fact that I ran away, isn't it? He's never going to forgive me for that.'

'If anyone can relate to not feeling like you're good enough, it's River. He does understand why you did it, but it's still hard for him to move past that. You hurt him when you left and I'm sure he's just trying to protect himself from getting hurt again. He was defending you this morning, it's obvious he still cares for you.'

Indigo approached the desk, placing a pen back in its holder. 'Where do I go from here?'

'I think you just have to give him time and, going forward, if something does develop between you, just be honest with him.'

Indigo nodded.

'And I have a question for you, and I want you to be completely honest with me when you answer it.'

'Of course,' Indigo said. She already felt bad. While she hadn't told any lies, she hadn't been honest about who she was and Meadow had been so lovely offering her a job. She didn't want her to think she'd made the wrong decision.

Silence stretched on for a moment as Meadow clearly thought about how to word what she wanted to say. This made Indigo feel a little bit uncomfortable. What on earth did Meadow want to ask her?

She was saved, momentarily, by Lucien walking into reception to collect his list of treehouses that needed servicing that day and she half hoped that the question would be forgotten. But as soon as Lucien was gone Meadow turned back to face her.

'I might as well come straight out and say it. Are you pregnant?'

Indigo felt like she'd just been punched in the gut as her breath caught in her throat.

Meadow nodded. 'I'm guessing, as you've just gone white as a sheet, that the answer is yes. OK, come on, sit down, before you pass out, take some deep breaths.'

Meadow rushed round to Indigo's side of the desk and, putting her arm around her shoulders, she guided her to a seat. Then she moved to the door, closed it and then grabbed a bottle of water. She came back to Indigo and handed her the bottle, crouching down in front of her.

'Are you OK? Seriously, my first aid skills are crap, I don't want to have to call you an ambulance.'

Indigo took a sip of water, her mouth suddenly dry. Tears welled up in her eyes. God, this was all such a mess.

'I'm sorry, I didn't mean to upset you,' Meadow said.

Indigo shook her head. 'How did you know?'

Meadow shrugged. 'I don't know. Our conversation yesterday about raising a baby alone gave me a clue, then you felt faint yesterday – I had that all the time when I was pregnant with Star – and then I find out that you're the famous Mindy and I kept thinking, why are you here? If you really just wanted a job, you'd have come before now. You said you've been unemployed for six months, if you were that desperate for a job and River had offered you one, you'd have turned up a few days after that night, apologised for running away and asked for the job he'd promised you. Why wait two months?'

'I don't think I'd have come at all if it wasn't for the baby. He had every right to be mad at me for running away the next day. I regretted leaving him so much but I was too scared to face him, I was too scared to face the man I had lost.'

'That's why turning up here after two months didn't make sense, so I thought why else would you come? It was a guess but turns out I was right,' Meadow said, standing up and sitting down on the desk next to Indigo.

'I swear, I came here specifically to tell him. I wanted to do the right thing, he deserved to know he was going to be a dad. I didn't want anything from him, I didn't want

196

marriage or money, I just wanted to let him know. I would have happily raised this baby alone if he didn't want anything to do with me. And then he didn't recognise me and I thought at first you two were married and I didn't want to come between the two of you with my baby and then...' she wiped the tears from her cheeks '...when I started having feelings for him again I selfishly wanted him to want me for me, not because of our baby. He married Danielle just because she was pregnant with Tierra and I didn't want to be another obligation for him.'

'Oh honey, I get that. But he is crazy about you, you have to see that.'

'I don't know about that. I hurt him and lied to him. I don't see any way past that. But I can't wait around for him to decide if he wants to date me again before I tell him about the baby. It was wrong to ever think that. He needed to know all the facts *before* he got involved with me, not for me to present him with a baby as a fait accompli if and when he'd fallen in love with me. That's not fair. I was going to tell him last night, when I planned to tell him who I really was, but he was so pissed off about the whole Mindy thing, and rightly so, I didn't want to throw a baby into the mix as well. And now he's going to hate me for not telling him about that too.'

'Look, I'm not going to get involved in this, I won't tell him or anyone else. How or when you tell him is up to you but, if you ask my opinion, the sooner you tell him the better,' Meadow said, gently.

Indigo nodded. 'I know.'

Meadow glanced at the entrance. 'And you have about ten seconds before he comes barrelling through that door, so if you don't want to tell him now, I suggest you wipe your eyes.'

Indigo looked over to see River approaching. She cast around for a tissue but it was too late, he was suddenly pushing the door open.

'Indigo, I...' River started but his face fell when he saw she'd been crying. He turned to Meadow. 'What the hell is going on? I told you I didn't want you to give her a hard time over this.'

Indigo shook her head. 'Meadow hasn't said anything to upset me, this isn't to do with her at all.'

'Then what? You better not be crying over me. I told you, I'm not worth losing any tears over.'

Indigo took a deep breath. 'Do you have time to talk?'

He nodded, looking thoroughly confused. He had no idea his whole life was about to change.

She glanced at Meadow who gave her a little nod of encouragement. Indigo got up and walked out the office and River followed her.

CHAPTER TWELVE

'Let's go down here,' River said and Indigo followed him down some steps into a tiny cove. The sea was out and the white sand sparkled in the sunshine. There was no one else down there, which she was thankful for. She slipped off her shoes, feeling the warm sand between her toes as they walked down to the shore. It was quiet here, only the sounds of the waves lapping on the wet sand. They looked out over the sea, the horizon lost in a pink haze. It was hard to believe the weather was going to change quite so ferociously later that day, maybe the weather report had got it wrong.

'I want to say something first,' River said, turning to face her. 'I reacted horribly last night and I'm sorry.'

'River.' She put a hand on his arm to stop him speaking. He had to know the truth before they went any further. 'You have nothing to apologise for. You are a wonderful man and I don't deserve your compassion. I've lied to you from the moment I arrived here.' She sighed. 'I lied to you when I said I came here for a job, although I am eternally grateful to have one.'

He frowned. 'What did you come here for?'

She swallowed the lump of emotion in her throat, wondering how to phrase it, whether to explain why she hadn't told him before now, but sometimes the simplest words were the most effective.

She took a deep breath. 'I'm pregnant.'

His eyes widened, his eyebrows disappearing into his hair. He was shocked now but in a minute he was going to get angry. He'd demand to know why she hadn't told him before now, which he was completely justified in asking. He'd probably shout at her and then storm off, furious at her deception.

He rubbed his hands across his face and turned away, pushing his hands through his hair.

'Christ,' he muttered.

'I'm sorry,' Indigo said, tears filling her eyes again.

He turned round to face her and she braced herself for his wrath.

'Oh Indy,' he said, softly. He reached out and pulled her into a hug.

She stood with her head resting on his chest, stunned into silence. He started stroking her hair and after a moment she tentatively wrapped her arms around him, a thick lump of emotion lodged in her throat. This was absolutely not the reaction she imagined or what she deserved. They stood like that for the longest time and she knew he was probably using this moment to process this massive piece of news.

'I'm sorry,' River said, eventually.

She looked up at him. 'What do you have to be sorry for? I was the one who kept it a secret from you.'

'For making you pregnant.'

'You can't take that on your shoulders. We're both responsible for that.'

He shook his head. 'We used a condom?'

'Every time.'

He pulled a face. 'I'm pretty sure those condoms were well past their expiration date. I haven't been with another woman for five years. I didn't even think of that when I was making love to you. Which makes this my responsibility. You trusted me to protect you and I didn't.'

'It doesn't matter. That's in the past. We're here now. There's nothing to gain from pointing fingers.'

He stroked a hair from her face. 'This couldn't have come at a worst time.'

She frowned and stepped back from him. 'I'm sorry this isn't convenient for you.'

He smiled slightly as he snagged her hand and pulled her back into a hug.

'I meant, for you. No home, no job and I come along and make things ten times worse for you.' He suddenly frowned. 'Have you decided what you are going to do?' He swallowed. 'I understand if… you don't want to keep it.'

'There is no decision. There never was. I'm keeping this baby. I didn't come here wanting money or expecting you to turn your whole life around to include our baby. I just came to tell you you're going to be a dad whether you want to be involved or not.'

River opened his mouth to speak but she silenced him with a finger over his lips. 'I'm sorry if that's not what you want to hear. Maybe other women in this situation might discuss it with the father and they'd decide together whether to keep it, but there is no way in the world I could ever...' she couldn't even say the words. 'I don't see this as a bad thing, River. You've given me this wonderful gift and I'm going to treasure it.'

River stared at her and then a slow smile spread across his face. To her surprise he bent his head and kissed her. It was only a brief kiss but she couldn't help melting against him. He pulled back slightly and kissed her on the forehead.

'You don't know how relieved I am to hear you say that. It's the strangest thing, wanting something so badly that I only found out existed ten seconds ago. When Danielle came to me pregnant with Tierra, there was a huge part of her that didn't want to keep our daughter, but I did. I was terrified that I couldn't possibly be a good father, I'd never had any good role models, but I wanted her to have that baby. I want you to have this baby too.'

Tears welled in her eyes. 'You don't know what it means to hear you say that. I came here with no expectations, I didn't need anything from you. I just thought you should know. But in my heart, I really hoped you'd want this baby. I wanted our baby to be loved, not something to put up with. I saw you with Tierra and Star and I wanted my child to have such a wonderful man in their life too. I know things with us are complicated and that's all my fault. I understand if you don't want to be with me. I'm a mess. As you said last night, maybe it's best that we draw a line under us but I would love it if you were a part of our baby's life. I can get a house nearby and you can see our baby as often as you want.'

River shook his head. 'You can move back in with me. When the baby cries in the middle of the night I want to help soothe it back to sleep. I want to help with the night feeds, the dirty nappies, I want to be there for all of it.'

The tears that had been threatening to spill over for the last few minutes finally did. Not only did he want her to have the baby, but he wanted to be involved to that extent too.

'That's… so incredibly generous of you. You don't have to do that.'

He gently wiped her tears away. 'Of course I do, I have a responsibility to you both. I want to be a proper father to our baby, not someone who only sees their child at weekends. I never had a father who cared about me or my brothers. I want my children to have that. Raising a child is a partnership and I want to help you with it. Actually, we should probably get married.'

She let out a little laugh at that. 'River, I'm not getting married to you just because I'm pregnant with your child. It might be old-fashioned but I'm only getting married for love, and as much as I'd like to believe that night we both fell in love at first sight, we know that isn't true. I certainly didn't come here hoping for a ring on my finger.'

'I think we could have something amazing. Don't you think we owe it to ourselves and our baby to try again? We can make this work.'

Her heart sank at those words. 'I think we're better off being friends.'

'But you said you felt that connection from that night when you first came here.'

'I did, I do, but if you did too then we wouldn't have to *make it work*. We would just be together and it would be incredible. Last night you said you didn't want to give us a second chance, you said that night we fulfilled a need for each other, it wasn't anything more than that. That is not something to build a marriage on.'

'Last night I was an idiot.'

'No you weren't. Not at all. You had every right to be angry at me for not telling you who I was. You have every right to be angry now for keeping this a secret from you too.'

'I'm not in the habit of shouting at pregnant women,' River said.

'The point is, when I came here and realised my feelings for you from that night were still there, I was hoping you'd want me for me, not out of duty or responsibility to our baby. Let's face it, after last night, you wouldn't be standing here now with your arms round me if I hadn't just told you I was carrying your child.'

'That's not true.'

'You were still pissed off at me over breakfast.'

'I can be pissed off and still care about you at the same time.'

She took a step out of his arms. 'We can work out a way for both of us to be involved in raising our baby but marriage isn't it. Thank you for being so utterly lovely about all of this. It's a hell of a lot more than I deserved. I better get back.'

She turned and walked away.

'Oi!'

River looked up at the half-finished treehouse to see Bear and Heath staring down at him.

'What?'

'You've been staring at that piece of wood in your hand for the last ten minutes,' Bear said. 'We've been talking to you and you've not heard a word since you got back from seeing Indigo. What gives?'

River climbed the ladder so he was level with them. There was no point in trying to keep something this big a secret. 'Indigo is pregnant.'

They were both silent for a moment.

'It's mine, before you ask,' River said. 'And she's keeping it.'

'Wow,' Heath said. 'How do you feel about that?'

'It's a shock of course and rather selfishly when she first told me, for a few seconds, I thought about how this was going to impact on my life and Tierra's. But then I turned around to see her on the verge of tears and I just felt this huge surge of protectiveness for her. This isn't about me, it's about her. She's about to become a mum for the first time, no home, no money, she must be terrified. And this is my fault. She trusted me to protect her and, in my drunken state, I used out-of-date condoms. What kind of ass does that make me? I care about her and finding out she is Mindy doesn't change those feelings, despite that she got scared and ran away the next day. If anything, those feelings are stronger than they were before because now I know why I felt so connected to her when she first arrived.

Why I felt an attraction that was so powerful, unlike anything I've ever felt before. It all stems back to the best night of my life. Last night, watching her laugh with Tierra and really take the time to talk to her, I felt those feelings deepen for her. And now I find out she's carrying my child. Well, I want to look after her.'

'That's very caveman,' Heath said.

'You're going to need a bigger treehouse,' Bear said, practically.

'I don't think she wants to move in with me. I said we should probably get married, she didn't like that idea.'

'Why not?' Heath said. 'Raising a baby on your own can't be any fun. Raising Star with Meadow was hard enough work, I can't imagine doing that alone. Christ, you know that better than anyone.'

'It wasn't easy and I don't want Indigo to have to do that. I don't want my baby to grow up without a father either, we've all been through that and it's not good,' River said.

'I thought she was crazy about you,' Bear said.

'I think I hurt her last night with my reaction to the whole Mindy thing. She thinks we're better off being friends.'

Heath shrugged. 'You can be friends and raise a baby together, you don't need love to do that. Look at me and Meadow.'

'She says she will only get married for love.'

'That's a bit of an old-fashioned notion, isn't it?' Heath said.

'So is getting married just because she's pregnant,' Bear said. 'I'm with Indigo on this. Your last marriage failed

206

spectacularly, and I'm not saying that's your fault, but marrying for love has got to be better than marrying someone you hate just because they're carrying your baby. That's a recipe for disaster.'

'I don't hate Indigo.'

'But do you love her?' Bear asked.

River was silent, remembering how he felt the night before, before everything had come tumbling out in the open. He sighed. 'I have feelings for her. But I don't think we know each other well enough for it to be love yet. But I think we could love each other eventually.'

'Christ, that's romantic,' Heath said, dryly. 'Please tell me you didn't say that to her.'

'No, well, I said that I think we can make it work.'

Bear and Heath winced.

'And you wonder why she turned you down?' Bear said. 'No woman wants to hear "We should probably get married."'

'Or "We can make it work," like it's some chore to finish,' Heath said.

'She thinks you only want to be with her because of the baby,' Bear said.

River knew he was right. Indigo had pretty much said the same thing herself. The frustrating thing was he'd come to see her because he'd wanted to apologise and ask her if she wanted to go to lunch. He was never one to hold a grudge for long and he didn't want to walk away from their incredible connection so easily. Now, if he asked her out, she'd think it was because of the baby, not because he wanted to go out with her.

'I've cocked this up,' River said.

'I don't think it's beyond repair,' Bear said. 'Show her your romantic side.'

'I don't think I have one of those.'

'I suggest you dig deep and find it,' Heath said.

River sighed. He knew they were right.

'Look, don't say anything to anyone about this yet. I'm pretty sure Meadow knows, but no one else needs to. I don't need this getting back to Amelia yet. And I need to figure out how and when to tell Tierra too.'

They both nodded. 'My lips are sealed,' Heath said.

'And if you need a babysitter while you sort this mess out, you know I'm always happy to have Tierra,' Bear said.

'Thanks, I might just take you up on that.'

Indigo was manning the reception while Meadow was putting some flowers, champagne and other treats in one of the treehouses for another honeymoon couple who were due to arrive that afternoon.

She'd been busy all morning planning the big opening ceremony in July. There was a lot to organise. As head receptionist in one of the finest hotels in the UK, she always went above and beyond for her guests, organising their every wish and need. From getting one of the best Chinese restaurants in Bristol, which never normally did takeaways, to deliver their food for one guest, to arranging for two llamas to be in the hotel gardens when one of the guests proposed, she'd done it all. But organising an entire party was a big task. The hotel had a whole conference and banqueting department that did that kind of thing.

Indigo had already spoken to Alex about providing food for the night. They weren't going to do a big sit-down meal or anything flash. They'd agreed to get a local farmer to do a hog roast and Alex was going to provide lots of bite-size foods and cakes as a bit of a buffet. Indigo had spent a long time finding some of the most influential bloggers and travel journalists and, because the bookings for the new treehouses didn't start until the Monday of the last week in July, she'd invited a few of them to stay the weekend before, which was when the party was going to take place.

She'd even discussed with Meadow about having fireworks but that was still a grey area as there were horseshoe bats living nearby which were a protected species and shouldn't be disturbed. She'd put a few emails out to firework display companies about silent fireworks to see what kind of thing they could offer. It was funny – living in a city, that sort of issue had never crossed her mind, but being here was a different way of life and one she could definitely get used to.

While it was quiet she sent a quick text to Violet and her friends, leaving Vicky out of the loop.

I told River this morning about the baby and he's been so utterly lovely about it. I don't know if we have a future together, but there is still a strong attraction between us. In the meantime, he's given me my own treehouse to stay in which is the most beautiful place I've ever seen. It has three floors, a bathroom with a roll-top bath and a gorgeous nursery. I feel happy here, which is something I haven't felt for a long time.

Suddenly she heard the familiar roar of the Lamborghini, which hopefully didn't disturb the bats too much. Her heart sank. She wondered if word had travelled as far as Amelia about her current predicament, or whether Amelia with her sixth sense suddenly somehow knew, as if the secret had been carried on the wind.

The car pulled up outside reception and Amelia climbed out looking as glamorous as ever. Today she was wearing a startling green Greek-style dress and she looked absolutely stunning.

'Indigo, my dear, how are you?' Amelia said, with false politeness, when Indigo knew what she really wanted to know was if there'd been any developments between Indigo and River. At the moment she was obviously trying to keep her end of the bargain she'd made with River and not pry any more. But at least one thing was clear, Amelia didn't yet know about her pregnancy. That would be the first thing she'd open with if she'd known that.

'I'm fine,' Indigo said.

'You don't look fine, or sound it. Did you and River have a little falling-out?'

'No, well… yes, but it's complicated,' Indigo said.

'What did he do?'

'It's more like what I did.'

'The course of true love never runs smooth. There are always complications, bumps in the road. Is there anything I can help with at all?' Amelia added eagerly.

Indigo couldn't help smiling at the subtle, or rather not so subtle, interfering.

'Why are you so interested in your grandsons' lives? I'm sure they are quite capable at messing it up for themselves without your help.'

'That's exactly why I want to help, I don't want them to make the same mistakes I did.'

'But that's what life is, we're supposed to make mistakes and then we learn from them, become better people. No one can lead a perfect life, even with the best of help.'

All humour faded from Amelia's eyes. 'Some mistakes are too big.'

Oh, that had Indigo intrigued.

Amelia sighed and pulled up a chair. 'I'm sure you'll hear it from River or one of the others anyway, so I might as well tell you my side of the story. When I was fourteen, I fell in love with an older boy. He was sixteen, not nearly a man, but I thought he was wonderful. My parents forbade me to see him, which just made sneaking out to meet him even more exciting. Long story short, I fell pregnant and he didn't want anything to do with me. Back then unmarried women were practically forced to give their babies up for adoption and teenage mums had no say at all. My parents made the final decision over what happened to my children.'

'Children?'

'I had twin boys, Michael and Joseph. Except they were the names they were given by their adopted parents. I didn't get to give them a name at all. Looking back, I probably should have fought harder to keep them. But I had no job, I was still living at home with my parents who wanted nothing to do with their grandchildren. I had no idea how to be a mother. In some ways it was something of a relief when they were taken from me. I thought they'd go to a better home. I grew up, got married, moved to Australia – never had any more children though. But I never forgot my babies. When I was a lot older, and when Michael and Joseph were both adults, I was able to track them down. They didn't have the better life I had hoped for them, in fact their childhoods were miserable. Our relationship was strained. I think they blamed me entirely. We kept in touch, I phoned them occasionally, they sent me the odd Christmas card.'

Amelia fiddled with a ring on her finger. 'Joseph had three children, River, Heath and Bear, and then abandoned them when they were still tiny children themselves, something I had no idea about until, well, after Joseph and his wife died actually. But I can't help thinking that it was history repeating itself – Joseph abandoned his children just like I abandoned him. Michael never had any family at all and I can't help feeling responsible for that too. River, Heath and Bear grew up without any parental love because Joseph had never been loved himself and don't get me started on the messed-up childhood his wife had gone through. And now, River is nearly thirty never having had any kind of serious relationship apart from with Danielle and she really doesn't count. Heath married his best friend, I think purely to have the family life he'd missed out on himself when he was a child, while Bear has a long list of failed relationships behind him, probably partly because none of them are Meadow, but maybe because none of them had a good role model in the relationship sense. And honestly, I just wonder if all of this is down to me. They come from a long line of failed relationships and a lack of love. And I would love nothing more to see all three brothers happily married and in love before I shuffle off this mortal coil. So yes, I'll keep interfering as much as I possibly can so they don't end up making the same mistakes I did.'

Indigo stared at her. 'Wow. That's…'

'Exactly, my dear. So if you want to give me some kind of nugget of hope for a happy ending for River, I would love to hear it.'

Indigo sat back in her chair as she thought. She didn't know if it was a happy ending for River. Amelia would probably think she was some kind of money-grabbing bitch, who was trying to trap River into marriage, just like Danielle did, at least in Amelia's mind. But the fact was Amelia was going to find out soon enough, so Indigo might as well get it out of the way now.

'I asked her to marry me.'

Indigo looked up to see River leaning against the door frame.

Amelia's face lit up as if all her Christmases had come at once.

'She said no, but I'm working on it,' River said.

Amelia's face fell and Indigo rolled her eyes.

River moved into the office. 'And we don't blame you for our upbringing. You were fourteen when you fell pregnant, you were still a child yourself. How could you have possibly raised my dad and uncle by yourself? Maybe Dad was a product of his upbringing and that indirectly had an impact on us, but that wasn't your fault. Besides, people can choose to let their past define them or they can choose to use that experience to become a better person, escape that loop, lead a better life. When Tierra was born, I knew there was no way she was going to grow up like I did, feeling unloved and unwanted. Dad could have made that choice for us too. And while it's true that I've never had a serious relationship outside of Tierra's mum, maybe that's because I've never met someone who I wanted that with before. Until now.'

Indigo's breath caught in her throat.

'What is going on here?' Amelia said, excitedly. 'Yesterday was Indigo's first day in her job and now you're proposing marriage and talking about having a serious relationship. You said nothing was going on between you?'

Indigo sighed. 'We might as well tell her. She'll find out soon enough anyway.'

'Tell me what?'

River gave a resigned nod.

Indigo took a deep breath. 'Well, River and I had a one-night stand two months ago that has led to me being pregnant with his child. I came here to tell him but he didn't recognise me, partly because I was dressed like a cat when we met and partly because he misheard my name that night.' She held back the fact River had been very drunk, she didn't want to discredit him in front of his gran. 'I decided to keep who I am and why I was here a secret for a few days so I could have a chance at getting to know him properly, but the secret's out now and River thinks the best solution to this problem is to marry me.'

Amelia, for once, was stunned into silence.

'Firstly,' River said to Indigo. 'I don't see you being pregnant with my child as a problem. Secondly, what we shared was way more than just some meaningless one-night stand, which is what you've just made it out to be. We shared a connection far deeper than that. Whether it was love or not remains to be seen but I won't dismiss it as some random drunken shag, because you deserve more than that.'

Now it was Indigo's turn to fall silent. Amelia still hadn't said anything either.

River carried on. 'I came to see you this morning because last night, while we were having dinner with Tierra, I felt things for you I had never felt before. Finding out you were Mindy has done nothing to change my feelings for you. This morning, I came to ask if you wanted to go for lunch today, so that maybe we could start again now I know the truth and we no longer have any secrets between us. That was before I knew you were pregnant. So to say I only want to be with you for the sake of our child is simply not true and, if you search your heart, you know that. That kiss last night was amazing, the night we met our connection was incredible… that has nothing to do with our baby, that's just us.'

Indigo couldn't help the huge bubble of happiness expanding in her chest. This was what she wanted to hear, but what a time to hear it. She wanted to step forward and kiss him but she couldn't do that with Amelia sitting next to her. She glanced across at Amelia, who had the biggest smile on her face. Indigo half expected her to get out a bowl of popcorn and watch the whole thing unfold.

Amelia finally found her voice. 'This is brilliant. Tell me everything. I want to know all the details. What was the sex like? How did you two meet?'

'I don't think you need to know those details. You know where we are now, that's enough,' River said.

'You promised me all the sordid details,' Amelia said,

like a child who'd just had their favourite toy snatched from them.

'I said that if we have sex in the future, I'd let you know all the details. Clearly now Indigo is pregnant there won't be any of that. I don't want to do anything to hurt our baby.'

Indigo frowned. That was a highly disappointing turn of events. And most likely not necessary either. A lot of couples continued to have sex throughout their pregnancy. This was something she would need to talk to him about if they started dating again. She couldn't imagine being with River and not being able to be intimate with him.

'I don't think that's right,' Amelia said, doubtfully.

'Our sex was definitely very… energetic. Look at the size of me. Sex with me is not going to be gentle.'

Except it had been. Not the first two times, that had been passionate and needful. He had taken her hard and fast and she'd loved every second of it, but the third time, after they'd dozed a little and then woken up and kissed, he'd made love to her with such gentle tenderness and affection, she had no worries at all about any future sex with him hurting their baby.

If they ever got that far again.

'I will tell you that me and Tierra had a wonderful night with Indigo last night and that when I kissed her, it felt like… coming home,' River said.

Indigo swallowed the lump in her throat.

'Oh go on, marry him, will you,' Amelia said. 'This is a beautiful story.'

'Indigo has said she will only marry for love and I understand that,' River said.

'Are you expecting the big bells and whistles proposal?' Amelia said as if Indigo was asking for the moon in expecting something a bit more romantic than *We should probably get married.* Maybe she'd read too many romance books and was now expecting the fairytale that didn't really exist.

'Not bells and whistles,' Indigo said, feeling like she was being railroaded.

'You could propose to him,' Amelia suggested. 'I did that to my second husband. If I'd waited for him to propose, I'd have been waiting a bloody long time. Then you can arrange the perfect proposal, exactly how you want it.'

'That's kind of the man's job,' River said.

Amelia snorted. 'That's very old-fashioned.'

'I have no problem proposing myself,' Indigo said. 'But you're kind of missing the point. It's not the big romantic proposal I want, I would only propose to a man if I was completely crazy in love with him. And that goes for saying yes to his proposal too.'

Suddenly Indigo spotted Kit Lewis approaching the reception area and she shushed Amelia and River, flapping her hands to get them to be quiet.

'Hello again,' Indigo said, snapping straight into professional mode, while River and Amelia were frozen like statues as if their very presence could give away what they'd just been talking about. Indigo smiled as a large overgrown puppy came bounding after Kit, all legs and flappy ears and bigger than an average dog. 'And who's this?'

'This is our puppy Moonstone, she's a Great Dane and will end up twice the size of this once she's fully grown.

She's only six months old and into everything. Zoey always wanted a Great Dane growing up, so of course we had to have one.'

'She's beautiful,' Indigo said, letting Moonstone sniff her hand, before stroking her under her chin.

'I haven't got long, Zoey will be here in a second. We're off to Tenby for the day so I said I was going to ask for directions. Have you had any more thought about where I could propose to her at the end of the week?'

'I have, me and River talked about it actually,' she indicated the man himself. 'There are lots of lovely beaches, Barafundle Bay, Manorbier, Skrinkle Haven. Church Door Cove has one of those spectacular sea arches which is very interesting and, even here, the little cove over there, Lilac Cove, is quiet and secluded, plus there's Pear Tree Beach further along. There's lots of nice restaurants, Pandora's is apparently very fancy. Or if you wanted something simpler and chose to propose here, we could help you with candles or fairy lights.' She looked at Moonstone who was gazing at her adoringly. 'Maybe you could even incorporate Moonstone somehow, tie the ring to her collar.'

Kit's eyes lit up. 'Now that's a wonderful idea. Let me look into some of these other places but using Moonstone is a lovely touch. I better go, thanks for your help.'

He turned to leave.

'Kit, the words you use are probably the most important thing,' Indigo said, recalling River's advice.

Kit grinned. 'Thanks, yes I should probably write some kind of speech to make sure I get it right.'

'From the heart is probably the best. Just make sure you

tell her you love her, no woman wants to hear a proposal without those words,' she said, meaningfully.

'Yes, thanks, sometimes we can get so caught up in the moment we don't say the words that are the most important.'

Kit gave her a wave and left, Moonstone bouncing after him.

Indigo looked at River who smirked and nodded. 'Message received loud and clear. But I feel we've gone off on a tangent here. Amelia, we're not getting married. Well, not yet.' He turned to Indigo. 'But I'd like to take you out for lunch as soon as Meadow gets back.'

'I'm here,' Meadow said, bursting into the reception area, obviously having heard the Lamborghini arrive.

'Thank goodness,' Amelia said. 'River's about to take young Indigo out on a date.'

'I'm asking her to have lunch with me, nothing more than that,' River said, firmly.

'Where are you going? Some place nice?' Amelia said, not to be deterred.

'Well, I owe you a meal at Pandora's so that seems like a good place to start.'

Amelia let out a low whistle. 'If you want to impress her, that would do it.'

'Indigo, would you like to come to lunch with me?' River asked.

She nodded. 'I'd love to.'

Amelia let out a squeal of delight and Indigo couldn't help but smile when River let out a small sigh of frustration. He gestured for him to follow her.

CHAPTER THIRTEEN

They walked round the back of the building to the car park and River opened the passenger door of a beaten-up old Land Rover.

Indigo spotted Greta getting into her car nearby and Greta gave her a wave. Indigo wondered what she would make of her going off somewhere with River, would that be cause for gossip? Although now Amelia knew Indigo was pregnant with River's baby, everyone who worked at the resort would soon know too so she shouldn't be worried about what they would think of her simply getting in the car. They now had much bigger news to get their teeth into.

River quickly dusted some wood chippings off the passenger seat into the footwell. 'I'm sorry, if I'd known I was going to take you out, I would have cleaned it up a bit.'

'It's no bother at all,' Indigo said.

He walked round the other side and got in.

'I expect, working for Crystal Orb Hotel and Infinity Hotels, things were just a bit neater and tidier.' River negotiated the car out of Wishing Wood and onto the road.

'The hotel was always clean and sparkling but Wishing Wood is charming and rustic. It's different but that doesn't mean it's a bad thing. You can't really compare the two.'

'No, they are in very different leagues,' River said.

'No, I mean it's like comparing ice cream to a burger. I love burgers, but I don't want that as my dessert, nor would I want ice cream for my main course and ice cream is one of my favourite foods in the world. This place is definitely ice cream in comparison to Infinity Hotel's forty-pound burgers.'

She watched River and he seemed to smile at this.

'I'm sorry about my family giving you the Spanish Inquisition about us too. I think you're a bit of a novelty to them. There's never been a woman I've been serious about before.'

'It's fine,' Indigo said. She felt warm inside that he was serious about her. Although Vicky was right, it was ridiculous to hope for the fairytale happy ending, she couldn't help doing just that.

'I'm sorry if I revealed too much to Amelia too but I've learned long ago she's completely insufferable unless you give her some morsels to get her teeth into. I hope you don't mind.'

'Not at all but I think you've whetted her appetite so much she'll definitely be back for more.'

'I don't plan on telling her anything else, what happens between us stays between us from now on.'

She smiled at that. Although she knew Amelia would have her means to squeeze information out of them.

They hadn't been driving for long when River pulled into a car park of a restaurant so posh it looked like it belonged on a high street in one of the most expensive parts of London.

'Wow,' Indigo said. 'Have you been here before?'

'No, never. This is not the kind of place I would go for dinner.'

He got out of the car and she frowned after him. If this wasn't his sort of place then why would he bring her here?

Together they walked inside into a reception area made entirely out of black marble. Gold lamps hung from the walls with subdued lighting and there was a woman in a very tailored black trouser suit ready to greet them.

The woman looked them up and down in disgust. Indigo was wearing a little summer dress more suited for the beach than posh restaurants. River was wearing very dusty clothes that were covered in paint and other things because he spent his days building treehouses. She could immediately see that he was uncomfortable with the way the woman was looking at him, brushing his clothes down and combing his fingers through his hair to try to make himself more presentable. Her heart ached for him.

'Can I help you?' the woman said, clearly hoping they'd made a wrong turn.

'A table for two please,' River said.

'It will be a fifteen-minute wait at least,' the woman snapped.

'That's OK, we can wait.'

River picked up two menus and sat down. Indigo sat down next to him and he handed her a menu. The woman walked off.

Indigo opened the menu and scanned the different dishes. The food was very fancy and over the top. She spotted a burger and her eyes nearly fell out of her head to see it was priced at fifty-six pounds.

She snapped the menu closed. 'River, this place is disgustingly expensive and they have a really bad attitude, or at least the maître d' does. I just want a burger and chips and to have some time to talk to you. I don't need you to pay a small mortgage to do that.'

'Do you want to go somewhere else?'

'Yes.'

'There's a clifftop café down the road that does a great burger.'

'Let's go there.'

'If we leave now, she'll think it's because we can't afford the prices.'

'I don't care what she thinks. This place isn't me and it isn't you and if we want to find out more about each other then this is not the place to do it.'

River stared at her for a moment and then took the menu off her, put it back in its stand along with his own, and gestured for her to follow him back out.

They returned to the car and drove a couple of minutes down the road. He pulled into the small car park of a restaurant with large glass windows overlooking the sea.

'This place has the most amazing burgers,' he said.

'That sounds great.' Indigo's stomach gurgled appreciatively.

He got out and Indigo did the same.

'What a wonderful location to have a restaurant,' she said. The sea stretched out in front of them and you could easily see for miles up and down the coast too. The golden sands below them looked warm and inviting and there were families playing on the beach and in the waves. This would be a wonderful place to raise a child. Maybe that was getting ahead of herself as things between her and River might not work out, but she could picture herself here, walking on the beach every day, playing in the sea with her young toddler. The bay below them was large but very sheltered, the waves, at least right now, were very gentle.

'What are property prices like round here?' Indigo said as she followed him inside.

'Expensive. You might struggle to buy anywhere close to Wishing Wood. Renting is expensive too. Most of our staff drive in from some of the bigger towns further inland.'

That dream of living by the sea quickly fizzled and died.

'But you don't need to worry about that. You can live at Wishing Wood, either with me or in Blossom Cottage. If we are going to raise our baby together it makes sense for you to live there.'

She smiled at that gesture. The possibility of spending the rest of her life in Wishing Wood was a lovely one. She could get excited about that.

They went inside and one of the waitresses – dressed in shorts, t-shirt and flip-flops – showed them to a table by the window, overlooking the sea. She offered out two menus but River shook his head.

'Two burgers and chips please.'

The waitress smiled. 'I love a decisive customer. No problem, I'll put that order in for you. And to drink?'

'Just water for me,' River said.

'Me too.'

She nodded and left them alone.

Indigo looked out over the waves. 'Now, if you wanted to impress me, this view is the way to do it, not some fancy-ass restaurant where you have to wear a suit and tie to enter.'

He smiled. 'I'm not really a suit and tie person.'

'Yeah, me neither.'

The waitress returned with two glasses of iced water and then left them while she dealt with some other customers.

'Thank you for agreeing to come to lunch with me,' River said.

'Thank *you* for asking me, I thought I had ruined everything.'

He frowned. 'What we have is too important not to explore it some more. I do have feelings for you—'

'I have feelings for you too.'

'But I want to be honest with you and say I am cautious about getting involved in a relationship. That doesn't mean I don't want that but this is all new to me.'

Her heart sank a little. 'What is it you're worried about?'

'I suppose mostly about what happens when it ends.'

'Why will it end?'

'Because… Because I have nothing to offer you.'

'That's not true.'

'As my dear gran said, I have never had a serious relationship. Why do you think that is?'

'I could make a guess.'

'Because I'm not the kind of person people fall in love with. I'm... nothing.'

Indigo felt her eyebrows shoot up. 'See, that wouldn't be my guess at all. I would say the reason you've never had a relationship is because your parents abandoning you hurt more than you're willing to admit and you've never wanted to let anyone in in an attempt to protect yourself from getting hurt again. The reason you're trying to push me away is because I already hurt you and you're scared I'm going to do it again.'

He stared at her with wide eyes and she guessed by his expression she'd probably hit the nail right on the head.

'OK, let's start with that. I don't know what's going to happen between us, whether we have a future or not, but I promise you I will never run from you again. If things don't work out we'll talk about it in a way that I hope means we can stay friends. But I feel very excited about where we are right now. I have feelings for you too that I've never felt before, not even with Luke. Now let's talk about the other thing: you are not nothing. You are the most incredible man I have ever met.' She looked at him, knowing he didn't believe it, and she decided to try another way. 'It hurts me that you think that about yourself. Because if you believe that then you must think I have no taste in men if I'm attracted to you, that I set the bar incredibly low if I want to be with you. So you don't have a very high opinion of me at all.'

'Indigo, I think you're wonderful.'

'If you think that then you have to trust in my decisions, you have to believe that I would only choose someone magnificent to be with and you are magnificent in every way. If all we had was one great night and we didn't have this connection, then I wouldn't be here now. I've already told you that I'm not marrying you simply because I'm pregnant. That should show you that I wouldn't just settle for you or for anyone. I'm a woman with extremely high standards. Don't doubt that.'

He stared at her for the longest time, taking in everything she'd said, and then very slowly a smile started to spread across his face. 'OK.'

She took his hand. 'I feel that this baby has brought me back to you, so we can have a second chance. I regretted running away and there hasn't been a single day since I left that I didn't think about you and wish we could try again.'

He turned his hand and entwined his fingers with her own. 'I've thought about you constantly too. I've thought about what I would do if I ever got a second chance with you and it certainly wasn't pick an argument with you. Last night, it threw me because I've always thought it was my fault you ran and it wasn't and I just didn't know what to do with that. So I'm sorry for being an ass about all of this.'

'Maybe we just put the past behind us now and start over?' Indigo said.

He shook his head. 'I don't want to forget the past. Our connection that night is something I want to build on, not pretend it didn't happen. Besides, our baby was conceived that night, that's something to be celebrated.'

She smiled, her heart filling with love for him.

'Look. I want to take things slow, really get to know each other,' River said. 'We jumped ahead to the dessert without taking the time to enjoy the starters and the main course. I know sex is off the table until at least after the baby is born but I would prefer that we waited until we were more comfortable with each other anyway. We can date, talk, learn to trust each other, then we can be intimate with each other in other ways that don't involve me pinning you to the nearest hard surface.'

She frowned.

'River, I'm happy to take this as slow as you want. I don't want to mess this up either. When I thought you didn't recognise me, that's what I wanted, time to get to know the real you, not just the passionate, crazy-good-in-bed you. We can date for as long as it takes for you to be sure you want a future with me but you know we can have sex, right? If you want to, that is. I know you're not ready to do that yet because things between us are still so… up in the air, but just because I'm pregnant, it doesn't mean we can't still have sex.'

He stared at her. 'I wasn't sure if you'd want to. When Danielle was pregnant, she made it very clear there would be no sex. Not that I wanted to, I couldn't stand her so I didn't really care. But I overheard her talking to a friend once about how horny she was feeling while she was pregnant and her friend asked if I wasn't delivering in the bedroom. Danielle pulled a face and then said that she didn't want to hurt the baby. I wasn't sure if that was just an excuse but, since I had no interest in having sex with her, I certainly didn't push it.'

'I'm not sure why Danielle didn't want to have sex with you but you don't need to worry about hurting our baby. Our little bean is about an inch big right now and tucked up safe and sound inside here. Sure, having hard and fast sex against the wall might be off the table but I have no worries about making love to you.'

He swallowed. 'OK.'

'When you're ready, of course. And if we never get that far and we just decide to stay as friends then that's OK too. I don't want you to feel like you have to date me or be with me to get me to stay. You are a wonderful father and I want my baby to have you in their life. Regardless of what happens between us, that's the most important thing to me. So if you decide that all it was that night was us fulfilling a need for each other, and you don't want to take it any further than that, then we can be friends and we'll raise this baby together as friends. There is no pressure here to force this into some fairytale ending if you're not comfortable with that.'

He was quiet for a moment. 'OK.'

Just then the burgers arrived.

She smiled. 'I'm going to eat my burger now. This baby is hungry all the time.'

He nodded and let go of her hand to pick up his own food, watching her as he ate, his eyes locked on hers, and she couldn't help but cross her fingers and toes that he would want that fairytale with her.

She looked out at the sea. 'This is beautiful. I love being near the sea. Whenever I had a day off, I would always head to the beach, even in the winter.'

'What did you do at the beach?'

'Surf mainly, sometimes I'd swim. My friends had paddleboards so I'd use them if it was calm enough. I had to sell my beloved surfboard when times got tough, which is a shame as I'd love to get back out on the water while I'm here.'

He looked out on the waves. 'The sea can be quite volatile round here. We see a lot of people underestimate it.'

She studied him. She hadn't expected an overly cautious attitude from him.

He glanced back at her and obviously saw the question in her eyes. 'I volunteer for the RNLI, lifeboat crew. Part time. I can't give as much time as I'd like as Wishing Wood takes up so much of my life but generally I'm on call one or two days a month. Heath and Bear do it too. I'm on call tonight actually.'

'Bear mentioned it before, I didn't realise you did it too.'

'Lots of us do it round here. Lucien and Greta volunteer too, and Felix. But we all do it at different times. We're rarely on call together.'

'That's... amazing. I used to make a monthly payment to the RNLI before I lost my job. When you use the sea as much as I did, knowing they are always there for you, it's important to give back. You guys are heroes.'

River shook his head, trying to dismiss it.

'No, you are,' Indigo said. 'You risk your own life to save other people's. Don't try to diminish that. I've seen them in action and I've never failed to be impressed. They are always so brave.'

'Ever needed them?'

'No, thankfully. But not because I'm any wiser or fitter than other sea users, just lucky, I guess. I know people who have far more experience than me who got caught unawares and had to be rescued. It can happen to anyone.'

He nodded. 'That's true. The people I've rescued have been of all ages and abilities. Some of it is about education and teaching people about water safety and what to do if they get into trouble.' He shook his head. 'Sorry, this is a heavy conversation.'

'No, it's not. We want to get to know each other, I think this is a wonderful thing to find out about you. What made you want to get involved?'

He took a sip of his drink. 'Well, that's a hell of a story.'

She watched him for a moment, wondering if he was going to tell it.

'I used to surf a lot when I was a kid,' River said. 'So did Heath and Bear. One day, when I was fourteen, I was surfing with my best friend, Will. He was a brilliant surfer, he'd been surfing since he could walk. The waves were big that day and we thought we could conquer the world.' He paused. 'The last time I saw him, he was right next to me, catching a big wave, stupid grin on his face as we raced each other to the beach. He always got there before me so I was surprised when I got there before him... He never made it to the beach. To this day, I have no idea what happened. He was right next to me and then he went off to the right and I went to the left and I never saw him again. The lifeguards went in, there was this huge search, helicopters, boats. His body washed up on the shore a few days later six miles down the coast.'

'Christ River, I'm so sorry. When you said it was a hell of a story, I thought you were going to tell me of a time you were inspired by them. I'm so sorry you went through that.'

'In many ways, Will's death did inspire me. I couldn't let go of that guilt, that maybe I could have saved him. I don't know if that was true, whether there was anything I could have done. The lifeguards on the beach that day said he must have been caught in a rip tide, so there'd have been very little I could do. But if I'd seen him go under, I could have... I don't know. I've replayed that day in my head a million times and I just couldn't let it go. One of the teachers at school encouraged me to learn some lifesaving skills so I could help someone else in the future. I joined my local lifesaving group at the swimming pool, did the whole swimming-in-your-pyjamas thing and diving down to retrieve a brick from the bottom of the pool. We learned CPR, mouth-to-mouth, other basic first aid skills too. I got various certificates to prove I was qualified to save lives, whatever that means. I became a volunteer lifeguard at the pool, then did some lifeguarding on the beach, and let me tell you all that training in the nice safe pool went straight out the window when faced with the unpredictability of the sea. That was a huge eye-opener. I did that for several years and, as part of that, I also helped to do water safety courses for children, not in the pool, but in the sea so they would know what to do if they got into trouble. Eventually I trained to be part of the lifeboat crew too. I suppose I thought that if I saved enough lives it would ease some of the guilt around Will's death.'

'Did it?'

'Not really. But it feels good now that I'm doing something rather than doing nothing.'

'You're doing something amazing.'

He shook his head and turned his attention to the view. She studied him and realised he didn't want people to think he was a hero because he hadn't been able to save his best friend. Nothing else mattered because he hadn't been able to save the person who mattered the most.

She reached out and took his hand. 'River, what you do is important and I know you don't believe that it is. But how many parents, friends, siblings will forever be grateful for what you've done? Not just saving lives, for being there when no one else was, but also for the education, for teaching people how to look after themselves. That's equally important. Can you imagine how many lives you've impacted on? How many people would not be here now if it wasn't for you? How many parents or siblings, just like Will's family, who would be going home from their day at the beach with one less member of their family, how many people have you saved from that heartbreak? Your debt, if you ever owed one in the first place, has more than been paid.'

He stared at her and she ploughed on.

'You forgave me for not telling you I was Mindy or about the baby so you're clearly someone who forgives easily, who doesn't dwell on the past, but you can't forgive yourself for something that wasn't your fault.'

'It's easier to forgive others, I guess. We are our own worst critics.'

'That's true. But you should be proud of the life you lead, raising Tierra single-handed, what you've done with Wishing Wood, being a member of the RNLI. The more I get to know you, the more I see what a wonderful man you are.'

'I think you see me through some very rose-tinted glasses. At some point the glasses will come off.'

She stared at him. He really didn't see his worth at all

and that made her feel so sad. She decided to let it go for now but she was going to make it her mission to make him believe it too.

∼

Bear walked into reception later that afternoon, while Meadow had gone to pick the girls up from school. Indigo braced herself for the worst. So far Heath and Meadow had been fine with her about her deception and Meadow had been totally understanding about the baby too. But if River had been defending her over breakfast, then it meant someone wasn't happy.

'Hi,' Indigo said, warily.

Bear smiled. 'You've been on an emotional rollercoaster the last few days, haven't you?'

'I… it wasn't what I expected when I came here. I thought at best River might want to be a part of our baby's life on some level and at worst he'd tell me to get lost and want nothing to do with me.'

Bear sat down, turning his chair to face her. 'I have to say when I heard you hadn't been upfront with River when you arrived, I didn't like it, but finding out you were pregnant does explain a lot.'

'I genuinely didn't mean to deceive anyone. I didn't think he knew who I was and blurting out that I was some random woman he'd slept with two months before and that I was pregnant with his baby wasn't exactly easy to bring up in conversation.'

'No, I can understand that.'

'So you don't hate me?'

He grinned. 'No, you're family now. No matter what happens between you two, you'll always be family.'

She smiled with relief. 'You're going to be an uncle again.'

'I know. But I already have two nieces, and somehow I always end up with glitter in my clothes and hair. So if you can do your best for a little boy this time, that would be great.'

She smirked. 'I'll try.'

'So I assume everything is OK with the baby? Have you been to a doctor yet?'

'No, now I'm staying here I need to register at one.'

'So you are staying?'

'As long as River wants me to. I never expected him to turn his whole life around for me and his baby but he wants to help raise his child so it makes sense to stay around here, even if I don't end up staying at Wishing Wood. He is a wonderful dad to Tierra and I want our baby to grow up having him in their life too.'

'But is that what *you* want, a life here, working in a treehouse resort surrounded by his weird family?'

She smiled. 'Three years ago my dream was to work in the Beverly Hills Hotel, or to travel the world working in some of the most exclusive hotels or resorts. But life can change in a blink of an eye and those dreams just don't seem important any more. I've had a few of those blinks recently. Meeting River was a great big blink, not just because I'm pregnant but because I do want a life with him. This place is great and I know I could be very happy here, and I'm rather partial to his weird family, but I've fallen a little bit in love with your brother and what I want more than anything is to have that fairytale ending with him. And I'm aware how silly that sounds, I've known him for such a short amount of time, but I know how I feel. I know I hurt River when I ran but I hope he can trust me again. I'm going to do everything I can to make this work, not just for my baby but for me too.'

'I have every faith you two can figure this out. He's smitten with you.'

'The feeling is very mutual.'

Bear fished out his phone from his pocket. 'I'll give you our doctor's number so you can get registered there. And my friend is a midwife actually. Maybe you should give her a call. It might take some time to register at a doctor's round here. And I know from chatting to her that it's important to get checked and screened for certain things early on in the pregnancy.'

'That would be great, thanks. I'll give you my number and you can send me the details. I need to get an appointment for an ultrasound in a few weeks' time too.'

'Now that will be exciting, seeing your baby for the first time.'

'It will be. But it will just be a relief to know the baby is healthy. I'm not sure if River told you but I was pregnant before and I lost the baby in a car accident. I did wonder if I'd be able to have another baby or whether the accident had done some permanent damage, so I'd like to make sure everything is OK sooner rather than later. But I only found out about the baby a few days before I got here so there's a lot to sort out.'

'I'm so sorry to hear that,' Bear said. 'That must have been devastating.'

'It was. But I feel like I've been given a second chance at happiness with this baby and with River.'

'I'm sure, if you mention to the doctors your concerns, they might arrange for an earlier ultrasound for you.'

'That would be good.'

Thunder suddenly sounded in the distance. The skies had been darkening ever since she'd got back from lunch with River. It seemed the weather report had got it right for once.

'The weather is not going to be good tonight,' Bear said, and she couldn't fail to notice the note of worry in his voice.

'River's on call, isn't he?'

'Yeah, the boat gets called out once or twice a week at this time of year, so chances are he'll have a cosy night at home and won't be needed. When the weather is bad, people tend to stay at home too so there's less chance of anyone needing rescuing. But I can't help worrying when Heath or River are on call when it's forecast bad weather. If they get the call they have to go out, doesn't matter if the waves are forty-foot high, they have to respond, people's lives depend on them being there. But of course it's a risk for them too.'

'I bet they worry about you too. Do you not worry for yourself when you get the call?'

'There's no time for that, we just have to get on with the job. But afterwards there's time to reflect, time to think how close we got to danger ourselves. Some call-outs are relatively simple, some are harder, some are life-threatening for all concerned. We get home from one of those, we hug our loved ones a little bit tighter that night.'

'I can't even imagine what that's like. You guys are heroes.'

Bear shrugged it off. 'But if he gets called out tonight, give him a big hug when he gets back, he'll need it.'

She glanced over at the painting River had done of the storm, the huge waves he'd painted crashing against the rocks suddenly looked foreboding rather than dramatic.

'Let's just hope it doesn't get to that.'

CHAPTER FOURTEEN

The storm clouds had got darker and heavier over the afternoon with the occasional distant rumble of thunder, but by the time evening had come round the storm was definitely above them. Thunder cracked and roared across the skies and intermittently there was a flash of lightning somewhere nearby. From Blossom Cottage Indigo had seen the big waves crashing over the rocks, the white horses pounding the shores of Pear Tree Beach. As she ran through the woods to get to Magnolia Cottage, dodging the puddles, rain was lashing down. The wind was roaring through the trees, whipping leaves and flowers through the air. It was a horrible night.

She raced up the steps to River's home and knocked on the door.

A few seconds later, he answered.

'Indigo! What are you doing out in this, is everything OK?' He quickly snagged her hand and pulled her inside.

'I'm fine, I'm here for movie night.' She wrestled herself out of her wet coat.

He stared at her in surprise.

'I… did promise Tierra I would be here,' Indigo said, uncertainly. 'But I can go if you'd prefer it to just be the two of you. I wouldn't want to intrude.'

A big smile spread across his face and he grabbed the thick fleecy blanket from the sofa and wrapped it around her, rubbing her shoulders to get her warm. He leaned down and placed a sweet kiss on her forehead. 'You are very welcome. Come and sit down, the movie is just about to start.'

Tierra came running down the stairs from her bedroom and threw herself into Indigo's arms. 'You came!'

'Of course. I love *Frozen*, I wouldn't miss it for the world.'

'We have chocolate popcorn. It tastes amazing,' Tierra said, taking Indigo's hand and pulling her over to the sofa. She sat down next to Tierra and River sat on the little girl's other side. Tierra grabbed the bowl of popcorn and plopped it on her lap. 'Daddy, you can start the movie now.'

'Right, of course,' River said, pressing a few buttons on the remote control.

The movie started with the ice-cutters doing their song and Tierra watched transfixed.

'How many times has she seen this movie?' Indigo asked River over Tierra's head.

'Probably over a thousand. When she was younger, she used to cry when it was finished and we'd end up watching it all over again. Thankfully she's grown out of that now, but we still watch it once a month.'

'Shhh! No talking,' Tierra commanded, not taking her eyes off the screen.

Indigo quickly zipped her lips, looking suitably chastised, and River suppressed a smirk.

They continued watching the film but she kept on glancing over at River who kept looking over at her. It gave her a delicious thrill.

They'd been watching the film for only about ten minutes when suddenly a beeping sound came from River's pocket. Indigo looked over and watched him grab his pager and study it, cursing under his breath. She felt herself go cold.

'I have to go,' he said, getting up, all humour suddenly gone.

'But Daddy, we've only just started watching it,' Tierra protested.

'I know but I have to go and help someone,' River said, giving his daughter a quick kiss on the cheek.

'OK, Daddy,' Tierra said, barely taking her eyes off the screen.

Indigo got up and followed him to the door. 'You're going out in this?' she said in alarm.

'I have to, someone is in trouble. Give Meadow, Heath or Bear a call, they'll come over and take care of Tierra,' River said, pulling on his coat and boots.

'We'll be fine, don't worry about us,' Indigo said.

'You sure?'

'Yes, please just be careful, I need you to come back to us.'

He smiled. 'I will, I promise.'

He gave her a quick kiss on the cheek and then was gone.

She stared after him as he disappeared into the darkness. The storm was raging out there, lightning illuminating the sky in a spectacular fork that made a knot of worry grow in her stomach.

She turned back to face Tierra in case she was worried, plastering on her best smile, but Tierra was too busy watching the film. Indigo glanced at the screen and saw they'd reached the bit where Elsa and Anna's parents die in a storm at sea. Their boat disappeared beneath the waves and did not come back up.

The knot in her stomach twisted into fear.

River still hadn't come back and that fear had turned to dread. The film had long since finished, and Indigo and Tierra had been making salt dough sculptures in the kitchen. The sculptures had just come out of the oven and were cooling down and Tierra was upstairs searching for paints to decorate them with.

Indigo had been trying to be upbeat and positive all night but now she let her mask slip for a moment. If Tierra wasn't worried about her dad, Indigo definitely didn't want to project her concerns onto her. But she couldn't stop fearing the worst. She couldn't lose him, not when things seemed to be starting to go so well for them.

For the umpteenth time, she picked up her phone to check for any messages or updates. There was nothing, well not from River.

The responses from her friends and Violet after her rather positive message early were mainly full of excitement and enthusiasm. She was glad they were no longer worried about her. They'd been worrying about her for the last two and a half years. Vicky's comments were still negative though. She read the latest one.

I'm not sure why you left the group chat last night, or why you're not replying to me. Getting involved with River is a big mistake. Take it from someone who knows, married life is not the utopia everyone thinks it is. If you walk away from your dreams for this man you will regret it for the rest of your life.

Indigo decided to send her a quick reply to try to put an end to this once and for all. **I'm happy here. Please let me figure out the rest by myself.**

She heard the thunder of feet come running down the stairs and quickly shoved her phone back in her bag.

'I found them,' Tierra said, waving a small bag in the air that looked to be filled with acrylic paints of every colour. 'I'm going to paint the T-rex first.'

'Good idea,' Indigo said. 'You'll have to make its skin look scaly and green and give him sharp pointy teeth.'

'Actually, no one knows for sure what colour dinosaurs were,' Tierra said, digging out a bright orange paint. 'Some people think they were green or grey but some scientists think that they might have had bright colours like purple or orange to attract a mate.'

'That's interesting,' Indigo said as the orange was smeared across the dinosaur's body. 'Where did you learn that?'

'In a book that Daddy read to me. What does attracting a mate mean?'

'Well, animals like to have boyfriends and girlfriends too. The male animals sometimes have bright colours on their bodies to attract the females. Imagine the females walking around trying to find a nice boyfriend – they might choose the one that has the brightest colours.'

'Daddy always says it doesn't matter what someone looks like on the outside, it's what inside that counts.'

'That's true, but animals behave differently to people. Female animals look for male animals that will be a good daddy to their babies. Humans look for people they can be good friends with, someone who they can talk and laugh and dance with. Animals don't do that kind of thing.'

'So animals look for a boyfriend or girlfriend to have a baby with?'

This felt like shaky ground. 'Yes. Are you going to try to do scales too?'

'I don't know if I can do scales. I might try some spots,' Tierra said and Indigo was relieved the subject had moved on.

'Spots are good.'

'So will you and Daddy have a baby when you're boyfriend and girlfriend?'

Christ, that was a tricky question to answer. She knew River hadn't told Tierra about their baby yet. While she wanted to be there to tell Tierra together, as long as River thought that was appropriate, she certainly didn't want to tackle it on her own. She couldn't say no now, for River to then tell his daughter a few days or weeks down the line that they *were* having a baby. But she couldn't exactly say yes either. Also, she didn't want Tierra to think having a boyfriend or girlfriend automatically meant that there would be a baby. Indigo and River were still at the early stages of getting to know each other but they had already skipped ahead a few steps with the unexpected news she was pregnant.

She attempted to play it safe.

'We're not really boyfriend and girlfriend yet,' she said.

That was mostly true. River had said he wanted to take things slow and there'd been no mention of them going out on a date. Nor had there been any kissing apart from on the cheek or on the forehead tonight. She didn't think she could really use that label.

'But when you are, will you have a baby?'

'Not all boyfriends and girlfriends have babies,' Indigo said, awkwardly. 'Some do, some don't.'

'But will you and Daddy have one?'

She clearly wasn't going to let this go.

'How would you feel if we did?'

That was safe, wasn't it?

Tierra started adding purple spots to her dinosaur. 'Sampson at school has a baby sister and he says she cries all the time.'

'Babies do cry sometimes,' Indigo said. 'But they also giggle and laugh and play.'

'Will your baby laugh or cry?'

'*If* we do have a baby, it will probably do a bit of both.'

'And the baby will be my sister?'

'Or brother. It could be a boy or a girl.'

Oh god, now they were talking about it as if it was definitely going to happen.

'And I'll be a big sister?'

'Yes, which means you'll have to help us look after the baby,' Indigo said.

'Will I have to change the nappies?' Tierra said.

'No, we will take care of that.'

'Will she share my bedroom?'

'No, *if* we did have a baby, she *or he* will most likely be in our room to start with because they will need a lot of feeding. But when they are older we will probably build them a room of their own. Unless you want to share with them.'

Tierra's eyes lit up. 'Sharing with her might be fun. Sometimes.'

'Well I'm sure she or he would like that too. Sometimes.'

'When will the baby come?' Tierra said, excitedly, clearly getting into the idea now.

'There might not be a baby. Me and Daddy are not boyfriend and girlfriend yet,' Indigo quickly back-pedalled. But Tierra clearly wasn't listening.

'When the baby comes, can I play with her toys?'

'Oh yes, in fact you can play with them first.'

Tierra grinned. 'I think I might like being a big sister.'

They finished painting and, as it was getting late, Indigo decided it was probably time for Tierra to go to bed. She had no idea what time her bedtime was but Tierra did have school the next day.

'Right, time to get into your pyjamas,' Indigo said.

'Will you put your pyjamas on too?' Tierra said.

'I... my pyjamas are at Blossom Cottage.'

'You can wear Dad's. He has lots of different ones you can wear.'

'Dad's pyjamas might be a bit big for me,' Indigo said.

'Let's go look,' Tierra said.

Indigo followed her up the stairs and Tierra went straight into River's bedroom and opened one of the drawers. 'You can wear any of these.'

'OK, you get yours on and I'll put these on,' Indigo said.

Tierra scampered off into her room and Indigo quickly got changed, pulling on a t-shirt and a pair of stripy bottoms. They were huge so she folded over the waist several times and rolled up the legs so they resembled knee-length shorts.

She heard Tierra cleaning her teeth in the bathroom and, when she came out, the little girl giggled to see Indigo wearing her dad's clothes.

'Come on, I'll read you a story,' Indigo said.

She watched Tierra climb into bed and Indigo covered her over with her duvet.

'Will Daddy be back soon?' Tierra said, showing the first signs of concern all evening.

'Yes, very soon,' Indigo said, hoping to god that wasn't a lie. 'And I'll get him to come in and give you a goodnight kiss as soon as he does.'

'OK. Will you be here until Daddy gets back?'

'Yes, I'm not going anywhere.'

'Good. Can you read me that story about the tiger who comes to tea?'

'I'd be happy to.'

It was nearly midnight when the door opened and River stepped inside, looking exhausted and battered by the wind.

Indigo felt relief flood through her as she ran across the room and threw herself into his unsuspecting arms. She kissed him hard.

'Christ, I was so worried about you,' she said, kissing him again. River instantly kissed her back, struggling to get out of his wet coat and then wrapping his arms around her. The kiss was urgent and desperate as he shuffled her backwards. She thudded gently against the wall and he lifted her, and she wrapped her legs around him as he pinned her to the wall.

'Daddy.'

River tore his mouth from Indigo's and they looked up to see Tierra standing there sleepily at the top of the stairs, rubbing her eyes and clutching her toy dinosaur.

'Hey sweetheart, go back to bed and I'll be up in a second to tuck you in and give you a goodnight kiss,' River said.

Tierra nodded and disappeared back to her room, seemingly not at all bothered by catching her dad in a compromising position.

River turned his attention back to Indigo. 'Well, that was the best welcome home I've ever had.'

Indigo let out a little shaky laugh. 'I was so scared for you, I was worried you might never come back.'

He smiled. 'I quite like that you were worried for me. I don't think I've ever had anyone worry about me before.'

'I'm sure that's not true.'

'I'm quite sure it is. I better go and see Tierra. Stay right here.'

She released her legs from around him and leaned back against the wall as he raced upstairs. He was back a few minutes later. She wondered if he would kiss her again but instead he pulled her into a big hug and just held her there, his head resting on top of hers. They stood like that, wrapped in each other's arms for the longest time.

'Tonight's call-out was awful,' River said.

'What happened?'

He pulled back from her slightly and shook his head. 'I'm so tired.'

'I should probably go then, let you get some sleep.'

He shook his head. 'No, because then I'll have to walk you back and then I'll have to wake Tierra up and bring her with us and I'm too tired for all that. Stay here, please.'

'OK.' It was no hardship for her to sleep up on the mezzanine again. She liked being here with River and Tierra.

He nodded and took her hand, leading her upstairs, but she was surprised when he walked straight into his room still holding her hand. He closed the door and started getting undressed.

He glanced over at her. 'I was going to ask if you wanted to borrow some pyjamas but I see you already have.'

She blushed. 'Sorry. I suggested to Tierra that she put her pyjamas on for bed and she said she would only if I put mine on. All my stuff is at Blossom Cottage so I kind of had to use yours. She suggested that too. Is it weird?'

'Not at all, there's something very sexy about you wearing them.'

She smiled at that.

When he was wearing only his tight black boxers, he slipped into bed and held up the covers for her to get in too.

She hesitated. He'd spoken only that day about taking things slow – now they were going to sleep together? But she knew it would just be sleeping, he didn't look capable of anything else.

She climbed into bed next to him and he turned off the light and immediately cuddled up to her, his head on her chest and his arm round her belly. She stroked his head. They were silent for a while.

'It was a family who got into trouble tonight. They were walking along the promenade after dinner, trying to get back to their hotel, and a wave crashed over them and pulled the mum and the little boy into the sea. Of course the dad immediately jumped in after them. By the time we got there they were already quite far off the land. We found the mum and dad fairly quickly but we couldn't find the boy.'

'Oh no.' Indigo's heart broke for the family and for River.

'We found him, eventually. But he wasn't breathing. I pulled him onto the boat and immediately started CPR. His dad was crying, his mum was wailing. I've never heard a noise like it, it was horrific, real agonising sobs. I fought for the longest time to bring him back to them, one of the crew was telling me the boy was gone and I knew that he was but I couldn't let him go. Suddenly he coughs up a ton of water and he's breathing again but he didn't regain consciousness. The kid was in a bad way, he'd clearly hit his head and he wasn't breathing for so long. We got the boat into shore where an ambulance whisked him and his family off to the hospital but I don't know if he's going to make it.'

She could hear the emotion in his voice as he spoke and she held him tighter.

'Oh River, I'm so sorry, but you did everything you could to save him.'

'I know. The ops manager is going to let me know later if the kid is OK. We try to remain detached. You kind of have to when you're doing this job because you can't let emotions take over. But this kid was so small, he has so much more life to lead. I just can't detach myself from that.'

'I don't think you'd be human if you could.'

She had no words at all to make him feel better, she could only hold him and hope it was enough.

'Try to get some sleep, I'll wake you if you get a call or text,' she said.

He nodded against her, holding her close, and she knew he was still awake, but eventually exhaustion took over and he drifted off to sleep.

Indigo was woken by the low buzzing of a message notification from River's phone. River was lying cuddled round her, completely fast asleep. The moonlight was streaming in through the windows, painting the room in a silvery glow; clearly the storm had passed for now. She debated whether to wake him. He needed to sleep and hearing bad news in the middle of the night was not going to make the situation any better but she had promised to let him know.

She stroked down his back and gave him a gentle shake.

'River, you've got a text,' she said.

He lifted his head to look at her, peering at her in the darkness with some confusion before his eyes cleared. He leaned over her to grab his phone and swiped his fingers across the screen. He stared at it and she stroked him, wanting to bring some comfort, and then heard a giggle coming from the phone, one filled with joy.

A slow smile spread across River's face and he turned the screen round so Indigo could see. There was a video of a small boy sitting in a hospital bed with a big bowl of ice cream on his lap, trying to shovel the biggest spoonful into his mouth. His mum was sitting next to the bed and it was her who was giggling at her son as he tried to fit all the ice cream into his mouth at once.

'Oh my god, River he's alive.'

River turned the phone to look at it again, watching the video three or four times over, and she could see he had tears in his eyes.

He eventually put the phone down. 'I can't believe it, I feared the worst and he's sitting up in bed eating ice cream.'

Indigo cupped his face. 'You did that. You saved his life. You fought to save him long after anyone else had given up. He is there eating ice cream right now because of you. And did you hear his mum's laughter? You gave that to her. You. You made the difference.'

He smiled and nodded. 'I did.'

'You are the most incredible, amazing man I have ever met.'

He stared at her and then bent his head and kissed her. She caressed his face, kissing him back. She stroked down his back and he moaned against her lips.

He pulled back to look at her, 'Christ Indy, I need you, will you let me love you?'

She nodded, without hesitation. It didn't matter that this was coming from a place of need rather than love for him. It didn't matter that they were supposed to be taking things slow and they hadn't even properly started dating yet. She had wanted to be with him almost since arriving at Wishing Wood and she wanted to be there for him in any way she could.

He kissed her again, his hands caressing her body and then dragging her pyjamas off with a desperate urgency. She pushed his shorts off with a need for him too. After fearing the worst tonight that he had been hurt or lost in the storm, she needed this connection to him more than ever.

He started trailing his hot mouth over her body, driving her insane with every gentle whisper across her skin. He kissed across her breasts, making her cry out for him. He traced his lips across her belly and gave her the gentlest of kisses there and she knew that was for their baby.

He shifted down the bed and kissed the insides of her knees before slowly inching his way back up her thighs. She trembled in anticipation and suddenly he was kissing right there, eliciting a noise from her that was purely animalistic. All thoughts and reason went clear from her mind. Her only thought was him.

He sent her flying over the edge within seconds, every cell in her body exploding with ecstasy.

He slowly kissed his way back up her body and then kissed her hard on the lips, catching the last breaths of her orgasm. He shifted so he was on top of her and a thrill of excitement shot through her.

He pulled back slightly to look at her. 'I don't have a condom but I'm guessing I don't need it.'

She laughed. 'That's what you call shutting the stable door after the horse has bolted.'

He smiled. 'Thought so.' He kissed her again, settling himself between her legs. 'And you don't need to worry, I'm going to go slow, I don't want to do anything to hurt our baby.'

She smiled with love for him.

He kissed her and slid carefully inside her, making her moan against his lips. She wrapped her arms around his broad shoulders and moved her legs around his hips. His touch, the feel of his body against hers, his intoxicating scent, it was complete sensory overload. He was slow, gentle, moving with tenderness, and it was complete and utter bliss. For the longest time it was just the two of them, the world outside forgotten, moving in perfect sync with each other, kissing, touching, caressing. It was heaven.

He pulled back to look at her as he moved against her, his eyes locking with hers. 'You have no idea how much I needed this tonight.'

'Sex?'

He frowned. 'You, I need you. You really have no idea what this means to me?'

She stroked his face. 'Show me.'

He kissed her, sliding a hand under her back, holding her tighter against him, and that glorious feeling started building inside her, tingles of pleasure bubbling through her entire body, every nerve, every fibre in her body exploding into tiny fireworks and then suddenly she was falling apart, shouting out all manner of words that didn't make any sense, and he fell with her, clinging to her as if she was the air he needed to breathe.

CHAPTER FIFTEEN

The next day River woke with the biggest grin on his face as he remembered the night before. He stretched out an arm to Indigo but couldn't find her. He sat up and looked around. His bed and room were completely empty.

Had he dreamed the whole thing? Except he knew that he hadn't. The memory of it was so vivid, so clear, unlike every sexual experience he'd ever had before when he'd been blind drunk. This was the first time he'd made love sober and it had been incredible. The scent of her was on his sheets, on his skin. He knew he hadn't imagined it.

Surely she hadn't run again. Worry and fear bubbled up in him. Had it been too soon? Had she misinterpreted what it was?

He grabbed his phone and blinked when he saw the time. Ten past nine.

Shit.

He scrambled out of bed, throwing on some clothes. 'Tierra,' he shouted as he got dressed. 'We're going to be late for school.'

There was no answer, no thud of footsteps as she ran into the room.

He burst out of his room only to see his daughter's bedroom door open and no one inside.

'Tierra, Indigo!' he called, but the treehouse remained silent.

He ran downstairs and stopped when he saw the note fluttering on the table. He grabbed it.

Taken Tierra to school.

He sank down into a chair in relief. There was a reason for Indigo's departure and Tierra was safely at school.

He looked at the note again. After what they'd shared the night before, should there not be some reference to it, some affection, even a kiss at the end?

He laughed to himself. He was being ridiculous. But after his big speech the day before about taking things slow, he wondered what Indigo must think of him. Making love to her last night had not been part of the plan at all. But after the night he'd had out on call, the storm, the waves, the search for the little boy, the worry the kid wouldn't make it, she had been there for him, holding him, stroking him, talking to him. And then when the boy was clearly fine, and she'd told him that he was amazing and wonderful, he'd really started to think he was actually worth something. For the first time ever, she'd made him believe that and he loved her for it.

He smiled. That was the crux of what happened the night before. He'd suddenly realised that he loved her with everything he had and he wanted to show her.

Now he just had to find it in him to tell her.

~

After dropping Tierra at school, Indigo rushed into the reception area.

'I'm so sorry I'm late,' she said, flopping down in her chair.

'Is everything OK? We missed you guys at breakfast,' Meadow said.

'Yes, River had a call-out last night, it was a hard one but everyone survived. He got back really late and was exhausted. We all ended up sleeping in late. I woke up at half eight and realised that Tierra was going to be late for school, we got dressed, hotfooted it over to the restaurant, grabbed some pancakes and fruit and Tierra ate them in the car on the way to school. River was still asleep when I left, I thought it was a good idea to let him recover.'

Indigo didn't mention that he probably needed to recover from the most incredible sex she'd ever experienced.

'So you were with River when he got the call-out?' Meadow asked innocently.

'It was movie night, Tierra made me promise I'd come. Ironically, we'd just got to the bit where Elsa's parents die in a big storm at sea when he got the call. He didn't get back until gone midnight.'

Indigo logged on to her computer, ignoring the fact that Meadow was watching her.

'Sooo, you ended up spending the night.'

'I was looking after Tierra so yes, I ended up staying over.' She glanced over at Meadow and laughed at the raised eyebrow. Meadow obviously wanted more detail

258

than that. 'Look, I'm not sure where your mind is going with a very innocent movie night but River wants to take things slow between us. We're not even officially dating yet and I don't know whether we'll ever be something more, we're just sort of friends.'

She let out a little sigh because what did that make what happened the night before, some kind of friends-with-benefits arrangement? Was that what they would have going forward, just sex without ever having any kind of emotional commitment?

She was relieved when she saw Mr and Mrs Andrews approaching the reception area so that she wouldn't have to talk about it with Meadow any more, and hopefully she could distract herself from those kinds of thoughts too.

'Good morning, how was Church Door Cove?' Indigo asked.

'It was wonderful, quite spectacular. Very rocky though, not sure it has the romantic vibe your potential fiancés are looking for.'

'Lots of steps down to it too,' Mr Andrews grumbled. 'My poor knees.'

'The exercise is good for you,' Mrs Andrews said.

'Are you off somewhere interesting today?' Indigo asked.

'Well, we heard Barafundle Bay was a lovely place to go to,' Mr Andrews said.

'It is, very beautiful,' Indigo said, despite not having been there herself. 'Voted one of the best beaches in Britain and the world. The sea is always a gorgeous shade of blue and you might find sea gooseberries on the beach, a type of jelly sea creature that looks like tiny eggs or balls.' She'd googled them after River had mentioned them so she was glad she had the opportunity to talk about them now. 'But it is a bit of a walk, I'm afraid. You can park in Stackpole Quay car park and then walk over the cliffs for about half a mile to get to it, but sadly there are quite a few more steps to get down there.'

Mrs Andrews looked at her husband hopefully and he smiled and nodded. 'Go on then, while we're here, we have to visit one of the best beaches in the world.'

'Let me just get you a tide timetable for the local area. Some of these beaches are best visited at low tide, though Barafundle Bay still has plenty of beach at high tide so you should be fine.' Indigo grabbed the tiny booklet and showed them how to see when it was a high and low tide for the local beaches.

'And we saw in the welcome book in our treehouse that you provide packed lunches, is it possible to get a couple of those?' Mrs Andrews said.

'Yes of course, let me phone through to Alex in the restaurant and ask her to make some for you. What kind of thing would you like on your sandwiches?'

She took their order and put a call through to Alex, who promised to have them ready in fifteen minutes.

'Well, have a fun day,' Indigo said. 'And let us know if you think it's proposal-perfect.'

Mrs Andrews laughed. 'We will.'

They walked out and Meadow smiled at her. 'You're very good with the customers. They like you. And well done on that information you gave them on Barafundle Bay. I always think it looks better if we know this stuff rather than having to look it up online in front of our guests.'

'Oh, I like working with people, guests. I enjoy trying to help them. I looked up that information after River told me it could be a good place to propose. I want to find out as much as I can about the local area so I can assist the guests with any questions they have.'

'The little detail about the sea gooseberries was nice.'

'Oh, River told me that.' Indigo smiled fondly as she remembered him telling her about finding them when he was a child. She wondered what he'd been like as a little boy before his parents had made him feel so utterly worthless.

And suddenly he was there standing in the doorway, looking gloriously sexy with that just-got-out-of-bed stubble. Simply looking at him made her heart soar.

'Can I have a word about… last night?' River said.

Her heart sank a little. Here was the speech about how it shouldn't have happened and that it didn't change anything between them. She suddenly didn't want to hear it.

Indigo glanced at Meadow. 'I, erm… I've literally just got to work five minutes ago after taking Tierra to school. I don't think it's appropriate that I—'

'Go,' Meadow said. 'We're OK here.'

Indigo let out a heavy breath and followed River outside. He led her to the shade of a large blossom tree, the pink blooms filling the air above them.

'Thank you for taking care of Tierra this morning.'

'That's no problem. She thought the whole thing was very exciting, going to school in my car. I didn't have a booster seat for her but it was only a few minutes' drive and I went very slowly.'

He smiled. 'I trust you with her. And thank you for being there for me.'

'I will always be there for you, if you'll let me.'

He stared at her, then cleared his throat. 'I wanted to talk about last night, about what happened between us. I don't want you to be under any false illusions about what it was.'

'River, it's OK. I know what it was. I fulfilled a need for you. And I'm totally fine with it. I kind of liked that you needed me like that. And it was no hardship for me, last night was magnificent.'

'See, I knew you'd think that's what it was, especially when I told you yesterday that I wanted to take things really slow. But the truth is…' he paused, then took a deep breath. 'The truth is I'm falling for you. Not because you're pregnant with my child, I'm falling for *you*, and I've never had these feelings before in my life. I know we still have so much to learn about each other but the more time I spend with you the deeper those feelings become. Last night was not just a need for sex, it was a need to reconnect with you, to be with you, because you are in here with every thought and every breath. This is not just lust and desire for me, this is something far far bigger and being intimate with you, making love to you, was a celebration of that.'

She stared at him in shock, she had no words at all to say to that.

'Look, if you don't want to make love again, if you want to hold back until we know each other better, then I respect that,' River said. 'But I think as we've already skipped forward to the main event twice—'

'Technically four times,' Indigo said, finding her voice.

He grinned. 'That's right. Well, personally I feel that being intimate with each other is also a good way to get to know each other.'

She swallowed. 'I do too.'

He nodded then cupped her face and kissed her. God, the taste of him was like a punch in the heart, her body responding to him instantly. She wrapped her arms around his neck and pressed herself against him. Right now, she couldn't be happier. This was the life she wanted, here in the most beautiful place in the world with this incredible man.

He pulled back slightly to look at her. 'And I plan to do a lot more of that.'

'I think I'll be OK with that.'

'Good. Now would you like to go out to dinner with me tonight?'

'Is it a date?'

'It absolutely is.'

'Then yes.'

He smiled and kissed her again, and she stroked down his back, relishing in the feel of his body against hers.

She reluctantly pulled back. 'I, umm… should get back to work.'

'Yeah, I need to as well.'

She stepped out of his arms and they started walking back towards the reception. Indigo smiled when she saw Meadow and Bear, who must have just arrived, quickly dart back inside as if they hadn't been watching them.

River slipped his hand into hers as they crossed the grass and it filled her heart because it wasn't just a gesture of his feelings for her, but it was also a sign to his family that this was something serious.

They walked back into the reception together, still holding hands, to find Bear and Meadow pretending to do some work.

'Can one of you two look after Tierra tonight?' River asked.

'I can,' Bear said.

'Thanks, that would be great. I'm taking Indigo out on a date.'

Indigo smiled and River leaned forward and gave her the briefest of kisses on the lips, before walking out with a big smile on his face.

Indigo sat down at her computer knowing she had an identical smile on her face.

'Just friends, eh?' Meadow said.

'I think I've just been promoted.'

There was a knock on her door later that night and when she opened it she found River standing there in jeans and a pale purple shirt open at the collar.

'Indigo, you look lovely,' River said.

'Thank you. You too, I think purple suits you.'

He reached out and took a strand of her purple hair, letting it run through his fingers. 'I think so too.'

She grinned and stepped forward and kissed him

briefly and it warmed her heart when he smiled against her lips.

Indigo closed the door behind her and they headed down the stairs. After a moment River held out his hand and she smiled and took it.

She looked around the wood as they walked through it. It looked enchanting in the dusky light, fairy lights hanging from every tree, even those that didn't have treehouses, but the treehouses themselves were like shining beacons, reaffirming the fairy-wood feel. With the twinkling lights around the windows and the lanterns hanging off the branches, it was completely magical.

Up above them it was a clear night, the stars sparkling through the canopy of leaves. It was warm and Indigo probably wouldn't even need the little cardigan she'd brought with her.

'What have Bear and Tierra got planned for tonight?' she asked.

'Video games, probably Mario Kart, and he always lets her win.'

'I bet she'll love that.'

'She adores Bear and the feeling is very mutual,' River said.

They walked through the woods until the trees cleared on the edge of the headland and Indigo realised they were heading for the beach.

He led her down the stairs to Lilac Cove and she gasped softly because it was clear he'd gone to a hell of a lot of trouble. On the white sand were a table and two chairs surrounded by a canopy of fairy lights that must have taken ages to rig up. There was a picnic blanket and hamper next to the table and a bunch of handpicked flowers sat in front of one of the chairs.

'River, this is lovely. You didn't have to do all this.'

'I wanted to.' He drew her chair out for her and she smiled and sat down.

To her surprise he pulled a bottle out of the ice bucket. The fact that neither of them would be drinking was a tiny problem.

'It's non-alcoholic,' he said, obviously seeing her confusion.

She laughed and held out her champagne glass. He poured out something fizzy and pink.

'Rhubarb and raspberry,' he said as he topped up both glasses.

'Sounds wonderful.'

He sat down and he offered out his glass. 'To us.'

She smiled and chinked her glass against his.

The inky sea was millpond calm, the moon sparkling across the waves, and Indigo let out a contented sigh.

'I have soup to start, the only hot part of the meal, I'm afraid.' He picked up a flask from the hamper and poured out the soup into two bowls. 'Picnicking on the beach does have its limits. Bread?'

She took a bread roll and started buttering it. She sipped a spoonful of the soup.

'This is delicious.'

'Thank you, an old recipe.'

'How did you have the time to make this, what with being in the middle of building twenty treehouses?'

'I work until five most days, but then I go home and spend my evenings with Tierra. This soup was made with her expert guidance. She loves helping me in the kitchen, mainly watching and tasting. So making this soup ticked two boxes tonight: making something good for you and spending time with her.'

'Well, you can tell her that I love it. And our dates don't always have to be just us, I'm very happy to have her along. She makes the whole thing very entertaining.'

'But not romantic.'

She laughed. 'Probably not. And I know this is a long way off but if we are going to work, as a family, it's important that me and Tierra have time to get to know each other too. I'd like to get to know all of your family, Heath, Bear, Meadow, even Amelia. These are the people who are important to you. You're very lucky you get to spend so much time with your siblings. Before I lost my job and moved in with Violet, sometimes months would go by without us seeing each other. We'd keep in touch, text or chat most days, but it's not the same as working alongside her or seeing her every day.'

'I can't imagine not having my brothers in my life. And I don't mean that in a soppy "they mean the world to me" kind of way, it's just that it's always been us three, we've lived together almost our entire life. I studied architecture in Bristol and I stayed there some of the time, but it did feel like I was missing a limb. I didn't like it. They drive me mad sometimes, well most of the time, as siblings do, but of course I love them. This place will always be home for me and I hope they feel the same way.'

'Do you think they might not?'

'I think Heath would stay here. He has Meadow and Star and he will always be a part of their lives, even when they're divorced. He loves building the treehouses, just like me, so I think he'd be happy to stay here. I guess it depends whether Meadow will stay because I think he would go wherever she went so he could be there for Star. But I think Bear might crave bigger and better things. He's so super smart and there's so much more he could do with his life rather than being stuck here fiddling around with our website or sorting out the electrics in the wood. When he was sixteen he was even offered an apprenticeship with Strawberry.'

Indigo felt her eyebrows shoot up. 'One of the biggest computer software companies in the world?'

'Yes, the very same.'

'That's huge.'

'Yes it is. He turned it down, I don't know why. He would have had to move to London for two years and then spend the final year of his apprenticeship in California. He was only sixteen and we'd already had so much unsettlement with our parents dying, and then Michael, so maybe he found the idea of that move too daunting. I do wonder if he regretted it though. Part of me wants him to find that job that will challenge and inspire him but I selfishly want him to stay here forever too.'

'Well, maybe he can do both, a lot of computer work can be done from home.'

'I think the best place for him would be somewhere like London, or some of the bigger cities around the world, but he's not really the city-slicker type, so I'm not sure what he'll do. What about your family, what do they do?'

'Violet works in a bakery, making cakes and other yummy delights. Blue is... I mean, Jake. I honestly have no idea what he does. We weren't close growing up, not after he turned ten anyway. He always seemed to be angry with the world, wouldn't let anyone in. He joined the army when he was sixteen and we barely heard from him after that, the odd postcard or letter just saying he was alive. I'd write to him all the time but I don't know whether the letters never got through or he couldn't be bothered to reply. He left the army when he was twenty-two and moved to Thailand to find himself. He never came back so I don't know if he is still trying to find himself. We don't keep in touch much, which is his decision not mine. I don't even have an address for him. I email him every few weeks. Occasionally he replies with very short answers, most of the time he doesn't.'

'That's sad that you don't keep in touch that often. He's about to become an uncle and he has no idea?'

'No, I'll mention it in the next email, but I'm sure he won't care.'

'Where did that anger come from?'

'Oh well, that's a crappy story for a first date. Blue was three when my dad died. He was in the car with him when it crashed, killing my dad instantly. Blue was fine. No one has any idea what happened, it looks likely that another car was involved because of the scuff marks on the side of the car but they never found the other car or the driver. The sad thing was that Dad was found with yellow paint all over his face, in his eyes. Blue was sitting next to him in his car seat and they found him with a yellow tube of paint in his hands. The police believe that Blue might have squeezed the tube of paint, it squirted Dad in the eye and that was the thing that caused him to crash.'

'Shit,' River muttered. 'So Blue blames himself for his dad's death?'

'I think so.'

'But he was three years old, how could he possibly remember that?'

'Oh he didn't. He was a happy little child until he was ten or eleven, always quiet and liked his own company a bit too much, but happy. Then someone, not sure who, probably some interfering neighbour or relative, told him how his dad died.'

'You're kidding?'

'No, I wish I knew who it was, but imagine putting that on a ten year old's shoulders. Blue did some research, found some newspaper articles on it, and sure enough it was mentioned in the article about Dad having paint in his eyes and Blue holding the tube of paint. It was such an unusual way to die that a lot of the papers ran with the story. Some of the seedier ones had the headline, "Toddler kills own father". When I looked into it myself later, the articles were horrible.'

She took another spoonful of soup as she thought.

'It was like a switch went off in his head and after that he was a changed boy, angry at everyone and everything. I didn't know the reason why at the time, neither did Mum. We just presumed he was going through the moody teenage phase a bit early. It wasn't until he was fourteen that it all came out. Mum was horrified that he'd taken on that guilt and responsibility for Dad's death. She never blamed him for it, it was just an accident. She tried to make him go to counselling but he wasn't having any of it. Went to a few sessions, refused point blank to talk to anyone.

Two years later he joined the army. I hope somewhere along the way he found peace with himself but I'm guessing that, as he never came back from Thailand, he's still struggling with that guilt all these years later.'

'That's awful.'

'It is. And my mum felt pretty crappy about it too, that she was never able to help him.'

'I can't believe he carried that guilt all his life. He was three, it wasn't his fault,' River said.

'I know, can you imagine someone feeling guilty their whole life about an accident that wasn't their fault? What must that feel like?' Indigo said, dryly.

He gave a small smile of acknowledgement. 'I guess guilt is not something any of us can control. It just eats away at us and there's nothing we can do.'

'We can choose to forgive ourselves and not let an incident from the past define our future.'

'I think that's probably easier said than done,' River said.

'Well, maybe you need a trip to Thailand.'

'It is one of the places on the bucket list. Maybe I'll get there one day.'

'Hopefully you'll forgive yourself before *one day*.'

'Actually, after last night, the guilt I feel over Will's death sits a little bit easier today. Thanks to you.' He took her hand. 'I'm not saying that I can completely let it go, but for the first time I can see that what I'm doing with the RNLI is something important and good. I've started thinking that maybe I have something to offer after all. You've made me start believing in myself and I'm so grateful for that.'

She stared at him. 'You are a wonderful man, I truly believe that, and I love that I'm helping you to realise that too. I will tell you every day until you know it and believe it as much as I do.'

He smiled. 'OK.'

She watched him start removing more food from the picnic hamper; pâté, which she knew she sadly couldn't eat, cold chicken, grapes, cheeses, nuts and crackers. It looked wonderful and her stomach gurgled appreciatively.

River looked up at her, 'So what's on your bucket list?'

'I found my old bucket list the other day actually, a list I wrote probably ten years ago. Twenty-year-old me wanted to go to base camp at Everest. I'm not sure why. That's something I would have no interest in doing now. I've climbed Snowdon and Scafell Pike and it was fun but I don't think I really thought that particular item on the list through. Both base camps on Everest are over five thousand metres high, that's significantly higher and much harder to get to than the top of Snowdon.'

'No train either at Everest.'

Indigo laughed. 'Now I'd definitely take the train up Everest if there was one. Get out at the top, quick photo opportunity and then get back on the train again.' She helped herself to some food. 'There are things on the list I've done and I'm glad I did, like seeing the Grand Canyon, whale watching in Canada, swimming with dolphins, typical stuff that's given me amazing memories. And there are things that I'd still like to tick off, like seeing the cherry blossoms in Japan or giraffes running in the wild or seeing the aurora borealis. I'd love to learn how to play the saxophone and learn a different language. I also wanted to work at the Beverly Hills Hotel. It's one of those incredible places that always ends up on the best hotels lists. And it's such a famous institution with so much history and glamour, I've dreamed about working there for years. But will I look back on those memories or accomplishments and say they made me truly happy? I'm thirty years old next month and, when I was a teenager, I kind of thought I'd have my whole life figured out by the time I was thirty.'

'What does *figured out* look like?' River asked as he spread some cheese on a cracker.

'To my teenage self, I would have been married, living in a house by the sea, five kids, wonderful husband, possibly running my own guest house. But instead I'm pregnant with my first child, unmarried, no job up until a few days ago and no prospect of getting one either, no home, friends I rarely see any more, my life is a bit of a mess. And I have to ask myself, what are the things that will make me truly happy in life, what do I really want? And it's not a trip to Niagara Falls, as amazing as that would be.'

'I think want and need are two different things,' River said.

She placed some cold chicken on her plate. 'I think you're right. I need job security if I'm going to be able to raise my baby.'

'Our baby and you have that. No matter what happens between us, you will always have a job here. And even if we end up hating each other, you are not raising this baby alone, financially, emotionally, physically. I will be there to help you with all that every step of the way. Blossom Cottage will always be yours too if you want it.'

She smiled. It was lovely to hear him say it. To know that her job and home here were not dependent on them being together was a huge relief. 'Thank you. Honestly, that means so much.'

'So what is it you *want*?' River asked.

'Well, if we take the job and home out of the equation, it would be lovely to have a partner to navigate life's adventures with, someone I could talk to at the end of the day, someone to share my hopes and dreams with. Great sex would be a bonus. But... I don't *need* a man to make me happy. I've been on my own for two and a half years and I've kind of got used to just ticking along, taking care of myself. Sure, I get lonely sometimes, but I can always get a dog.'

She took a bite of the chicken as she thought. 'That's why I said I don't want to get married to you. Getting married needs to be for love, that great big life-changing kind of love, the kind that means being with the other person for the rest of my life *would* make me completely and utterly happy. Otherwise there's no point.'

'OK,' River said. 'So what would make you happy?'

'I want a child. As far back as I can remember I always wanted children. Me and Luke tried for years to conceive, and when I finally got pregnant, I was so happy. And then I lost it in the car accident and to have that thing I wanted so much within my grasp and then be snatched away was utterly devastating. And then by some gift of fate, I'm pregnant again. I can't tell you how completely overjoyed I am to be pregnant now. The only thing I really want is for this baby to be born safe and healthy.'

He nodded. 'I can understand that. Our priorities

change as we get older and some of that amazing stuff we add to our list just becomes frivolous and meaningless. My priority is making this place work, not just for me but my family. And most of all keeping my children happy.'

She liked that he had included her child in that statement, not just Tierra. God, she knew she was falling in love with this man and despite what she'd just said about not needing a man to make her happy, she knew she would happily cross off everything else on her bucket list in return for a life here with him. She just hoped he was on the same page.

CHAPTER SIXTEEN

River watched Indigo across the table as she finished off the Eton mess. Licking the cream off her fingers was probably the sexiest thing he'd ever seen and she wasn't even trying to be flirty. He had loved talking to her tonight, there'd been no awkward silences between them, they'd switched topics with ease, and he felt like he could keep talking to her forever.

The conversation about her hopes and dreams had left him with a tiny seed of doubt. She'd had big dreams before the accident. Going to Everest, however impractical, was a big adventure, even if it was only base camp. Visiting Niagara Falls, seeing the cherry blossoms in Japan, going on safari to see the giraffes, he wasn't sure he could ever give her those dreams. And she'd talked about wanting to work at the Beverly Hills Hotel with such passion and excitement, how could he possibly compete with something like that with his treehouse resort? The two were in very different leagues. She'd said the only thing she wanted was for her baby to be born happy and healthy, but would she still have those big dreams once the baby was born. He'd told her he only wanted to keep his children happy but he wanted her to be happy too. Would this life here be enough for her? Would he be enough?

'That was all wonderful, thank you,' Indigo said. 'And our baby thanks you, too. I feel like I'm constantly hungry lately but for once I feel full.'

He pushed those doubts away. 'Well, you're eating for two now and it's my responsibility to look after you both.'

She smiled and looked around the cove. 'This place is lovely, I'm surprised more of your guests don't use it.'

'There are three beaches that lead from the woods. This is Lilac Cove and Pear Tree Beach is further along. That's much bigger and tends to be the one that the guests enjoy. There's also Chestnut Bay too. This one is actually a nudist beach so that puts a lot of people off. The majority of British folk don't want to get their bits out and feel embarrassed looking at other people's naked bodies so they stay away. You get some coming here out of curiosity but I can count on one hand how many times I've actually found naked people down here so there isn't a lot to see.'

'River Brookfield, did you bring me to a nudist beach for our first date?' Indigo said, pretending to be shocked.

'Well, technically it's our second as last night with Tierra was our first. And surely that's how all good dates should end, with a bit of nudity,' River teased.

Indigo let out a laugh of outrage.

'I'm joking—'

Words stalled in his mouth as Indigo stood up and whipped off her dress in one swift movement. He watched as she stripped off the rest of her clothes.

'I think I might go for a swim. You can join me if you like,' Indigo said as she walked the short distance to the shore.

He stared at her as she slowly waded out into the water, the moon dusting her skin like pure silver. He had never seen anything so beautiful in his entire life. She dipped down, covering her shoulders with the water, and then turned back to watch him, her eyes dancing with amusement.

He smiled at the challenge. She didn't think he would.

He stood up and started unbuttoning his shirt, his eyes locked on hers the whole time. He quickly got undressed and then waded out to join her. The water was icy cold and it made him gasp as he went deeper. He gathered her in his arms as he drew close. She slid her arms round his neck.

'You're incredible, do you know that?' River said.

'I think you're pretty bloody fantastic too.'

He ran his hands down to her waist and relished in the feel of her body against his as she moved closer. 'So... tonight has gone well, I think, are you willing to have another date?'

'Oh, I'm very much looking forward to our next date, and many more after that.'

He smiled in relief and bent his head and kissed her. Christ she tasted wonderful. Every time he kissed her, feelings he'd never experienced before exploded through him. He'd had plenty of sex in his life so he was well aware what lust and desire felt like but this was so much more. He slid his hands up her ribs and touched her breasts. Her lips trembled against his mouth and he paused. Was she cold?

She pulled back slightly to look at him. 'You know,

being pregnant makes me incredibly horny. You can't start something like that and then stop.'

He frowned. She was pregnant. Of course he hadn't forgotten – the fact she was carrying his child was at the very forefront of his mind – but he needed to be more considerate. Bringing pâté to dinner earlier, something pregnant women couldn't eat, was a bad move, and kissing each other in the freezing cold sea probably wasn't good for the baby either.

He stepped back from her and took her hand. 'Let's take this some place warmer.'

He started walking back towards the beach and she followed him. They made their way back to the table and their clothes and he cursed not having had the foresight to bring a towel with him. Although he hadn't expected the date to end up being so wet.

They both quickly got dressed but, being soaking wet, their clothes rapidly became wet too. River grabbed the picnic blanket and wrapped it round her.

'Come on, let's get back to yours and get you warm.'

'What about all this?' Indigo gestured to the table and chairs.

'I'll sort it all out tomorrow.' He took her hand and led her back up the steps.

It didn't take them long to reach Blossom Cottage and she quickly let them inside.

As soon as the door was closed, she kissed him again.

'Let's get you out of these wet clothes,' River said, against her lips.

She laughed. 'That old chestnut. If you want to see me naked again, you just have to ask.'

She stepped back from him and stripped naked in seconds. He moved towards her and she giggled as she ran upstairs away from him.

He pulled his shirt off and followed her up the stairs, no longer feeling the cold at all.

～

Indigo watched as River ran up the stairs. She was leaning against the door frame and he stopped when he saw her, his eyes drinking her in. God, he made her feel so beautiful.

They stared at each other and then suddenly they closed the gap between them and before she could utter a word they were kissing. His lips tasted so good, she pressed herself against him, desperate to feel his skin against hers. He moved his hands to her body, exploring her, stroking and caressing her with the gentlest of touches.

She ran her hands over the muscles in his back. He cupped her face, kissing her hard, and then his hands slid down her chest stroking over her breasts.

'Oh god, River.'

He smiled against her lips and kissed her again. He lifted her and she wrapped her legs around him as he carried her to the bed. He laid her down as he lay next to her. The rest of his clothes were quickly removed and then he was touching and stroking everywhere. He moved his hot mouth to her shoulder and she let her head fall back onto the pillows, watching him as he adored her body with loving kisses.

'I want you to understand, this is purely an act of altruism.' He carried on kissing her body.

She laughed. 'How so?'

'I have a responsibility to look after you. You need a job or a home, you've got it. You start craving chocolate milk-shake at three in the morning, I'll drive the ten-mile trip to the nearest twenty-four-hour McDonald's to get you one. You need sex because your baby hormones are making you horny, I have a responsibility to take care of that too.'

She laughed hard at that and she could see the smile on his face as he continued to trail hot kisses across her stomach.

'How completely selfless of you.'

'I thought so.'

She giggled but the laughter died on her lips as he suddenly slipped her breast into his mouth, and she gasped at how good his tongue felt against her skin. All manner of words slipped from her mouth, none of which made any sense. He moved his hand between her legs and she cried out as soon as he touched her there. He knew exactly where to touch her to make her go weak and within seconds that feeling was building and then exploding through her. Her breath was ragged as he moved over her, capturing her moans on his lips. He gathered her hands and pinned them over her head as he moved inside her and she tightened her fingers around his.

He pulled back slightly to look at her and she could feel that connection between them, so strong and powerful it was like a solid thing she could reach out and touch. She stared at him in wonder. How could two people who'd randomly bumped into each other on a night out be so intrinsically linked after just one night?

'River, none of this makes sense.'

'What doesn't?'

'This thing between us. I feel like I've just been to a magic show and watched the most incredible illusion, only it's real and amazing and beautiful. I've never felt like this before.'

He grinned, releasing her hands. 'Oh, I think we make perfect sense.'

'You do?'

He continued to move against her, slowly and gently. 'We're two halves of a whole.'

She smiled and stroked his cheek, running her thumb across his lips and he kissed it. 'I like that.'

'I don't believe in fate or destiny or that our lives have a predetermined path but I can't help believing we were supposed to meet that night.'

'I think so too,' Indigo said, holding him tighter against her as that feeling inside her started to build.

He kissed her and she knew nothing in this world would ever be so completely and utterly right as this.

He pulled back to look at her. 'So you'll marry me?'

She smiled. 'Maybe one day I will.'

He kissed her hard. 'I'll take that,' he said against her lips and then kissed her again.

While it was true what she'd said on the date – that she didn't *need* a man to make her happy – the thought of marrying this man did make her very happy indeed. And as every cell in her body exploded with the most incredible sensations, as that feeling built, taking her higher and higher, it was that thought of forever with him that sent her crashing over the edge.

Indigo woke up in the early hours of the morning to find she was almost nose to nose with River, his arm slung over her belly, his legs entwined with hers. He was so utterly beautiful and even more so when he was asleep and he didn't carry that angst with him. He seemed to hold the weight of the world on his shoulders and she wanted to help him lighten the load. Although she had probably doubled it with the news he was going to be a dad again – it was quite obviously going to turn his world upside down – but she couldn't fault him for his reaction to it.

As if he knew she was awake, he stirred, opened his beautiful eyes and smiled when he saw her.

'Hi,' he said, his voice sexily husky.

'Hello.'

He leaned forward and gave her the sweetest kiss. 'God, making love to you is incredible,' he said. 'I'm trying to decide whether it was because it's sober sex or whether it was just you, marvellous, wonderful you.'

Indigo grinned. 'Let's go with it being me.'

He stroked her face. 'I think it was.'

She stared at him, her heart filling with complete love for him.

She leaned forward, cupped his face and kissed him. He moaned softly against her lips. She rolled on top of him and shifted so she was straddling him. She sat up and looked down at this magnificent man, knowing fate had brought her back to him, where she belonged.

He sat up and kissed her, caressing his hands down her back. He moved his hands up her sides, gently caressing her breasts as the kiss continued. She stroked round his shoulders and teased the hair at the back of his neck.

He moved his fingers between her legs and that feeling seemed to build suddenly inside her but River was slow and careful with his kisses and touches, making the feeling subside then build again then subside until she was desperate for a release, clawing at his shoulders.

'River, please.'

'It's OK, I've got this.'

She gasped with relief as he touched that spot and then she was spiralling out of control, falling apart, crying out all manner of words and noises.

He lifted her slightly and then, with his hands on her hips, he guided her down on top of him and moved deep inside of her. She moaned and let her head fall back.

'No, look at me. I want to see how much you want this,' River said.

She gazed at him, her eyes locking with his as she started to move against him, pouring everything she felt for him into how she touched and kissed him.

'Sex is amazing between us, but it's not this I want, it's you,' Indigo said.

He kissed her and held her tighter against him. As that feeling started to build inside her once more she stared at him and in that moment as their eyes connected, she knew she was in love with this man. And while she couldn't say the words, she wanted him to feel it. He stared at her in wonder and suddenly they were both falling over the edge together, clinging onto each other with a desperate urgency. As their moans and cries died down and they tried to catch their breath, he pressed his mouth to her throat with such tenderness she wondered if he felt that too.

~

River pulled on his shirt as he watched Indigo hurry round the room nervously getting ready, trying to find the perfect outfit. He'd asked her to join him and his family for breakfast and for some reason this seemed to be a big deal for her.

God, he loved this woman. He didn't care that she had only arrived here a few days before, he didn't care if any of his family thought it was too soon, he knew how he felt about her and he was starting to believe she felt the same for him too.

He was happy, for the first time in his life he felt content.

Indigo moved to stand in front of him. 'Will I do?'

He wasn't even really aware of what she was wearing as he stepped forward, cupped her face and kissed her. 'You look perfect,' he said against her lips and kissed her again.

She giggled. 'You didn't even look.'

'I know you're perfect, no matter what you wear.'

He stepped back to appraise her, knowing it was important to her. She was wearing a cute blue dress that shimmered in the sunlight.

'You look lovely. Come on, let's go see the family. They already like you so it's not like you have to impress them.'

He escorted her outside.

'I know, but things are different now.'

They carried on walking through the woods and he slipped his hand into hers. It felt so completely right.

'If you want, you can stay with me tonight, at Magnolia Cottage.'

She grinned at him. 'In the mezzanine bedroom?'

He smirked. 'Not much room for both of us up there. Whereas my bed has plenty of space.'

She smiled. 'OK.'

River watched her as they walked through the woods towards the restaurant. She looked happy too.

They walked into the restaurant and predictably it was empty apart from his family, sitting in their usual spot in the corner. He held Indigo's hand tighter for moral support.

They were almost at the table when Tierra spotted them and let out a little shriek of joy, running across the last few metres to meet them and throwing herself into River's arms. He lifted her, holding her tight with one arm, still gripping Indigo's hand with the other. He couldn't help the huge grin from spreading on his face when Tierra reached out an arm and brought Indigo into the group hug too.

'Are you two boyfriend and girlfriend now?' Tierra asked.

'Yes we are,' Indigo said and his heart soared at the complete confidence she had in them.

Tierra gave them another big hug and he smiled and placed a kiss on Indigo's forehead.

A cheer went up from Heath, Bear and Meadow and he looked over to see all three of them grinning inanely at him.

He shook his head and rolled his eyes but he couldn't help the smile on his face. He didn't know what the future held for them but things couldn't be more perfect right now. His life had changed beyond recognition and he couldn't be happier about it. He just hoped that she would be happy here too.

CHAPTER SEVENTEEN

River walked into the reception area later that afternoon. Indigo had contacted him over the walkie-talkie asking if he could spare fifteen minutes to watch reception as Meadow was picking up the girls from school and Bear had gone to collect some more electric cabling.

Her face lit up when she saw him and that warmed him from the inside. He leaned over the desk and kissed her and she smiled against his lips.

'Thanks for coming. Kit Lewis, the man who wants to propose to his girlfriend, has finally decided to do it in their treehouse. He says she loves it so much, it makes sense to do it there. He's asked if I can put some candles and fairy lights inside and on the balcony. They're out now and then when they come back he's going to pop the question. So I need to make it look extra romantic. I'm going to pick some flowers in the woods too but I won't be too long.'

'I could have done all that for you,' River said.

'Oh, it's no bother and you did tell me you're not really

the romantic type. Plus, I feel invested in this proposal now, I'm going to enjoy making the place look perfect for them.'

He smiled. 'Go for it. I'm happy to watch over things here.'

'Oh by the way, is there any chance I could get a tiny advance of my wages? Say fifty pounds, so I can get some petrol? Taking Tierra to school yesterday, well the tank was so empty I was practically driving on fumes, and if I have to take her again, or go anywhere else, we might not actually get there.'

'That's no problem, write down your bank details and I can transfer some over to you now,' River said.

She quickly scrawled her account number and sort code on a piece of paper. 'But this has to come from my wages, I don't want money from you.'

He smiled. 'It's OK, I'll make sure it comes from your wages.'

She gave him a quick kiss on the cheek and with a wave left him alone. It was pretty quiet, no phone calls, no guests needing help. He glanced through their upcoming bookings, noticing that the twelve current treehouses for guests were pretty much fully booked throughout the rest of the year. There were a couple of bookings for the new ones but River had told Meadow not to take any more until they knew for sure the treehouses would be finished on time. But they would have to start taking bookings soon to ensure they would be full once they were ready. He looked at Blossom Cottage. He logged in to their website and removed it from all future bookings. That was Indigo's home now and, with a bit of luck, he and Tierra would soon be moving in there too.

Just then the phone rang.

'Hello, Wishing Wood,' River answered it.

'Can I speak to Indigo please?' said a woman on the other end of the phone.

'I'm afraid she's not available right now, can I help at all?' River said.

'I'm her friend, Vicky.'

'Oh hello,' River said, warmly. 'I'm her boyfriend, River.'

He wondered if it was too soon to label himself as that to her friends, but Indigo had said yes to Tierra when she'd asked if they were boyfriend and girlfriend that morning.

'Boyfriend?' Vicky said in disbelief. 'You barely know her.'

He frowned. 'I know enough.'

'I presume she's finally told you who she really is and that she's pregnant with your child,' Vicky said.

River felt his eyebrows shoot up. 'It's a good thing she has because me finding out when one of her so-called friends blurts it out to me wouldn't be appropriate, would it?'

'I just thought it was so dishonest and deceitful,' Vicky said.

'Actually, I understand why she did it. And I didn't exactly make it easy for her when I didn't recognise her.'

'Oh yes, because you were so drunk you could barely remember your own name,' Vicky said, distastefully.

'I don't normally drink. Someone spiked my drinks which was why I got so drunk so quickly. And to be fair, she was dressed like a cat.'

Why was he even having this conversation? He didn't need to justify or defend himself to anyone. He knew what he had with Indigo. But he didn't want to alienate her friends either. He wasn't sure what conversations she'd had with them over the last few days but he supposed they had every right to worry about her. She was pregnant and, up until a few days ago, had no job and no home. They'd want to ensure her happiness. He would be patient and answer any questions her friend had, even if they were rude. If he had to prove he was worthy of Indigo's love then he would do it.

'Look, we're all worried about her,' Vicky said. 'Since the car accident she's spent the last two years keeping her head down, keeping to herself. She's been quiet, withdrawn. And then suddenly she gets fired for stealing, loses her home. She goes out, gets drunk and has a one-night stand. That's not like her. She's never had a one-night stand in her life. She gets herself stupidly pregnant, insists on keeping it and drives up there expecting you to look after her.'

'I take full responsibility for making Indigo pregnant,' River said. 'That's why I want to take care of her and our baby. She has a job here and a home; even if things don't work out between us, she will always have that. She'll be well looked after.'

'So she'll be living in a treehouse, with a baby?' Vicky said, the disdain dripping from her voice.

'The treehouses are very classy and luxurious,' River said, defensively. 'They have heating, hot and cold running water, lighting. It's not just some shaky shack in a tree.'

'I'm sorry, I'm sure they're lovely,' Vicky said, scornfully and not sounding sorry at all. 'But I can assure you this eco-warrior tree-hugging life is not what she wants. It won't be enough for her. This is a security thing, nothing more. No job or home, baby on the way, and someone offers to take care of her and with no better offer on the table she decides to stay. But living in a treehouse is not who Indy is. She worked for Infinity Hotels, one of the finest hotels in the world. Did she tell you about her job offer last week from the Beverly Hills Hotel?'

'She was offered a job at the Beverly Hills Hotel?' He frowned in confusion. That had been her dream, why would she turn it down?

'She didn't tell you? Now that is weird. She's always wanted to work there because of its glitz and glamour. As far back as I can remember, she's had a dream of working in the best hotels around the world and the Beverly Hills Hotel was the cherry on the cake. She applied for a six-month secondment-type thing there and she was offered a place starting in a few weeks. Many of these secondments lead to permanent work offers so this was a huge deal for her. But because she's pregnant and had no money, she's deferred it for a year. So this time next year there's a good chance she'll be taking her baby and swanning off to Los Angeles, probably to never come back.'

His mouth was dry. Why wouldn't Indigo have mentioned this to him? She had told him her dream was to work at the Beverly Hills Hotel, but she hadn't said anything about this job offer or the fact she would be leaving in twelve months' time.

'It is funny she didn't tell you,' Vicky went on. 'Unless she wanted to keep that a secret too. I think she's still trying to decide what to do. Maybe I shouldn't have said anything.'

He cleared his throat. 'I'm glad you did.'

'I'm grateful you understand. I'm sure we both want her to be happy and I'm worried she's considering throwing away an amazing opportunity. Right now she's seeing everything through very rose tinted glasses but I know her and I know if she doesn't do this, she will regret it for the rest of her life.'

His mind was a whirl of emotion and all words stalled in his throat.

'Tell her I called, will you?' Vicky said.

'I will.'

And with that she hung up.

River put the phone down and rubbed his hand across his face. This was what he'd feared the night before, that this place wouldn't be enough for her and one day she would follow her dreams and leave. But why would she go on dates with him, make love to him and let him and Tierra fall in love with her if the plan was always to leave the following year?

Unless… that was no longer the plan. In twelve months' time there would be a five month old baby taking over every waking and sleeping moment. If she took the job next year would she really be able to enjoy it? Would she resent that she had missed out on the opportunity to do it now? Would she even be able to go at all next year? He knew from experience that raising a baby, for the first year or so at least, was an all-consuming thing. Was she giving up that dream? Was she settling for an ordinary life here instead?

Suddenly he wanted her to take this opportunity and fulfil that dream. He knew if she went to Los Angeles now there would be a huge chance she wouldn't come back. She might love the job and the place and decide to stay there. Although that thought broke his heart it was better that she led a life that made her happy than one where she never realised her dreams.

$$\sim$$

Indigo bounced back into the reception half hour later. Kit and Zoey's treehouse was now bedecked with candles in storm lanterns, twinkling fairy lights and flowers. It looked perfect. All Kit had to do was get the words right and Zoey would be putty in his hands.

'Hey, I'm all done. Thanks for looking after this place,' she said to River as she sat down.

'Your *friend* Vicky called,' River said.

Indigo sighed. 'God, she won't leave me alone. She phoned me on my mobile three times but I didn't pick up. And she's not my friend. More like an acquaintance.'

There was silence from River and she glanced over at him. He looked absolutely miserable.

'Did she say something to you?'

'She had quite a lot to say.'

'She always does, none of it nice. She has no social boundaries at all, just blurts out whatever comes to mind. And she always sees the negative in everything. Unlike my friend Joey who always sees the sunshine. What did she say to you?'

He paused. 'Are your friends happy about... us?'

That was a bit awkward to answer. 'I think they had their concerns over how fast things were happening between us, but most of them are happy now because they know I'm happy. But either way, I don't care what they think. They don't understand what we have.'

He was silent for a minute.

'River, are you OK?'

'Your friends do want you to be happy and Vicky doesn't think this place will tick that box for you. She actually thinks it's hilarious you're living in a treehouse and she says that this "tree-hugging" life would never be enough for you.'

'Well that isn't true. I love it here.'

He turned his chair to face her and it was painful to see how upset he looked. 'Do you want to tell me about the Beverly Hills Hotel?' he asked softly.

She stared at him in confusion. 'What about it?'

'That you have a job offer there.'

'Oh that. It's not really a job though, it's a "work-enrichment opportunity to invest in my future,"' she quoted from the Living the Dream website.

'Which you've deferred for a year?'

She frowned. 'Well technically yes but… What the hell has Vicky said to you?'

'According to her, you have much bigger and more glamorous dreams than staying here,' River said. 'She said you want to work in the finest hotels in the world and it's always been your dream to work in the Beverly Hills Hotel.'

'Well that part is true. That has always been my dream. I told you that. But that all changed when I met you.'

'Because I got you pregnant?'

'No, I told you last night, this baby is my dream and now you are too.'

He shook his head.

Indigo's heart was racing; she was suddenly feeling like their whole relationship was tumbling down like a house of cards. Could it really be that fragile? She'd thought they had something strong and unbreakable, that forever kind of love. She was furious at Vicky, her own marriage was miserable and now she was attempting to ruin what Indigo had with River with her stupid meddling.

'But you have deferred the job?' River asked.

'I deferred the job when I found out I was pregnant. I had no money to get over there anyway so it would have been impossible. But having my baby was the most important thing so I deferred it.'

'You didn't just say no?'

'No, because at that time I had no idea where I'd be in a year's time.'

'You were still holding out hope that you might be able to go?' River said.

'I guess at the time that I deferred it, before I came here, there was still a tiny part of me that wanted to go but now I know I belong here with you,' Indigo said.

'Have you told them now you won't be going?'

'Well no, not yet.'

He nodded, sadly. 'Because you're not sure.'

'Because since meeting you again I haven't given it a moment's thought.'

'So your dreams have changed overnight?'

'Yes, why is that so hard to believe?'

He was silent for a moment. 'You have such big dreams, Indy, Niagara Falls, Japan, Africa to see the giraffes. And having a baby won't stop that thirst for adventure pumping through your veins. I want you to be happy. This life, this place, me, it will never be enough. If you stay you'll grow to resent me for it, just like Danielle did.'

'Don't put your issues on me,' Indigo snapped. 'I know you've grown up believing you are worthless and unlovable but that's not what I think of you. I've told you time and time again that I think you're a wonderful, magnificent man but you continue to doubt yourself. How can we ever move forward if you don't trust me?'

He stared at her. 'I don't know.'

They were silent for a moment and she suddenly realised he was breaking up with her.

A sob escaped her throat.

'I've transferred some money into your account. Five thousand pounds.'

'What? I don't want that.'

He rubbed a hand across his face and when he spoke his voice was broken. 'You wouldn't be here now if it wasn't for our baby and the fact you have no money, you'd be on a plane to America. So go to Los Angeles. Follow that dream. Use the money to invest in your future.'

He stood up to leave.

'Wait? That's it? We're over? One stupid phone call from some bitch who calls herself my friend and you're finishing with me? You said you were falling for me. How can you say that when it's so easy for you to walk away?'

He stared at her incredulously. 'Letting you go is the hardest thing I've ever had to do. I never wanted to let anyone in for fear of falling in love with them and then have them leave just like my parents did. I let my guard down with you. Indy, I am falling for you. And more than anything I want you to be happy even if that isn't with me.'

Indigo stared in horror as he walked out the door.

CHAPTER EIGHTEEN

Indigo was still crying when Amelia turned up. She tried to wipe her tears but more kept coming.

'Oh my god, what's happened? Is it the baby?' Amelia said, rushing in as soon she saw Indigo was upset.

'River has just broken up with me.'

She explained briefly what had happened and Amelia shook her head. 'There is something a bit romantic in that weird, twisted logic of his. He wants you to follow your dreams. There's that quote that says something like, "If you love someone, you let them go." He's letting you go so you can be happy.'

'*He* makes me happy. A life with him is the dream I want now. I told him that but he won't listen. I've told him time and again how wonderful I think he is. I don't know what I can do to reach him.'

'His confidence is so damaged from his upbringing, it would only take something tiny for him to start thinking he's worthless again,' Amelia said.

'But I don't see him as worthless. I love him.'

'Have you told him that?'

'No.' Should she have said that to him? Would that have made any difference?

'You need to fight for him. Don't let him get away with feeling sorry for himself. This is too important to throw away. Show him you have something worth holding onto.'

Indigo sighed. 'He gave me five thousand pounds to leave. Told me to invest in my future. That's a great big push out the door.'

'Or a sign of how important your happiness is to him.' Amelia said. 'Even if that means watching you walk away. He loves you, you know that. And you love him. Wouldn't you do the same for him if you could?'

'Give him a load of money to leave?'

'Give him the thing he wants the most.'

Indigo sighed. 'I don't want his money.'

A light sparked in Amelia's eyes. 'No, you should use it. He told you to invest in your future. You should invest in the future that you want.'

Indigo stared at her, suddenly knowing what she had to do.

'Can you watch reception until Meadow gets back? She won't be long.'

'Go, go,' Amelia urged, practically pushing her out the door.

Indigo took off at a run with her ideas bubbling over. She only hoped it would be enough.

'You did what?' Bear said, after River had told Heath and Bear what had happened.

He'd sat in Lilac Cove for over an hour, replaying the phone call from Vicky and the conversation with Indigo in his head. He just wanted her to be happy but he felt horrible about what he'd done. The look she had given him when he'd walked out was as if he'd ripped out her heart and taken it with him. He had hurt her and that wasn't his intention at all. He should never have made that decision for her. They should have talked about her dream together and come up with a plan. He loved her, he should be fighting for her not pushing her away. He'd wanted to prove to Vicky that he was worthy of Indigo, that he would look after her, and instead he'd ended up asking Indigo to leave. She was pregnant with no home and he'd told her to go. It didn't matter that his reasons had been selfless. He had let her down. He wasn't worthy of her after all. He had to find her. He knew she'd never forgive him, and he didn't deserve that anyway, but he had to tell her she would always have a home and a job here, no matter what.

He'd come back to reception only to see that Indigo had gone and Amelia was there. He didn't dare go inside, he didn't need to hear from his grandmother that he'd made the biggest mistake of his life. He already knew that. He'd been to Blossom Cottage but Indigo wasn't there, then he'd gone to Magnolia Cottage but she wasn't there either. He'd raced across to the restaurant, checked out the beaches and now he'd bumped into his brothers in the woods and poured out the whole sorry story. He normally wouldn't talk to them about his problems but right now he needed all the help he could get.

'I gave her five thousand pounds and told her to leave,' River said, quietly.

Bear stared at him incredulously.

'You're a dick,' Heath said.

'I agree,' Bear said.

'She's the best thing that's ever happened to you,' Heath said.

'You love her and I'm pretty sure she loves you. Why would you ruin that?' Bear said. 'She told me about her dream to work in the Beverly Hills Hotel the other day and she said that changed the second she met you. She said all she wanted was a fairytale ending with you.'

River felt sick. 'I just wanted her to be happy and I didn't think I could give her that.'

'Shouldn't she be the one to decide that?' Heath said. 'You don't get to make decisions for her. Or live her life for her. She chose you, that should be enough for you.'

'Listen, I know I'm a dick. We can stand here all day and talk about my faults. But what can I do to make this right?' River said.

'You tell her you love her,' Heath said. 'We all make mistakes and do and say stupid things, but if you love each other, nothing is unforgiveable.'

'There's quite a lot that's unforgiveable actually,' Bear said. 'Sleeping with someone else would be high on my list, this is nothing in comparison to that. This is just your insecurities, she knows that. You being an idiot will not change how she feels for you. But I agree with Heath: as soon as you see her, the first thing you should say is that you love her.'

River knew it would probably take a lot more than that to fix what he'd done.

Suddenly the walkie-talkie crackled into life. 'River,' Meadow said. 'Indigo has said there are some problems in Blossom Cottage she needs you to look at.'

'Is she there?' River said.

'Yes, she's waiting for you.'

He tucked his walkie-talkie back on his belt. 'I have to go.'

'Don't come back here until you've sorted it out,' Bear said.

He started jogging through the trees, but the jog very quickly turned into a run.

Indigo was upstairs in the kids' room when she heard River arrive, bursting through the door like there was some kind of emergency. Her heart was pounding against her chest.

'Indigo!' he called.

She moved to the top of the stairs. 'Up here.'

He thundered up the stairs and was suddenly in the room. 'Indy I—'

'No, I get to talk now. You've already had your say about my future, now it's my turn. You gave me money to invest in my future, so I have.' She gestured at the room and he looked around, his eyes widening. 'As this will be Tierra's room, she needs books, beanbags to lie on while she's reading those books, more soft toys because a little girl can't have too many of those, and fairy lights above the bed because she clearly loves a bit of sparkle in her life. I put fairy lights and beanbags in here too.' She opened the secret cupboard to reveal a magical playroom, twinkling with tiny lights and a few more soft toy animals presiding over everything.

River stared at it in wonder and she moved to the stairs and started down them. 'Come on, I have more to show you.'

She didn't wait for a reply. She walked straight into the nursery. He followed her in.

'Our baby needs toys too.' She gestured to the large teddy bear sitting in the cot. 'And a night light.' She switched it on and tiny rainbows danced around the room. 'I've also ordered a changing table. It will be delivered next week. I couldn't lift that on my own. There's more, come on.'

She moved to the door.

He snagged her hand. 'Indy, I love you,' he said, softly.

Tears smarted her eyes and she nearly faltered in her big speech but she needed him to know she was in this for the long haul.

'I know, which is why I'm not letting you push me away. Come on. I have one more thing to show you.'

She went back out onto the landing and pushed back the room divider to show the easel she'd set up next to the window. 'So you have somewhere to paint, because this treehouse was never just about my dreams but about yours too. I told you before that our dreams change and evolve, our priorities change too. I would get rid of every single thing on my bucket list to spend the rest of my life here in Blossom Cottage with Tierra, our baby and the man I love, so completely and utterly. I never told you about the Beverly Hills Hotel offer because, from the moment I came here and met you again, that dream wasn't important any more. You are the only thing that matters to me now and that's not me settling for less, that's me choosing a magical life here in Wishing Wood. You make me deliriously happy. No one will ever understand what we have and I don't care because we know what we have is real. River, I think you are the most incredible man I've ever met. You should be proud of the life you have. You're raising a brilliant little girl, single-handed, you've made this place a huge success and you have saved hundreds of lives. That's something to shout about, not be ashamed of. And that's the man I love.'

'You love me? After what I said before, you still love me?'

'With all my heart.'

He stared at her and then kissed her hard. She kissed him back, tears falling down her cheeks.

He pulled back slightly. 'I am so sorry for everything I said. I gave you that money because I wanted you to be happy, not because I wanted to get rid of you. I'm sorry for giving up on us so easily.'

'It's OK.'

'I don't deserve your forgiveness. I have baggage and insecurities and—'

'And none of that scares me. We will fight, we will say things we don't mean and then we'll have incredible make-up sex. Because a love like ours will weather the harshest storms. What we have is that big, life-changing, forever kind of love and that won't go away with a few silly words.'

He smiled. 'Indigo Bloom, you are a magnificent woman. I love you so much. The first time we made love, I knew then we had something incredible, something life changing.'

Her breath caught in her throat to hear that.

'I know you're proud of me for saving lives, and I am too, but *you* saved me. You've made me see my own worth. So yes, I was scared to hear your friend say that our life here would not be enough, I was scared that you would suddenly start thinking like that too. But I should never have doubted you or the connection we share and I'm so sorry for that. I love you. I want this life with you.' he gestured round the treehouse. 'I want forever.'

He kissed her again and she sighed with relief against his lips.

He pulled back again. 'I don't want you to turn down that offer from the Beverly Hills Hotel,' he said. 'Not yet. I know right now your priority is our baby but if you want to go and work in America next year, then I will support you. Me and Tierra can come out and stay with you while you're there. I don't want you to miss out on an amazing opportunity.'

'I won't be missing out on anything. I have everything I want right here with you.' She placed her hand over his heart.

He smiled. 'Let's make that decision next year. Now, about that make-up sex?'

She grinned and took his hand and led him into the bedroom. He kissed her and slowly started to undress her.

Everything really could change in a heartbeat. But the second she had met River Brookfield her life was entwined with his and she knew he was her happy ever after. Life was a funny thing, it had its ups and downs, but it had led her to here, and this was where she belonged.

EPILOGUE

Indigo looked around the small clearing in the middle of the woods, surrounded by many of the new treehouses. The sun was setting, leaving cranberry clouds across the sky, and fairy lights were twinkling in the dusky evening. People were lounging on chairs and beanbags on the ground as they ate, drank and chatted. Even some of the staff were there to support the event. She spotted Lucien chatting with Alex as they ate together, Greta was with her husband on a different picnic blanket, and Felix was feeding his boyfriend strawberries.

She couldn't help feeling a huge sense of pride. The opening weekend for the new treehouses seemed to have gone without a hitch. It had proved so popular with the bloggers and travel journalists that they had opened the new treehouses for one cohort to stay on Friday night and then for a second cohort to stay on Saturday night. Already Wishing Wood had been tagged on various social media posts in some brilliant videos and photos after they'd taken them on tours of the place.

Initially, River hadn't wanted to do any of the tours himself, saying Meadow or Indigo would be better at that kind of thing than he was, but Indigo had been really pleased that on the day he'd stepped up and done it and had excitedly shown all the fabulous treehouses and their unique features. She'd wanted him to be proud of what he and his brothers had achieved in such a short amount of time and see people's reactions for himself when he took them around this magical resort because those reactions were nothing short of wonder.

Every treehouse was pretty much sold out now for the rest of the year, it was a wonderful achievement.

She looked around for him now so he could see how happy everyone was but she couldn't spot him.

The event had taken a lot of organising. For something that on the surface appeared to be a laid-back, simple affair it had still taken a lot of planning but it had given Indigo a thirst to do more event planning in the future. Already she had ideas for holding weddings in the woods. They could build an archway for couples to get married under, hang fairy lights in the trees to create a space around the ceremony and the guests. She'd even wondered about building a large hall-type treehouse that could fit around thirty-odd guests for a ceremony in the trees. It was something she would need to talk to River and the others about but she was bursting with ideas about holding different events here in the future. And with the fields and beaches nearby, there were a lot of options open to them in terms of location.

She saw Bear, Heath, Amelia, Meadow and Star sitting together on the other side of the clearing, eating and chatting, and she wandered over to join them. They had completely accepted her into their family now as if she had been there all along and, for someone who had felt so adrift and lost over the last few years, it felt lovely to feel such a huge sense of belonging.

Heath and Meadow's divorce had finally come through the week before and their relationship, or rather friendship, had not changed at all because of it. They were still as close as ever. But it did make Indigo wonder how that would impact on their future relationships with other people. Whoever Heath and Meadow ended up with would have to be completely accepting of this third wheel in their relationship. Heath had meals with Meadow and Star every day; if Meadow got a new boyfriend, they'd have to put up with Heath turning up on a daily basis to spend time with Star. But the two of them currently seemed very content with their arrangement so she wasn't going to interfere.

In her own personal life, Indigo couldn't have been happier too. Her relationship with River had really bloomed in the last few months. Violet, Joey, Etta and Tilly had all been to visit and were absolutely charmed with the place. Etta had already arranged to come back with Marcus later in the year and Violet and Max were booked to stay in a few weeks. River had wrapped them all around his little finger and she knew they couldn't be happier for her. Vicky still thought Indigo was making a huge mistake *settling* for a life with River, although Indigo knew that was mainly due to Vicky's own unhappiness with married life. Indigo had had stern words with her about interfering and her rudeness and, although Vicky still didn't agree with the life Indigo had chosen, she'd agreed to keep those opinions to herself. Indigo knew their relationship would always be strained from now on but she hadn't exactly lost a friend because Vicky had never really been that. Although some weird loyalty meant that she still wanted to be there for Vicky if and when her marriage ended, which it undoubtedly would given how miserable Vicky was.

But regardless of Vicky's opinion, Indigo knew that what she shared with River was that big forever kind of love. He and Tierra had moved all of their belongings into Blossom Cottage the week before, much to Tierra's delight, and she knew they would all be blissfully happy there.

Suddenly her walkie-talkie crackled into life and she heard River's voice.

'Indigo, can you come to Magnolia Cottage?'

Indigo frowned in confusion. Magnolia Cottage had been stripped out of all their personal items and redecorated slightly so it was a bit more neutral for guests. Their first guest in what was River's old home was due to arrive on Monday so she had no idea what he would be doing over there.

'Is there a problem?'

'Yeah, kind of. You better come and take a look,' River said.

She moved off through the trees and soon arrived at Magnolia Cottage, which would always hold a special place in her heart. She climbed the steps and walked over the little bridge, letting herself inside. Everything looked neat and tidy in here, if not a little flat without all of their personal effects to bring colour to the place.

'River!'

'Up here,' River called.

She climbed up the stairs and noticed straightaway that the hatch to the roof terrace was open.

'Are you on the roof?' she called out.

'Yeah, come on up,' River called and Indigo was sure she heard Tierra giggle.

'You do know I'm five months pregnant. Me and ladders don't really mix when I'm carrying a watermelon,' Indigo said.

'Good point,' River said, and hastily came down the ladder.

That was another thing that had changed over the last few months. Despite being four months off her due date, she was really starting to show now and it already looked like she was ready to pop at any stage. River Brookfield's baby was obviously going to be huge. They'd told Tierra once Indigo had passed that important three month threshold and she'd taken it really well; she was clearly looking forward to being a big sister. Surprisingly, there'd been no awkward questions about where babies came from or how the baby had got in there.

River got to the bottom. 'I'll follow behind you, make sure you get up there OK.'

She looked at him. 'Why are you dressed in a suit?'

'For tonight's party. And Tierra coerced me into wearing one.'

Indigo smiled and started climbing the ladder, River following close behind her. She climbed out onto the roof and noticed Tierra there in her best gold dress.

'Hello beautiful,' Indigo said as the little girl ran over to hug her. Indigo bent down and held her tight.

She stood back up and looked around. Everything

looked completely normal so she was a bit confused why she was here and not enjoying the party.

Tierra ran over to the switch and flicked on all the fairy lights which twinkled against the pink sky above them.

Indigo turned to look at River in confusion but the way he was looking at her made her breath catch in her throat.

He moved towards her and took her hand, placing a kiss on her wedding ring finger, and then suddenly she knew.

'I love you,' River said. 'I want to make sure I say that before anything else, I love you with everything I have.' He bent to whisper in her ear. 'And later tonight, when Tierra is in bed, I'll show you the many many ways that I love you.' He straightened, looking at her with eyes that were dark with need.

She smiled. 'I'll look forward to that.'

'That first night you came here, when we lay here on this roof looking at the stars, I knew then you were going to change my life forever and you did. You *have* changed my life for the better and every single day I will count my lucky stars that we stumbled into each other at the bar that night. We were meant to be together, I know that now, and I will spend the rest of my life trying to make you as happy as you make me.'

'You already do,' she said simply. 'You are the future I want, you are my happy ever after.'

He grinned. 'Indigo Bloom, will you marry me?' Tierra came over and took his hand and he bent and picked her up, propping her on his hip. 'I mean, will you marry us?'

Indigo smiled. 'I love you both so much. Of course I will marry you.'

She stepped forward and kissed him, briefly – the big celebration could come later – before hugging them both.

'Daddy, you forgot the ring,' Tierra said.

'Oh god, I did, I was so intent on getting the words right that I forgot the important part.' He rummaged in his pocket.

'The "I love you" was the important part,' Indigo said. 'The rest is just bells and whistles.'

River opened the box and offered out the ring. It was a square-cut, deep purple amethyst, with tiny diamonds either side.

'Oh, it's beautiful.' He slid it onto her finger and tears filled her eyes, knowing this was her forever. 'River, this baby you gave me is a gift because it brought me to you and your wonderful family and this magical place. I can't wait to start the rest of my life with you.'

He kissed her hard.

'Daddy, how did you give Indigo the baby?'

They broke the kiss to look at Tierra and Indigo quickly swallowed down the laughter that was bubbling in her throat. She'd wanted a few bells and whistles for her proposal but she'd never envisaged it would end with a talk about the birds and the bees. But, as River awkwardly began to try to explain, she knew she wouldn't change it for the world.

***

If you enjoyed *The Blossom Tree of Dreams*, you'll love my next gorgeously romantic story, *The Wisteria Tree of Love*, out in July

STAY IN TOUCH…

To keep up to date with the latest news on my releases, just go to the link below to sign up for a newsletter. You'll also get two FREE short stories, get sneak peeks, booky news and be able to take part in exclusive giveaways. Your email will never be shared with anyone else and you can unsubscribe at any time

https://www.subscribepage.com/hollymartinsignup

Website: https://hollymartin-author.com/
Email: holly@hollymartin-author.com
Twitter: @HollyMAuthor

Jewel Island Series

Sunrise over Sapphire Bay

Autumn Skies over Ruby Falls

Ice Creams at Emerald Cove

Sunlight over Crystal Sands

Mistletoe at Moonstone Lake

The Happiness Series

The Little Village of Happiness

The Gift of Happiness

Sandcastle Bay Series

The Holiday Cottage by the Sea

The Cottage on Sunshine Beach

Coming Home to Maple Cottage

Hope Island Series

Spring at Blueberry Bay

Summer at Buttercup Beach

Christmas at Mistletoe Cove

Juniper Island Series

Christmas Under a Cranberry Sky

A Town Called Christmas

White Cliff Bay Series

Christmas at Lilac Cottage

Snowflakes on Silver Cove

Summer at Rose Island

Standalone Stories

The Summer of Chasing Dreams

The Secrets of Clover Castle

(Previously published as Fairytale Beginnings)

Tied Up With Love

A Home on Bramble Hill

One Hundred Proposals

One Hundred Christmas Proposals

The Guestbook at Willow Cottage

978-1-913616-33-5 Paperback
978-1-913616-34-2 Large Print
978-1-913616-35-9 Hardback

Cover design by Emma Rogers

Printed in Great Britain
by Amazon